How Deep is the Darkness

A Charlie McClung Mystery

Mary Anne Edwards

Publisher: Kindle Direct Publishing Platform

ISBN-9781987523966

Cover Design by Fergus Splotch

www.MaryAnneEdwards.com

To my husband, Jeff, the best of the best.

In memory of my mother, Peggy Gonzales.

I want to give a special thank you to Gina, my best friend, for her unending friendship and superb medical knowledge. Also, thank you to Melissa for her pathology and forensic wisdom; to my father-in-law, retired Chief Mike Edwards; and to my father, Mingo Gonzales, for his prayers. A special thank you to the University of Georgia College of Agricultural and Environmental Sciences. My beta readers, I love you!

Also by Mary Anne Edwards

Brilliant Disguise

A Good Girl

Criminal Kind

Sins of My Youth

Flirting with Time

This story begins on Monday, June 20, 1983,
in Lyman County, Georgia.

Chapter 1

Chief Charlie McClung stared at the pale, bloated body of Myron Wagstaff lying next to his own swimming pool. He'd seen enough bodies to know when dead is dead. And Myron was dead.

McClung glanced at his wife standing near the diving board at the far end of the pool. Marian's white tee shirt clung to her body and her wet hair was plastered to her head and neck. Hugging herself, she managed a pitiful grin.

Not only was Myron Wagstaff a neighbor and the president of their Homeowners Association, but he was also Marian's archnemesis.

McClung knelt beside Myron, grabbed his thick wrist, and checked for a pulse. His fingers sank into doughy flesh. Myron's waterlogged polo shirt looked as if it had been spray painted on his belly, now bloated more than normal.

While McClung held his fingers in place waiting for a beat, he scanned the area. The patio furniture was jumbled together with the garden hose, snaking between the chairs, and stopping at the spot where Myron lay.

That, combined with the fact there weren't any signs of bruising on Myron, perhaps meant this was an accidental drowning.

"Boss?" Sergeant Thayer asked as he stood behind McClung.

He shook his head as he moved aside for the paramedics to perform their magic. But McClung realized not even Doctor Frankenstein could reanimate poor Myron.

As the emergency team worked on Myron, Charlie hurried toward Marian.

"Are you okay?" He kissed her forehead and pulled her into his arms.

Marian's body trembled against his chest.

"Thayer! Get Marian a blanket."

The young sergeant ran full blast and quickly returned.

"I'm okay just, um, just, um." Marian fought hard to keep her tears in check.

"Here." Thayer's breath pounded the back of Marian's neck as he laid the blanket across her shoulders.

Charlie released Marian, secured the blanket then blotted a tissue under her eyes and nose. "Here's a clean one."

"Love the magical tissues." A weak chuckle tumbled from Marian as she pulled the blanket tighter. "You'd think I'd be sweating in this June heat."

"Well, it's not even ten o'clock. It's cloudy, and you're soaking wet." Charlie glanced at her feet. "Where are your shoes?"

"They were muddy, so I took them off before I went into Myron's house to call 9-1-1 after I failed with CPR." Marian sighed. "I was afraid that if Myron survived, he'd send me a bill to have the muddy floors cleaned."

Pointing at the patio doors, she winced. "My shoes are over there."

"What's wrong?"

Marian massaged her lower back. "I guess I hurt my back getting Myron out of the water. I'll be okay."

Charlie squeezed her hand. Ever since Marian had the terrifying encounter with the Paper Heart Stalker and fell from a second-floor balcony last year, he worried about her health.

When McClung came face to face with the Paper Heart Stalker, Marian almost lost her life to save his but unknowingly sacrificed their unborn child.

He crossed over to the diving board and beckoned for her to follow. "Sit down. Here. Back toward me."

She eased down on the hard plank.

Charlie's strong hands ran across her shoulders and down her back.

"Does it hurt?"

"No, not really."

"I guess nothing's broken, dislocated, or cracked."

He crossed over the board and sat down. "When I get home tonight, I'll give you an intense massage once you've soaked in a tub of hot Epsom salt water."

"Sounds good." Marian watched the paramedics work on Myron.

The team's jaws were tight as they knelt over Myron's body. One paramedic rubbed the back of his neck as he stood in defeat while the other one closed Myron's eyes and pulled a blanket over his face.

"I didn't think they'd have much luck reviving him. I'd hoped, but…" Marian's voice trailed, her head heavy as she leaned on Charlie's shoulder.

"You did everything by the book. I still don't see how you got Myron out of the pool."

Marian sighed. "I did what I had to." She studied Charlie's face, then swallowed hard and grimaced. "I tried to revive him. CPR but maybe if—."

"Don't even go down that path." Charlie scratched his eyebrow. "Dispatch said you saw a man run from the scene."

She sat up. "Yeah. Do you think he had something to do with this?"

"Possibly, but we won't know for sure until we've gathered the facts." Charlie shrugged. "To me, every death is suspicious. Been fooled before but never again."

A year ago, two weeks after Charlie McClung had moved to Lyman County, he was called to the scene of a fatal shooting, Dianne Pannell. Without an investigation, the then chief of police ruled Dianne's death a suicide, but Charlie proved it was murder after Dianne's irritating neighbor, his now wife, Marian, pressed him to look further into the case.

"Yeah." Marian murmured.

Charlie stood. "Could be the guy got spooked when he saw Myron in the pool and ran away." He held out his hand. "Come with me. The paramedics need to give you a quick check."

"Why? My back isn't hurting that bad."

His hand cupped her cheek. "Sweetie, please just humor me."

Marian avoided looking at Myron and let her husband guide her to the ambulance.

They met officers Willard and Marsh at the gate. Photographer Sam Goldstein wasn't far behind.

"Ma'am, are you okay?" Marsh's voice quivered, and his eyebrows drew together.

Marian looked at him for a moment. "I'm fine. Just a bit damp." She bit her bottom lip and blinked several times. "Maybe a little shaken."

Both officers were like sons to Marian.

A tentative smile eased the furrow between Marsh's eyes. "Thank goodness."

Willard scratched his head. "Where are your shoes, ma'am?"

McClung answered. "They're outside the patio door. One of you get them for Marian."

"Consider it done, Boss." Willard took off.

"Marsh, I want you and Willard to help Thayer process the scene."

"Yes, Boss."

Willard returned a few minutes later, holding the less-muddy sneakers. His hands were filthy. "Here you go. I cleaned them up the best I could."

"Thank you, Willard." Marian took the shoes.

"No trouble."

"You two. Go assist Thayer." McClung barked.

"Wait." Marian held up her hand. "I scratched the running guy's tag number on the sidewalk."

"Marsh go find it. Willard, you report to Thayer." McClung directed his trusted men.

The two young men hurried off on opposite paths.

"Sam, how did you know I needed you?"

The silver-haired man tapped his temple. "Didn't take me long to figure you out. You're a cop that sees murder everywhere."

"But Sam, how did you know to come here?" Marian blurted.

Charlie and Sam answered. "Police scanner."

Marian frowned. "Just anybody can have one?"

"Yep!" Charlie sighed. "In this case, it's a good thing but mostly it's not."

Sam coughed. "I'll just take a picture or two of that tag number."

"Yeah, do that. Plus, there's a lot going on behind the house." Charlie watched the older man trudge down the sidewalk. Camera bags banged against Sam's body with each step he took.

One of the paramedics joined McClung and Marian at the ambulance.

"Ma'am don't fret. There wasn't a thing you could've done for that guy." The bear of a man shook his head. "I ain't no coroner, but I've been at this job for a long time. He's been dead too long to be revived."

The reassurance that she wasn't a factor in Myron's death didn't make Marian feel any better.

"Mel, do you mind giving my wife a quick once-over to make sure she's safe to go home?" Charlie stroked Marian's back as he spoke.

"Sure."

Mel removed his latex gloves and put on a fresh pair. He tilted his head toward the rear of the ambulance. "Just sit there."

"Boss." Thayer called to McClung from the open gate.

Charlie looked at Marian.

"Go on. Do your job." Marian kissed her husband's cheek.

8

He didn't move from her side.

"I'm fine, just a tweaked back. Besides you're making me nervous watching me like a hawk."

"Boss." Thayer repeated more urgently.

Charlie smiled and gave her a casual salute. "As you wish."

McClung hurried toward Thayer. "Found something?"

"I think I figured out what happened."

McClung disappeared behind the fence.

◆◆◆◆◆◆

"What is it, Thayer?" McClung followed him into Myron's house as he pulled a pair of latex gloves from his pocket. "I was hoping I could go a whole year without having to use these."

"Makes for a mundane job." Sergeant Thayer said flatly. "Here sir, in the kitchen. There's a half-empty bottle of whiskey and one glass."

McClung arched an eyebrow as he leaned over to study the bottle of Four Roses Single Barrel Bourbon Whiskey. About three fingers of liquid was left inside the bottle, a few drops coated the bottom of the tumbler.

He walked to the sink and smelled the drain. No lingering odor of alcohol. Then he carefully picked up the tumbler. "Thayer, flip on the overhead light."

The fluorescent tubes buzzed to life.

McClung held up the tumbler to the harsh light. On the rim, was a faint lip print. "Hmm, make sure you dust this for prints and bag it." He set it back in its original position.

Marsh squinted as he entered the kitchen. "Boss, put me to work."

"Where's Sam?"

"Taking pictures of the deceased before they cart him away."

McClung rubbed his earlobe. "Tell Mel to instruct the hospital not to release the body until I say so. I want Jack Jackson to do the autopsy, if he's available." He snapped his fingers. "And tell Sam I'll need him in here when he's finished."

"Will do." Marsh headed outside.

McClung studied every inch of the kitchen: the floor, inside the cabinets, oven, and refrigerator. He examined everything as he searched for possible clues. There was no hint to what may have led to Myron's death.

"Boss, I don't think it's murder."

McClung raised an eyebrow and replied sarcastically, "Yeah? Well then, enlighten me with your hypothesis of poor Wagstaff's watery demise." He strolled toward the open patio door and headed for the pool.

As Thayer spoke, McClung studied the jumbled furniture.

"Myron was drunk, got tangled up in the patio furniture, stumbled around, and then fell into the pool. He was too drunk to get himself out of the water."

McClung pushed out his bottom lip and nodded. "Hm. He was in the shallow end. All he had to do was stand up."

Thayer rubbed the top of his head. "Maybe he hit his head on the bottom. Knocked himself out."

McClung wandered around the pool. He stopped where the garden hose lay beside the pool.

The concrete was soaked, and the grass drenched to the point that a small stream had flowed down the incline, out the gate and onto the street.

"What do you think Myron was doing with the hose?"

Thayer hunched his shoulders. "Topping off the pool?"

"Yeah, sounds right." McClung pointed to the water-logged grass. "The hose had to be on for a long time to have created that miniature creek rolling down the hill and into the street."

"That goes to show I'm right. He was drunk standing here. The hose got tangled in the furniture. He yanked it. Lost his balance. Dropped the hose. Hit his head on the concrete and fell into the pool. Accidental drowning." Thayer crossed his arms and grinned.

McClung pulled on his bottom lip. "Plausible." Something on the concrete caught his eye.

"What does this look like to you?" McClung knelt close to the spot.

"It looks like blood. Must be where he hit his head."

"Yeah, and what about this?"

McClung touched a hard, yellowish, rectangular-shaped chip, like a half of a Chiclet. He looked around for Sam Goldstein.

The EMTs were talking to Sam as he photographed Myron's body.

McClung yelled over his shoulder. "Sam, get over here."

The paramedics began moving Myron's body.

"What do we have there?" Sam held the camera to his eye, snapping pictures as McClung pointed toward the areas.

"That appears to be blood." McClung pointed to the yellowish object. "And that, my friend, doesn't belong here. Possibly a clue."

Thayer knelt beside McClung. "Yep, could be. It looks like old ivory?"

McClung thought the odd chip looked familiar, but the vague memory faded away.

Sam zoomed to get a few tight shots of the chip and the blood spatters.

McClung glanced at the EMTs. "Thayer, bag it and look for more spatters and anything else in this area. I want a chat with Mel."

"Mel, where's Marian? Is she all right?" McClung moved out of the way of the paramedics while they loaded Myron onto the stretcher.

"She's fine. Just hurt her back. Understandable." Mel groaned as they lifted Myron's body. "Even for me this guy is hefty. I'm surprised your wife got him out of the water. She's a tiny lady. What 5'3'' and 125 pounds?"

McClung snorted as he nodded. "Yep, but she's stubborn. If she's got it in her mind to do something, consider it done."

"Is Marian still sitting in the back of the ambulance?" McClung followed the gurney.

"No, sir. She's sittin on the front stoop waitin on you."

Officer Billy Crawford met them inside the gate.

McClung couldn't help but smile at his oldest officer. Crawford was always in a jolly mood.

But not this morning.

"Boss, sorry it took me so long to get here." Crawford wore a rare frown.

"What's the matter?" McClung waved the paramedics to go on.

Crawford shifted the criminal investigation kit from one hand to the other. "Ah, the missus got news her favorite uncle isn't doing so good and her dad's not taking it none too well. If her uncle dies, my father-in-law will be the last one left in his family."

McClung gripped Crawford's firm shoulder. "I'm sorry to hear that. Are you sure you should be here? Your wife needs you."

"Thanks, but I'm not much help. Best thing for me is to stay out of her way."

"Okay, but don't be shy about asking for time off. Understand?"

"I appreciate that, Boss."

"If there's anything we can do, don't hesitate to ask." He shook his index finger at his officer. "I mean it. Ask. Marian will make sure you're fed, you got that?"

"Yes, Boss. But I saw her sitting out front, and she doesn't look so good."

McClung's eyes widened. "What?"

"You didn't know she's here?" Crawford pulled back his head.

"Yeah, but she said she was fine." McClung patted the officer's back. "Let me go speak with her. I'll catch up with you later."

Charlie hurried to find his wife, but stopped a few yards away to observe her.

So many questions he needed to ask, but he was worried about her. Marian didn't need this stress. Not now.

Marian looked like a triangular-shaped lump of coal. The dark gray blanket was wound tightly around her body and she was resting her forehead on her knees, which she'd pulled up to her chest.

Charlie wondered how she was able to breathe. He sat beside her and rubbed her back. "Sweetie?"

Marian's head popped up. "Hey! I didn't hear you come up. I must've dozed off as I was praying."

"Yeah? Are you sure you're okay? You don't look so hot." Charlie wrapped his arms around her.

Marian winced. "You're such a sweet talker."

Charlie released his embrace. "Sorry." His fingers massaged her lower back.

"That's okay." Marian pulled off the blanket and neatly folded it. "I'm tired. I want to lie down. Is it okay for me to walk home, now?"

"Nope, it's at least a mile and a half. I'm driving you home."

She straightened her legs. "Might as well. These sneakers are ruined. Not good for anything but stomping around in the yard."

Marian tucked the thin blanket under her arm. "What about the investigation? Aren't you going to question me?"

"Your well-being is more important to me. Besides, Thayer's opinion is this is an accidental drowning. My best team is on this. They don't need me telling them how to do their job. And you can tell me what happened when you feel like it."

"Now?"

"Do you honestly want to talk about it now?"

Marian whispered. "I need to, but—"

"But means later. Tonight?"

"Yeah, tonight."

Charlie held her hand as they walked toward the gate. "Let me tell the guys I'm taking you home."

McClung passed the EMTs as he disappeared behind the fence.

Marian shuddered as she watched the paramedics load Myron's body inside the ambulance. "I've witnessed this scene too many times in the past year."

Chapter 2

McClung sat in silence, massaging his earlobe as Sergeant Thayer maneuvered the patrol car through the busy town square. Lunchtime was always a game of musical chairs with cars. Fortunately, Thayer didn't need a parking space. He drove around the square on his way to the hospital.

Informing the next of kin was never a pleasant task, and it couldn't be done by phone. McClung wondered how Sheila Gerber, Myron's stepsister, would react to his death.

Seven months ago, while investigating Sheila and Myron as possible suspects in the Paper Heart Stalker case, he discovered there wasn't any familial love between the two step-siblings.

And who could blame Sheila for total disdain for her evil, sadistic stepbrother?

McClung's thoughts turned toward Marian. When he left her at home, she appeared to be in a good frame of mind, messing around the kitchen and worrying about what to make for Officer Crawford's family.

But he knew that finding Myron's body, coupled with the past year's events, weighed heavily on her mind.

Maybe she needs a break from being a copper's wife?

The crackle of the radio disturbed McClung's thoughts.

Penny Parkinson, the receptionist at the police station, broadcasted. "Chief? Are you there?"

"Yeah, go ahead."

"Got a hit on that tag number."

McClung and Thayer's heads whipped toward one another.

Thayer shot up a thumb.

A wide grin cracked McClung's face.

"The car belongs to a doctor, a psychiatrist. His name is Arnold James Carter. Lives at 1366 Cardinal Terrace, here in Lyman."

McClung's grin melted. "Are you kidding me?"

"No, Boss. That's in your subdivision."

♦♦♦♦♦♦

"I can believe this!" McClung growled as he squeezed the back of his neck.

Thayer backed the squad car into the sole parking space designated for the police at the Lyman County Hospital. "Well Boss, your subdivision is the largest and most affluent one in the county."

McClung cringed. The word affluent annoyed him. He flung the seatbelt aside as he exited the car and stomped toward the three-story building.

A blast of arctic air veered McClung's attention back to the task at hand, informing Sheila Gerber her stepbrother was dead.

McClung and Thayer followed the familiar path through the maze of hallways to Shelia's department.

Their footsteps echoed as they entered the vacant waiting area for the hospital lab.

"Hm." McClung stepped into the hallway and read the sign posted beside the door. "Yep, it's still the lab."

Thayer pounded several times on the call bell.

Sheila emerged from the *Employees' Only* door. "I'm so sorry…" Her eyes narrowed as she assessed McClung and Thayer. "What's the matter?"

"Please, sit down. I have some bad news." McClung murmured.

She sighed. "I'd love to. I'm exhausted."

Sheila walked around the above-the-waist counter and plopped down on one of the uncomfortable waiting room chairs. "But I can't think of any news that'll make me faint."

McClung sat next to her not sure how Sheila would take the news. "I'm sorry to inform you that your stepbrother, Myron Herbert Wagstaff, was found dead this morning."

"Are you serious?" Sheila's lips curved upward. She shook her head. "I'm sorry. I shouldn't be happy, but you of all people should know I have not a smidgen of love for him."

McClung shoved the tissue he had ready back into his coat pocket. He was relieved she didn't cry. Seeing women cry always made his gut churn.

Sheila sat up. "I guess you need me to identify his body. Where is it? Here or the funeral home?"

It. Shelia referred to Myron as *it*. Definitely no sense of loss there, McClung thought. "He's here."

She sniffed. "Well, the sooner this is over, the sooner I can get my rightful inheritance." Sheila rubbed her red, chapped hands together. "Let me tell my assistant to cover the front."

McClung watched her practically skip around the counter. Strange. He wondered if she was overcompensating to hide her real feelings.

Sheila opened the employees' door and yelled. "Hey, cover the front. I'm going to the morgue. Fill you in later."

A bright-eyed young man wearing blue scrubs covered with a white lab coat appeared. "What?"

Sheila waved at him from the hallway. "Later, I said."

McClung and Thayer shrugged, then followed her as she led the way to the morgue.

"Aren't you the least bit curious how he died?" McClung quickened his strides to keep up with Sheila.

Her sensible shoes squeaked on the linoleum floor.

"What difference does it make? Dead is dead. But if it'll tick off an important box, please, tell me how the miserable little man died."

McClung looked at Thayer and grimaced then mouthed, *cold as ice*.

"We're still waiting on an autopsy report, but it appears that Myron drowned in his swimming pool." McClung reported.

Sheila froze and jerked around to face the two cops. "What? Drowned?" Her eyes flicked toward Thayer then back at McClung. "I don't believe it. He was a waddling armadillo on land, but he was like a hippo in the water."

"He was drunk." Thayer blurted.

Sheila snorted. "Figures. Don't tell me, Four Roses, right? That's what his father drank. All the time." She shook her head. "Like father, like son. Only thing missing from Myron was his father's bright red nose. I guess he was working on that."

McClung took note that she used the term *his father* not *our father.* "We found a mostly empty bottle of it, but we won't know if Myron was drunk until we get the autopsy report."

"It doesn't matter." Sheila continued toward the morgue.

Once there, she swiped her card key and entered a small waiting room. She tapped on a frosted sliding windowpane.

A startled gasp echoed from the other side of the glass. The window flew open.

"Hey, Sheila! I wasn't expecting you." The pale young man leaned over to get a look at the two men standing behind her. "What's going on?"

McClung and Sergeant Thayer flashed their badges.

The freckled-face man nodded.

"I came to verify my stepbrother's body."

The young man's face fell. "Oh, I'm so sorry for your loss."

Sheila waved away his condolences. "Thank you, but we weren't close. At all. Can we come on back?"

"Sure." The window closed without a sound.

A heavy metal door to the left of the reception station opened. The young man held the door open and introduced himself. "I'm Tim Flynn. I usually work the night shift."

McClung shook Tim's unusually warm hand. "I'm McClung and this is Sergeant Thayer."

Tim grinned. "Yeah, I heard about you. All good." He walked toward a wall with a series of square metal doors and stopped at the one on the far right.

"He's here." Tim studied Sheila's face.

She nodded. "Go ahead. Open it."

McClung put his hand on the cold metal door. "Wait, a minute. How do you know you have the right one? We didn't tell you his name."

Tim pointed at the door. "He's the only one in here. The funeral homes just made their pickups. My instructions were to hold this one for an autopsy."

"All right then." McClung removed his hand as he smirked at the carrot-top young man.

The door handle release clicked. A metal-on-metal scraping sound bounced off the stark white concrete walls as Tim pulled out the stainless-steel bed where Myron Herbert Wagstaff rested.

"Ready?"

Sheila nodded.

Tim pulled back the thin cotton sheet, exposing only Myron's face.

Sheila pulled on the loose skin on her neck as she stared at her stepbrother. A sniff echoed in the quiet room. "Uh, yeah. That's him. That's Myron." Her voice trembled.

McClung offered her a tissue.

"Thanks." Sheila dabbed the inside corners of her eyes as she chuckled. "I don't know why my eyes are tearing up. Allergies, I suppose." She pivoted and marched out of the room.

Chapter 3

McClung, the solitary figure in the war room, straddled a backward-facing chair. His elbows rested on its back, a fist on each cheek supported his head as he stared at the collage of photos posted on the long whiteboard.

His men had done an excellent job collecting evidence even though Myron's death hadn't been ruled a murder. Yet.

The Wagstaff case was being investigated as a suspicious death even though Sergeant Thayer thought it was a waste of time. Everything at the scene pointed toward an accidental death

But McClung's gut whispered otherwise ever since he learned from Myron's stepsister how agile he was in the water.

Then there was Marian's answer. The one question he had asked her after taking her home and before he went back to the scene. He didn't want to ask her, but he had to know.

Did she think he'd been drinking?

Marian said that while she was blowing air into Myron's mouth to save his life, she didn't smell or… taste any alcohol.

That image of Marian trying to save Myron sprang into his head.

McClung stood. His whole body shook as he tried to get rid of the gross feeling crawling over his skin.

"What's the matter, Boss?" Thayer sauntered toward him.

McClung's cheeks pinked. "Nothing." He walked toward the coffeepot. "Want some coffee?"

"Yeah." Thayer stood with his fist resting on his holster as he studied the whiteboard.

The aroma of coffee put McClung at ease. "Do you still see this as an accidental death?" He leaned against the table as he waited for the last drip from the coffeemaker.

Thayer nodded. "I'm afraid so."

"I think you're going to be proved wrong." McClung smiled as he watched his sidekick pull on his bottom lip. A habit Thayer had picked up from him.

"Sorry, Boss. I just don't see it."

"Fortunately, things are slow at the GBI which means our buddy, Jack Jackson, is going to able to do Myron's autopsy tonight. Then you will."

McClung couldn't wait for the last drip and poured a cup.

Thayer stood beside him for the next cup. "Well, we cordoned off Myron's house and yard. We'll remove it when Wagstaff's death is ruled an accident."

"You're just praying that your old boss will be proved wrong, aren't you?" McClung blew on his coffee then took a sip.

Thayer smirked and tilted his head. "Would be nice to be right for once."

McClung laughed. "You'll get there one day. Still got a lot to learn from this old copper." He walked toward the whiteboard.

"Just in case I'm right," McClung looked over his shoulder and caught Thayer rolling his eyes, "I've asked Stewie and Jenny to delve deeper into Myron's life. We have an extensive dossier on him since he was one of the suspects in the Paper Heart Stalker case."

Thayer nodded as he stirred his coffee.

"What about the witness Marian saw running away?"

"Mm." Thayer swallowed a mouthful of coffee. "Arnold Carter. Turns out he's a local psychiatrist. Marsh went to his office. Doctor Carter said he'd stop by the precinct today after his three o'clock patient."

Thayer looked at his watch. "So hopefully, we'll see the good doctor within the hour."

McClung opened his mouth.

"Before you ask, I asked Stewie and Jenny to work up a file on Carter." Thayer grinned.

"You're a good man." McClung tapped one of the pictures on the board. "Why is the morning paper resting against the front door?"

"What do you mean?" Thayer leaned in to get a better look. "You think the doctor put it there?"

McClung shrugged. "Someone did. Was it before, during or after Myron drowned?"

"Boss, why worry about it? All of this will most likely be a moot point." Thayer sighed. "I have a pile of paperwork to do."

McClung tugged at his earlobe, keeping his focus on the whiteboard. "You'll see. The autopsy will prove me right."

"Sure thing, Boss." Thayer's voice faded as he walked out of the war room.

McClung was thankful for the solitude. He scanned each photo, his finger skimming the surface as he searched for the tiniest clue.

He was impressed with Sam Goldstein's skills and insight as to what the police would consider photo-worthy.

The zoom shots of the newspaper proved it was today's morning edition.

McClung lined up the photos of the mini river that had flowed from beside the pool, down the front yard and onto the street. The ground was completely saturated. Someone had shoved a yardstick into the ground near the pool. Close to seven inches.

He massaged his chin. "Interesting." McClung took out his pen and pad and jotted a note to contact the Lyman County's extension agent.

The next set of photos were around the pool. McClung followed the trail of turned over patio furniture, blood spatter, and water. The blood spatter was iffy at best. Could be the red Georgia clay. His instinct said blood.

He tapped the picture of the small yellowish chip and leaned closer. "Could it be?" His eyes widened. "Yeah, it is." McClung stepped back and then ran out of the room.

◆◆◆◆◆◆

McClung made a sliding stop and plopped in his worn black leather chair he inherited with the job promotion. The corrupt chief before him had excellent taste.

He picked up the phone and punched in the two-digit speed dial number for the hospital.

"Hello, this is Lyman's Chief McClung. I need the morgue."

His fingertips kept time with *Raindrops Keep Fallin' On My Head* as he waited for someone in the morgue to answer.

"Flynn speaking."

McClung smiled and sat up. "Hey, Tim. This is McClung. I was in earlier today."

"Yes, sir. I remember. Funny, I was about to call you. I've had a request to prepare Myron Wagstaff for transport to Gibb's Funeral Home."

"From who?" McClung said in a husky voice.

"Got it right here." Tim Flynn flipped over a few sheets of paper. "Dr. Jack Jackson. Said he's with the Georgia Bureau of Investigation." Tim cleared his throat. "Is he for real?"

"Yes, he's real all right. You can release the body."

"Yes, sir. Will do."

McClung heard a loud buzz.

"Holy crap!" Tim juggled the phone in his hands. "Stupid buzzer scares me every time. Geez! Gibb's must be here already."

"Tim, before you go, did you by any chance examine the body?"

"No way! I just store them. Not interested in forensic pathology, or whatever it's called. I'm just doing this until I can get my business degree."

Whoever it was that wanted Tim's attention was unrelenting. They held the buzzer making a loud, intrusive, maddening sound.

"Sorry, sir, I've gotta go."

As he hung up, McClung heard Tim cursing loudly at whoever it was on the other side of the door.

"A little man with a dynamite temper. I guess it's the Irish in him." McClung made a mental note to never get on the wrong side of Flynn.

He hoped by the time Dr. Carter's interview was over, Jack would be finished with the autopsy. McClung had to know if he was right about the chip he'd found.

McClung decided to return to the war room. Maybe the pictures would reveal the true story. Maybe Thayer was right. He may be wasting his time. Either way, he had time to kill and coffee to drink before Arnold Carter, the running man, arrived for the interview.

He jogged down the back stairwell and at the last minute decided to check in with Stewie and Jenny, his faithful admins.

"Hey! How's the Carter file coming along?" McClung leaned against the door jamb.

Stewie kept his focus on the computer monitor, his narrow back toward McClung. "Jenny, give him the lowdown."

Jenny's round face glowed with excitement. "Oh, I've found some juicy stuff on our dashing doctor."

McClung chuckled. "Good one."

Jenny's pug nose wrinkled then she laughed as the light bulb came on inside her brain.

She giggled. "Yeah, it is a good one. Dashing. Because he was running away from the scene and because he's handsome."

Stewie's head flopped toward his chest. "Oh, brother."

Jenny ignored her co-worker. "I found a few interesting news stories. Thank goodness for the society section in the Lyman County daily paper. More like gossip but what the hey. Right?"

McClung hunched one shoulder. "I suppose."

"Anyway. It appears the dishy doctor got a divorce right before he moved his practice here from Atlanta. And it seems he's considered the town's most eligible bachelor."

"Really?" McClung pushed away from the doorjamb.

As he pulled the worn visitor's chair next to Jenny, he made a mental note to see how much money was left in the office supply budget. Everyone in the building needed new chairs. Except for himself, he liked his leather chair.

"Got any pictures?"

Jenny bobbed her head. "Yep. Lots. Got three years' worth." She pulled copies of newspaper articles from a manila folder and lined them up on her desk. "See? Looks like a different woman on every occasion. There's a couple you'll recognize."

McClung studied the grayscale photos. The clean-shaven man with dark slicked-back hair looked rather familiar.

"Hm. Do you think he's handsome?" He stared at Jenny's face to make sure she wasn't lying.

"Yeah. Although, I prefer a man with a little more meat on his bones. Not fat, but the doc is too thin, not enough definition. If you know what I mean."

Jenny looked at Stewie. "He's in better shape than that skeleton at the keyboard."

"Ha. Ha. I have a high metabolism. You're just jealous."

Stewie pulled a large bag of peanut M&Ms from his right-hand desk drawer. He poured a mound next to his keyboard.

"Would offer you some, Jenny, but I need all of them to put some meat on my bones." He popped one in his mouth.

"Pfft." Jenny rolled her eyes. She jerked open the bottom drawer of her desk, shoved several hanging file folders back, and retrieved a brown bag. "I prefer plain M&Ms."

"Can we get back to Arnold Carter?" McClung pointed to one of the women. "Is this Chief Miller's ex-wife, Wendy?"

"Uh-huh." Jenny pointed to the date. "Right after Chief Perry Miller got tossed in the slammer."

He pointed to another one. "That's Shelia Gerber. When was it taken?"

Jenny squinted at the date. "That was last year. Hmm, that's odd." She wrinkled her nose. "It was right after her husband died."

McClung leaned back and rubbed his earlobe. "So, two women who were dealing with difficult circumstances. Who most likely needed to talk to someone to work through their pain. Interesting. I wondered if our prominent doctor was dating all of his patients."

"Eww. That's not right." Jenny screwed up her face.

Stewie whipped around. "I should say so, especially if they were patients at the time those pictures were taken."

McClung stood. "See what you can find out." He held out his palm. "May I have one or two of your M&Ms, Stewie?"

Stewie twirled his chair around and grabbed the bag of candy as his chair continued to spin. Planting his feet, he stopped, facing McClung. "Here you go, Boss. Take as many as you want."

Stewie ignored Jenny as she stuck out her tongue.

McClung jiggled the yellow bag until his hand was full. "Thanks." He tossed a green candy into his mouth. "I'll be in the war room."

As he walked down the hallway munching on candy, McClung almost choked on an orange piece as he remembered where he had seen Arnold Carter.

He'd grown a beard.

It was three months ago at the Homeowners Association meeting. McClung slapped his forehead. The fight. Myron had pushed one of the homeowners too far. A bearded man rushed toward Myron. If McClung hadn't grabbed the angry man, Myron would've seen a fist, close-up.

The enraged bearded man was Arnold Carter.

Chapter 4

Marian sighed as she eased into the soaking tub filled with peppermint-scented Epsom salts.

Her goal?

Forget about the morning's horrible events and relax. She closed her eyes and planned the menu for supper.

Nothing sounded good.

She'd baked two lemon poppy seed cakes. One for Officer Billy Crawford's family and one for dessert.

Maybe a pot of chicken tortilla soup would hit the spot. Or cheesy potato soup with cornbread.

As she enjoyed the hot water loosening her muscles, Marian pondered the question, potato or chicken soup.

The word chicken turned her mind to the crows at Myron's house.

"I wonder why they were there. They're attracted to shiny things. Hmm. I don't remember seeing anything sparkling in the water."

She splashed water over her bare shoulders. Then she remembered something her mother used to say. Crows hanging around meant someone in the house would die.

Myron.

That's what the crow was looking at, Myron.

The water had cooled.

Marian opened the drain and blotted just enough water to keep from dripping on her way to the shower. She jumped in, washed her hair, and scrubbed the Epsom salt from her skin.

Once finished, she smoothed lotion over her entire body. She thought of the crows as she tapped anti-wrinkle cream around her eyes.

She slid into a colorful spaghetti-strap sundress and walked barefooted to the kitchen.

Opening the pantry door to get cornmeal and potatoes, Marian thought about calling Charlie, but she didn't want to bother him at work.

She stood at the kitchen sink as she peeled potatoes and glanced out the bay window. Marian stared at the space where Dianne Pannell's house once stood.

You can get rid of physical reminders, but you can't erase the memories, she thought.

"Not going there." Marian reminded herself. She sighed. "At least the pain dulls with time."

So much had happened in the past year, beginning with Dianne's murder the night she had met Charlie. If it had not been for him coming to her rescue, she'd more than likely be dead too.

"Good sometimes comes from bad." Marian mumbled and continued to peel potatoes. With each peeling that slapped against the bottom of the Corian sink, a memory popped into her head.

She smiled as she thought of Ma and Da, Charlie's parents.

Marian not only gained a practically perfect husband but a loving family to boot.

The smile faded.

Three months after she and Charlie met, they traveled to Virginia to meet his family.

The first person she met in Charlie's hometown was a dead girl lying in the bottom of an armoire that had been delivered to the antique shop owned by the McClung family.

The trip began with murder but ended with a wedding.

A naughty smile played with Marian's lips as she remembered their first night as husband and wife.

She shook her head as she remembered their honeymoon cruise. One they'd tell their—.

The metal ting of the peeler and the thud of the half-peeled potato echoed in the kitchen as they tumbled around the bottom of the sink.

Marian's empty hands suspended in the air.

Her knuckles turned white and her knees wobbled as she clutched the edge of the counter.

Tears spilled as she collapsed onto the floor. The memory of the horrible night she lost their baby gripped her heart.

Marian leaned her back against the dishwasher. The cool chrome on her naked shoulders was surprisingly soothing.

Her hands caressed her belly, flat instead of swollen.

Marian banged the back of her head against the metal. She stared at the ceiling, fearing there wouldn't be another baby. They hadn't planned on a baby this late in their lives. It was a total surprise.

She pulled down the dishtowel dangling from the counter and ran it over her cheeks. Pressing the damp towel on her eyes, Marian resigned herself to being childless.

"It's not fair!" She yelled and then stood.

Leaning over the sink, she splashed her face with cool water.

"Well, there goes the mascara." Marian groaned at the sight of the jet-black smudges on the olive-green dishtowel. She strolled into the laundry room and tossed the dirty towel into the hamper.

As she wandered through the living room toward the master bedroom, Marian yanked a tissue from the box she kept on one of the end tables.

Just as she buried her nose in the tissue, the phone rang.

Marian ran to the bedroom to answer it.

In her best cheery voice, she chirped. "Hello."

Marian didn't need Charlie or Joan, the only two people who called her, to grill her about her tears.

"Hey, darling."

"Charlie, I was just thinking about you." She wiped her nose.

"Mm, what kind of thoughts?"

Her husband's flirtatious innuendos pushed aside her melancholy. "Well, maybe you should come… wait, are you alone?"

"But of course."

"So, what's going on?"

"I just wanted to hear your voice to make sure you're okay. Why does your nose sound stuffy?"

Marian's cheeks flamed.

"Pollen. How does cheesy potato soup and cornbread sound for supper?" She hoped food would lead her husband down a different path.

Silence.

Charlie grunted. "Pollen, huh?"

He hesitated.

"Sure, fine. Soup sounds good. Do you mind if I ask Jack to join us?

She instantly thought of Joan, her best friend.

Joan and Jack had been spending a lot of time together since they joined the McClung clan for Thanksgiving in Virginia.

"That's okay but if Jack is in town, don't you think he'd rather be with Joan?"

"You haven't told Joan what happened this morning? You've been at home all day dealing with it by yourself?"

Marian bit her bottom lip.

"I needed time to gather my thoughts, to calm down. I had a hot soak and I'm de-stressed now. Okay?" She snapped. "Besides, I'm not a delicate little flower."

She pinched the bridge of her nose and giggled to soften her harsh tone. "You know how I rebound, right?"

Her defensive tone surprised Charlie, but he let it slide. "Yeah. Just making sure you're okay."

"I'm fine." A twinge of guilt poked at her. "What time will you be home?"

"I'm shooting for six o'clock. Only one interview scheduled for today." He shrugged. "We can't do anything else concerning Myron's death until Jack finishes the postmortem and files his ruling."

"Yeah, it makes sense."

Marian glanced at her reflection in the dresser mirror and was startled to see her mascara smeared like Alice Cooper, the macabre, theatrical rock star.

She pressed her fingers on her mouth, stifling her amusement, then coughed quietly and turned her back toward the mirror.

"Don't need to be wasting manpower for an unfortunate accident."

"Yep." Charlie leaned his forehead into his palm. "Are you sure you're up for having company?"

Marian murmured. "I love you, Charlie."

"Yeah?"

"Yeah. Thanks for putting me first."

Charlie grinned. "It's my job, ma'am, as a practically perfect husband."

"You always know how to make me feel better."

"Well, like I said, it's my job, my perfect little bride."

Marian shook her head. "Yeah. Yeah. Let's get back to the reason you called."

Charlie sighed. Back to the real world.

"You're the boss. Back to dinner. If you're sure you don't mind having Jack over, do you mind giving Joan a call and asking her what her dinner plans are tonight?"

"I'm positive."

"All right, then. I have to speak with Jack tonight and I don't want to hang around the office all night."

"I'd rather you be here then at work talking shop. Count on me to have Joan here for dinner no later than seven o'clock. How does that sound?"

Charlie knew Marian would gussy up the dining room. Just because she was serving soup and cornbread didn't mean that the dining experience had to be ordinary. There'd be flowers, candles, crisp white linens, and fine china. His wife loved to entertain with panache.

"Sounds good. Gotta go. Thayer's here and I don't like his expression."

"Charlie."

"Yeah?"

"I love you."

"I know. Love you, too."

◆◆◆◆◆◆

McClung motioned for Thayer to sit.

"What's wrong?"

Thayer shook his head. "You're not gonna like this, Boss, but the shrink called. He's not coming."

"Why's that?" McClung stood and gestured Thayer to follow him from the office. "Let's take the elevator."

McClung stared at their reflections on the shiny elevator doors.

His image betrayed his emotions, eyebrows were squished together, jaw muscles bulged, and his lips tight.

McClung didn't believe Marian's claim that pollen was making her nose stuffy.

A few weeks back, he'd arrived home early and discovered her crying on the screened back porch. After much consoling, she admitted that she was thinking of the baby they'd lost.

Even though they had never thought of having a child so late in life, he knew she now longed for a baby.

"Boss?"

McClung realized he wasn't staring at Thayer's reflection.

"Sorry." He stepped next to his sergeant. "I missed what you said."

Thayer scratched his head above his left ear. "Everything okay?"

"Yeah. What were you saying?" McClung forced his thoughts back to Arnold Carter.

"He claims he had a last-minute patient. An emergency."

"Is that so?" McClung exited the elevator and headed toward the front door. He paused at the front desk.

Thayer took a quick sidestep to avoid smacking into McClung's back.

"Penny, we're heading to Dr. Arnold Carter's office."

Chapter 5

McClung admired the precisely mowed lawns and graceful landscaping of the 1920s homes that were just off the town square and a few miles from the police station. A handful of the stately homes were now offices for lawyers, doctors, and a prestigious spa.

His main interest was the one Dr. Arnold Carter's psychiatry practice occupied.

Thayer pulled into a wide driveway that snaked its way behind a craftsman-style house. An eight-foot-high fence, painted creamy-white to match the trim of the house, surrounded the backyard.

The parking area had spaces for four cars, two were taken. A big black Cadillac and a sporty little 1960 Corvette convertible. A serenity garden took over from the edge of the concrete pad and drifted around two well-established oak trees.

"Marian would love this yard." Thayer backed into the spot farthest from the two cars.

McClung released his seatbelt and exited the car. "Yeah, I was thinking the same thing." He pointed to the far corner of the quarter-acre yard. "She'd go crazy over that water feature."

Water spilled down three terraces composed of mossy boulders and flat rocks then splashed into a shallow pond. Tall swaying grasses contrasted against bushy dark green ferns and Hostas, a few edged in white, others in yellow. Pink, yellow, red, and orange flowers peeked in between the greenery and rocks.

"It's too big for this yard but ideal for yours."

McClung massaged his chin. "I'm thinking it'd be perfect for her birthday coming up soon."

He envisioned Marian lounging alongside the sound of falling water with a book on her lap as butterflies flitted around, paled by her beauty.

Thayer cleared his throat. "Boss?"

"Sorry, just thinking about the water feature."

"Yeah, sure." Thayer smirked.

McClung looked at the two cars and headed to the open convertible.

Thayer followed. "Think of the brownie points you'd score if you got her a fancy water feature."

"Don't care about points." McClung leaned over the open-top car. "Must belong to a woman." He tilted his head toward the milky white leather passenger seat. A bright orange scarf lay puddled in the seat, its edges fluttered in the light breeze.

Thayer picked up the silky scarf and sniffed. "Yep, reeks of perfume." He wrinkled his nose and dropped it on the seat. "You'd think I'd remember seeing this car with a woman wearing that scarf cruising around town but for the life me I don't."

"Me, neither." McClung scribbled down the tag number then examined the rear bumper of the Cadillac.

"Scraped?"

McClung shoved the notepad in his shirt pocket. "Yep. We should head inside."

They stepped into the screened back porch. It was like Marian's but not as elegant. A reader's paradise she called it.

An ornate sign hung on the backdoor. It said, *Doctor in Session.*

McClung tried the doorknob.

Locked.

"Huh." McClung smirked. "Let's try the front door."

Thayer peered through the back window. "Can't see a thing. All the blinds are closed."

"Secrets. That's what psychiatrists do. Harvest people's deep dark secrets, problems, and idiosyncrasies. Can't let the world learn about them." McClung wagged his finger.

"Yeah, but you'd think at least one would be open." Thayer shrugged. "Must have lots of secrets to hide."

"Let's check out the front."

They strolled around the house and onto the long, well-maintained porch. Three white wicker rockers sat under a double-wide window. On the opposite side of the porch, a swing suspended from the planked ceiling made a nice balance.

Next to the front door was a simple sign that gave the good doctor's name and phone number, no hours of operation. Just the words, *Call for an appointment.*

"Looks like Carter is very accommodating." McClung tapped the wooden plaque. He tipped his head toward the windows.

"I see overflowing bookshelves." McClung cupped the sides of his eyes, shifting his head side to side. "Not much else of any significance. What do you see?"

Thayer pressed his ear against the glass. "Can't see a thing. I think I hear giggling. A woman."

"Hm, let's hope the front door is unlocked." McClung pulled on the elaborate wooden screen door that matched the craftsmen style front door.

It opened.

He tried the oil-rubbed doorknob.

It turned.

"Well, what do you know?" McClung grinned.

They stepped into the house. It smelled of fresh paint. The hallway led straight to the back of the house. To the left was an intimate library. To the right was a closed door. A small entryway bench sat in the hallway.

McClung leaned close to the four-paneled door with a stained-glass transom window above it. He motioned for Thayer to listen.

Definitely two people behind the closed door. A woman and a man.

McClung put his finger to his mouth then pointed to Thayer and himself. Next, he used two fingers and pointed to his eyes then pointed toward the long hallway.

After checking each room, they sat on the bench and waited for the closed door to open, trying their best to ignore the whispers, moans, and thumping noises.

When McClung heard muted conversation, he relaxed and smiled knowing he and Thayer would be an interesting surprise for Dr. Carter.

With the sound of a smack, a female giggling, and the click of the door lock, the door cracked open.

An attractive blonde with curves in all the right places filled the open space. She leered at someone behind the door. Her delicate hand raised and disappeared behind the door.

"Arnie, baby, you've got lipstick on your neck."

"Thanks, Shellie girl." A man's voice. The good doctor?

The blonde puckered then leaned forward. "Mwah. Air kiss." She giggled. "When can I make another appointment?"

"Just call me. I'll squeeze you in anytime."

She moaned. "I can't wait. Dinner. Tonight. My place."

"Time?"

"Seven."

"I'll be there."

"Mmm, maybe dessert first." She snickered.

The door swung open revealing the man. "Sounds like an excellent plan."

The blonde turned. Her silly grin vanished. "Oh." She looked back at the doctor. "Your next appointment or are they here to arrest you?"

Dr. Carter gritted his teeth. "No. Neither. Ms. Culbertson, I'll see you at your next appointment." He gripped the woman's elbow and guided her out of the office.

"Hey." The blonde frowned and refused to be frog-marched out of the house. "Ms. Culbertson? Really? Aren't you going to introduce me to your handsome friends?"

"Yes, Arnie, introduce us to your patient." McClung smirked.

The blonde snorted. She jerked her elbow free from the good doctor and then extended her slender hand. "I'm Shelby Culbertson."

As McClung cordially shook her hand, he wondered how her thin finger could support such a large diamond ring. "I'm Chief McClung and this is Sergeant Thayer."

"My pleasure." Shelby purred. She glanced over her shoulder at Dr. Carter. "See you tonight, baby." Then she sashayed out the front door.

"You've a little red right here." McClung tapped the side of his head.

Carter rubbed his left temple removing the red stain Shelby had overlooked.

"Is she your patient? The *emergency*?" McClung rubbed his earlobe.

Dr. Carter's Adam's apple bobbed a few times as he ran his hands over his jet-black hair and smoothed out his wrinkled shirt and trousers.

"Yes. I mean no. She used to be." He snapped.

McClung arched his eyebrow as he looked at Thayer and then back to Carter. "I see. Well, okay. Let me get to the point since you're apparently in great demand."

Carter pursed his lips and narrowed his eyes.

"We need to ask you a few questions about Myron Wagstaff." McClung walked toward Carter. "Shall we talk in your office?"

Carter glanced into his office and then stepped aside for them to enter.

45

He motioned for them to take a seat. "How long have you two been waiting?" Carter sat behind a contemporary wooden desk.

"Long enough." Thayer replied as he made himself comfortable in one of the two leather-tufted club chairs in front of Carter's desk.

He tented his fingers in front of his mouth and stared at McClung and Thayer.

McClung was curious why Carter didn't ask why they wanted to speak with him about Wagstaff. That's usually the first question an interviewee asks. Interesting.

"What were you doing at Myron Wagstaff's house this morning?"

Carter shrugged and opened his hands. "I don't know what you're talking about."

McClung sighed and thought, so we're going this route.

"Don't make matters worse. You were seen fleeing from Wagstaff's backyard and then driving off in that black Cadillac parked outside." McClung tipped his head backward.

Carter scoffed. "This morning." His index finger punctuated the air.

"Yes, this very morning." McClung slid forward in his chair. "Now, I need you to think very carefully before you answer. We have an extremely reliable eyewitness. Besides, I can arrest you for not reporting it. But we might be able to work things out if you tell us everything."

Carter's eyes widened. "I see. Your wife. I'd hoped the flash of a figure was just a figment of my imagination."

He slid back into his chair and waved his hand. "Everyone in the subdivision knows the infamous Marian Selby, excuse me, Marian

McClung. Yep. She's one of the few people to go against Myron and win."

"Your point?" McClung snarled.

Carter puffed out his cheeks, then exhaled noisily. He pulled on his chin hairs as he studied McClung and Thayer.

"Fine. You've probably figured it out after seeing Shelby."

He coughed. "Wagstaff was blackmailing me. The guy's a blood-thirsty leech. I couldn't take it anymore."

Carter's body relaxed like a wilted flower. "It feels good to get that off my chest."

"You killed him." Thayer said dryly.

Carter found his backbone and sat straight. "God, no! When I saw him at the bottom of the pool, I hightailed it out of there. Didn't want anyone accusing me of putting him there and that's exactly what's happening. I swear I didn't do it."

McClung, for some odd reason, believed him but he wasn't going to let Carter know. "Is that a fact? If you didn't kill him, why didn't you call for help?"

Carter's eyes shifted between Thayer and McClung. "Honestly?"

McClung grunted. "That would be preferable."

"I was only thinking of saving my hide, not Myron's." Carter continued to pull on his beard.

"So, Myron was blackmailing you because of your affair with Ms. Culbertson?"

Thayer grunted. "Sounds like reason enough to kill him."

"I said I did not kill him." Carter blinked a few times, took a deep breath and then cleared his throat. "Well, you see." His gaze dropped to the items on his desk. "You see, I uh, well."

Carter squirmed in his well-padded chair. "Can I get you something to drink?" he asked as he stood up.

"Nope. But it looks like you could use one. You're a little pale." McClung stood with Carter and accompanied him to a side table.

Thayer jumped up and blocked the office door just in case the good doctor decided to make a run for it.

Carter opened a cabinet, took out a bottle of sherry, El Candado. The bottle had a miniature gold padlock on the cap.

"That must be some good stuff." McClung flicked the lock.

"You're sure you don't want a glass?" Carter pulled a tiny key from his front pants pocket.

McClung shook his head. "I'm at work but it's tempting."

Carter poured a small amount of the deep caramel-colored sherry into a cordial glass. He held the glass toward McClung. "You can at least enjoy the nose."

McClung inhaled. "Hmm, sweet. Raisins. Figs. Honey and a hint of cinnamon. Nice."

Carter took a small sip. "The best. I'll get a bottle for you."

"No, but thank you." McClung waved away the offer and backed up a few steps. "Let's get back to business."

The good doctor downed the sherry and poured another glass.

"Myron found out that all my patients are women and he put two and two together." Carter sipped the sherry. "You saw Shelby. How can any man resist?"

"You're sleeping with your patients." McClung scratched his forehead above his right eyebrow.

Carter nodded. "I love women." He shrugged. "It was the downfall of my marriage."

"Sounds like you need therapy." Thayer stated.

McClung stifled a laugh.

The good doctor sneered at Thayer. "For the life of me, I don't know how Myron found out."

"His stepsister was one of your patients."

Carter blanched. "What? Who?"

"Huh, I'm surprised she didn't tell you. Sheila Gerber." McClung trailed behind Carter as he returned to his desk.

"Sheila is his half-sister? Why didn't she tell me? She came to me after her husband died." Carter's tongue ran around the back of his teeth.

"Stepsister. Not half." McClung corrected him.

Thayer sat next to McClung. "If I were her, I'd be embarrassed for anyone to know."

"Thayer." McClung warned.

"Sorry, Boss, but we're all thinking it."

Carter found his voice. "How did you know she was a patient of mine? Did she tell Myron?"

"There's a blurb in the newspaper about you two at a fundraiser with pictures." McClung shrugged. "Sheila may not have told Myron anything."

He wiggled his thumb between himself and Thayer. "We figured it out."

"Pfft. You set yourself up for blackmail. Taking them to public events and getting your picture taken." Thayer said flatly.

Carter stroked his beard as he nodded slightly and stared at the space between Thayer and McClung.

"You realize what you're doing is unethical."

Arnold Carter wobbled his open hand. "Well, that depends."

McClung grunted and leaned forward. "Yeah. On what? Whether it was consensual? You're treading on dangerous ground preying on vulnerable women."

Carter's tongue darted in-between his dry lips, making them glisten. "Now wait a minute. You've got this all wrong."

"Yeah, well enlighten me." McClung spat out his words. Realizing his temper was getting out of control, he relaxed in the chair and took a deep breath to calm his flaring nostrils.

Beads of sweat dotted Carter's forehead. "You see. I counsel them until they feel they don't need me. Uh, how do I say this with sounding arrogant?"

McClung dreaded what the good doctor would say next. He snapped. "Just say it."

Carter flinched. "Well, all right. I'm extremely good at my profession. You see, a few of the women that sought my counsel only need someone to listen to them. No mental issues. A little reassurance was what they required. If you know what I mean."

McClung rolled his eyes. "Are you kidding me? None of that explains why it's not unethical. Having an affair with them is not the way to reassure them."

"You didn't let me finish." Carter held up a hand to stop McClung's tirade. "Just let me finish."

McClung threw up his hands, then crossed his arms. "Fine. Go on."

"I don't have affairs with all of them."

Thayer snorted. "Just the attractive ones?"

Carter glared at the young sergeant, opened his mouth but decided not to react to Thayer's snide remark.

"I usually see them, professionally, for a few months. Of course, there are others that need intense therapy. But let me stress this. I do not have affairs with every patient. I want to make that perfectly clear. Got it?"

McClung and Thayer didn't respond.

"Look. The ones I had affairs with didn't need me. They wanted someone to make them feel good about themselves after their husband abandoned them for younger women. I only saw them as a patient a few times, a month or two at most." Carter said in one short breath.

Still no response from McClung and Thayer.

Carter stood.

McClung and Thayer grabbed the arms of their chairs.

Carter rolled his head on his shoulder. "For Pete's sake, I'm not making a run for it. Just more sherry."

Thayer hopped up and stood in front of the door.

"Sheesh." Carter filled the empty glass. "At ease, Sergeant." He then returned to his desk.

The good doctor continued with his explanation. "As far as Sheila Gerber goes, I saw her for maybe three weeks. Then she and I attended a fundraiser for the hospital where she works. She invited me."

"So, no affair with her?"

"No. I ran into her at lunch a couple of times but purely by accident. I swear. Well, maybe a dinner or two. Nothing sexual. I can attest to that."

"Okay. The blackmail. When did it start?" McClung removed a notepad from his jacket.

"You're not going to arrest me, are you?"

"Depends how detailed you are." McClung stared at Carter. "It's a fine line you're walking with your patients. But I understand why you paid the blackmail. Scandal. Bad for business even if things are above board."

Carter nodded. "All right." He paused. "Come to think of it, it was around the time that guy was murdered at The Primrose."

"November? Before or after you last saw Sheila Gerber?" McClung poised his pen over the pad.

"Yes. November. After I last saw Sheila Gerber."

"Before Shelby Culbertson became a patient."

"After."

"Any affairs with patients before Sheila Gerber or after, besides Ms. Culbertson?"

Carter sipped the sherry. "What difference does it make? Wagstaff was blackmailing me, not my patients. I'm not going to give their names to you. That's treading on patient-doctor privileged information."

McClung nodded. "How much money did you pay Wagstaff?"

"In the whole scheme of things, I guess it wasn't that much. Just a thousand dollars a month, but he called me yesterday demanding more. That's why I went to see him this morning."

"So roughly seven thousand dollars."

Carter bobbed his head. He lifted the tiny glass to drink. "The creep wants, correction, *wanted* twice that much."

McClung studied Arnold Carter as he sipped the fine sherry, then looked around the office. Everything was high-end, including the sherry. "Did Myron say why he wanted more?"

The doctor shrugged. "All he said was pay up or suffer the consequences. Then hung up."

"You know I have to question Ms. Culbertson and Sheila concerning this affair thing. Anyone else you can think of that may have a motive to kill Myron?"

Carter moaned. "I understand." His face paled. "Do you think one of my patients did it?"

McClung stood. "Everyone is a potential suspect."

"That's it?" Carter grinned.

"No. I'll need you to come into the station for further questions and make an official statement. Clear your calendar for the rest of the day. You're coming with us."

"I don't think I can drive." Carter grinned and tossed back the sherry.

McClung looked at Thayer.

Thayer smiled.

"What's so amusing?" Carter asked.

Thayer removed the glass from Carter's hand, then grabbed his elbow and shoved him toward the door. "We don't mind playing chauffeur."

"Am I under arrest?"

"Do you want to be?" Thayer released him and pulled his handcuffs from his belt.

"No need for handcuffs, Thayer. Carter, all we want is your written statement after you've had a few cups of strong coffee and sobered up. But you need to make it at the station. Now. What do you say?" McClung blocked the doorway.

"Fine." Carter trudged forward.

The front door opened.

A brown-headed woman froze. "Dr. Carter?"

"Everything is okay, Robyn. I have to go with these nice gentlemen to the police station."

McClung stepped toward the doe-eyed girl. "I'm Chief McClung. And you?"

The young woman dropped a bucket filled with cleaning supplies, then rubbed her hands down the sides of her jeans. She pulled a card from the breast pocket of her dark blue bib apron and handed it to McClung.

"I'm Robyn Konopka. I clean Dr. Carter's office." She cast her eyes on her beat-up sneakers.

McClung glanced at the card then gave it to Thayer.

"Yes, she does." Carter confirmed. "But you're a little early Robyn."

Her head popped up. "Oh, I'm so sorry. Really. I am. I've got to take my grandmother to her heart doctor, then pick up her medicines. This was the only time I had. I don't like being out when it's dark."

Dr. Carter waved away her apology. "Perfectly fine. Just lock up after you leave. I shouldn't be gone long."

She scurried aside to let the men pass. "Is it about Mr. Wagstaff?"

"What?" The three men chimed.

McClung stepped toward Robyn. "Why did you ask Carter that?"

The young woman pressed herself against the tan-colored wall. "The whole town is talking about him murdered or drowning. Oh, I don't know exactly. I get confused." She squeezed her eyes closed and held her breath.

"Relax, no one is going to hurt you." McClung softened his tone.

Robyn exhaled and cracked opened her eyelids. Seeing his smiling face, she opened them completely.

"Who's talking? What did they say?"

She shrugged and murmured. "I heard people talking about it at the Darlington Diner. I don't know who started it. Everyone had their own theory. I just listened that's all."

McClung made a mental reminder to stop by and have a chat with Peggy and Frank Darlington, the owners of the local diner. "Thank you for that information. We'll be on our way."

Robyn shut the door behind them and locked it, then picked up her bucket of supplies. Dancing down the hallway, she whistled, *It's Money That I Love* by Randy Newman.

Chapter 6

Charlie washed the last dish and gingerly placed it to dry with the mound of china in the dishwasher. He smiled as he listened to Marian and Joan laugh. It was good Marian had friends here to help her forget the day's events.

Jack and Joan were their best friends in the world. And Marian was stellar at playing matchmaker and she was right about Jack and Joan being perfect for each other. He wouldn't be surprised if Jack and Joan weren't married before year's end.

In the past year, the four of them had become quite a team and had gone through more drama than most people experience in a lifetime. Marian was attacked twice with Charlie coming to her rescue. And Charlie was attacked twice with Marian recusing him. Jack's wife divorced him. Joan was accused of murdering her first ex-husband. Now Jack and Joan were an item.

Jack nudged Charlie on the shoulder. "What are those two conspiring about in there?" He tilted his head toward the living room.

Charlie took a dishtowel away from Jack's chapped hands. "Who knows?" He opened the cabinet under the sink. "Here put this on your hands. Don't go rubbing those scaly claws on Joan. A sure-fire turnoff."

Jack took the bottle of Jergens hand lotion, opened the cap and sniffed. "Not too girly." He rubbed a generous glob on his hands and forearms.

Charlie picked up the lemon poppy seed cake Marian made earlier in the day. "Grab that tray and follow me. I'll come back for the coffee."

Jack picked up an oval-shaped, silver tray laden with cups, saucers, plates, silverware, linen napkins, everything needed for the coffee.

"Tada." Charlie set the intricately cut crystal cake stand on the coffee table.

Joan sat with her bare legs tucked up on the sofa, her tiny shoes on the floor, and her arm stretched across the back cushion. The modest knee-length floral sundress she wore, and her true blonde hair made a striking contrast against the brilliant red loveseat. She leaned forward to get a better look at the dessert. "Oh, Marian, the cake looks amazing."

The Bundt cake had a simple, luscious lemon glaze. Candied bachelor buttons and marigolds encircled the base of the cake.

Marian beamed. "Thanks. The flowers are edible, but I've never eaten one." She wrinkled her nose.

Charlie poured out the coffee as Marian sliced generous pieces of cake.

Jack snuggled next to Joan.

Marian and Charlie grinned at each other, pleased to see Joan and Jack such a happy couple.

58

"Marian, you have surpassed yourself. Who knew soup and cornbread could be a gastronome delight? That swirly design in the soup and unbelievable salad. The cornbread. It's the best I've ever eaten." Jack held up his chunk of cake. "And this." He broke off a piece, and slid it into his mouth.

Marian laughed. "Thank you. But I can't take credit for the salad dressing. It's Joan's recipe. And as far as the cornbread, it's onions and…" She looked at Charlie. "Should I tell him?"

He nodded with a sly grin.

"Cracklings."

Jack dotted the air with his fork. "I've heard of them and thought they were gross, but now I'm a big fan of cracklings."

Charlie patted Marian's knee and kissed her temple.

Joan sipped coffee from a Royal Doulton Rossetti cup. "Marian, I have to compliment your presentation. My mother had fine china, linens, candelabras, and such that she saved for special occasions. I think I saw her use them once. I always thought what a waste."

"My mom was the opposite. Almost every day was a special occasion. Not that we ate off the best china every day, but she'd have candles or flowers, something to make it unique."

Charlie glanced at his watch. "Okay, ladies, it's getting late and Jack and I need to discuss Myron's autopsy. I don't think I need to ask if you want to stay." He draped his arm across Marian's shoulders then squeezed her tight.

"Staying." Marian looked at Joan. "Is that okay?"

Joan set down her empty cup. "I'm game. Besides, I want to know more about your work." She playfully punched Jack's bicep.

"Before we talk about the autopsy, can I tell you what I saw?" Marian bit her bottom lip.

Charlie knew Marian wanted to get it off her chest. And he also knew it wouldn't be a short story. But he'd get details that may be important. "Sure. It's probably best to let our food settle before we get to the gory details.

Marian held the coffee cup with both hands, then nestled against her husband.

"Get comfortable. This could take a while." Charlie pointed at Joan and Jack then he rested his chin on top of his wife's head.

Marian rolled her eyes.

"I was walking up the steepest hill in the subdivision."

Joan interrupted. "Myron's street or the clubhouse?"

"Myron's, but now that I think about it, the clubhouse street is steeper. Don't you think?"

"Yes, I think so." Joan gasped. "Oh, have you seen the new loungers and umbrellas at the pool?"

"Yeah. Those have to be the widest umbrellas I've ever seen. And the lounger cushions have to be at least this thick." Marian held her hands six inches apart.

"I know. Beautiful colors, too."

"Un-huh." Marian paused. "Where was I?"

Charlie kissed the top of her head. "You were walking up the hill."

"Oh, yeah. As I was walking up the hill, my mind was far away thinking about our first year together."

She stopped and looked at Charlie. Kissing his cheek, she whispered, "Thanks."

"For what?"

"Everything." Marian grinned and resumed her position.

"My legs felt like they were about to give out. I was huffing and sweating like crazy. I thought about my forty-eighth birthday coming up. I pushed on as I thought about what Dr. Vanderbloom told me at my last visit."

Marian took a sip of coffee then in a mimicking voice said, "Remember, Marian, you're not a spring chicken anymore."

"Dr. Kimberly Vanderbloom?" Joan frowned.

Marian nodded.

"Tut. She needs to work on her bedside manner."

"Exactly. Anyway, I stopped to catch my breath at the top of the hill under that huge Bradford pear tree on the corner. That's when I noticed water streaming down the road. Lots of it."

Charlie held her at arm's length. "That's when you noticed it. Marian, I'm disappointed in you. The water ran past our street." He clicked his tongue.

"I had a lot on my mind." Marian flopped back onto his wide chest.

Charlie grunted.

"As I was saying, I followed the stream and realized it was coming from Myron's house.

She sighed. "I didn't want to knock on his door to tell him he was violating one of the covenants."

Marian leaned forward and set her cup on the coffee table. "That's when I saw the bearded man running from Myron's house."

Charlie interjected. "Who we now know is Dr. Arnold Carter."

Joan shook her head. "He thinks he's God's gift to women."

"You know him?" Charlie asked.

"Yeah. We'll talk later. I want to hear Marian's story."

"Thank you." Marian cracked her knuckles. "I see this guy, Carter, running from Myron's backyard. I squatted beside the overgrown hydrangea bush at the edge of the neighbor's yard. The guy jumped into a long black car parked in Myron's driveway. The car shoots backward. The bumper scraped the asphalt, and the tires squealed. I could smell burnt rubber. Then the car flies right past me."

Joan rubbed her forearms. "Oh. Gives me goosebumps."

"A piece of gravel bounced against the curb. I grabbed it and scratched the tag number on the sidewalk."

"I wouldn't have remembered to do that." Joan looked at Jack. "Would you?"

Jack shook his head. "I don't know."

Marian jerked. "Charlie, I believe someone else saw what happened."

"Why do you say that?" Charlie's eyebrows crunched together.

"Because I looked around at the other houses. The curtains from an upstairs window from the house across from Myron's moved liked someone snatched them closed."

"Hm." Charlie looked at his watch. It was too late to send someone now. He'd have an officer look into it after the morning war room meeting. "Do you remember if there was a car in the driveway?"

"No, there wasn't. I thought about going over there myself, but I didn't think you'd be too keen about it. Besides, I really wanted to see what had happened in Myron's backyard. You know. What made that man run for his life?"

"I looked around for a heavy stick or something to use for a weapon. All I had was the piece of gravel." Marian made a fist.

"Hey, better than nothing I suppose. Look at David. He killed Goliath with a stone." Jack reached for the coffee carafe. "Anyone else want another cup?"

Marian continued as Jack poured everyone a cup.

"I walked through Myron's front yard. The grass was soaked, that's why my shoes got all muddy. The back gate was wide open. I peeked around the fence and called out for Myron."

Marian took a gulp of coffee. "I heard running water and the hum of the pool pump. And I noticed the patio furniture shoved together, one chair turned on its side."

"Not a good sign." Joan shuttered.

"Right. I called out to Myron, again. I saw a garden hose lying next to the pool. Water gushing everywhere. I went to the spigot and shut it off."

Charlie shifted and groaned.

"Okay. I promise I'm almost finished. The sliding glass door stood halfway open." Marian shrugged. "So, I poked my head inside and yelled for Myron. Nothing. Not a sound. I thought about exploring his home but if he caught me, there'd be hell to pay."

"That's when you called 9-1-1?"

She gawked at Charlie as if he'd lost his mind. "No. I didn't know he was dead or even around. Besides, I didn't want Myron to catch me in his house. I decided to go home and call you."

"This is the really creepy part. When I turned around to leave, a big, black crow strutted at the edge of the pool. It stopped and stared into the water. The crow tilted its head side to side. Then it looked at a stand of pine trees."

Joan pressed against Jack.

He held her tighter.

"Four crows were perched on alternating limbs on two trees. The big crow on the ground opened its beak and cawed. Then it focused on the water for a few seconds, flapped its wings, and soared toward the four crows. It banked and flew over Myron's house. In secession, each of the crows followed the path of the big, black one." Marian rubbed her forearms.

Charlie felt his wife tremble. A lap blanket lay next to him. He wrapped it around her bare shoulders.

"Thanks." She smiled at her husband. "I wondered what it was looking at. I walked to the spot where the crow had stood."

Marian's hair on the back of her neck prickled as it did earlier that day. "There was something in the shallow end."

"Myron." Joan whispered.

Marian nodded. "I jumped into the pool, took a deep breath, ducked my head under the water and kneeled to pull him out of the water."

Joan's mouth fell open. "I would've run away screaming."

"He was dead weight. Extraordinarily heavy. I remember thinking Dr. Vanderbloom was right." Marian hunched her shoulders.

"I struggled to get him to the edge of the pool and the whole time I screamed for help. I managed to get half of his body out of the water."

Marian was silent. She held the blanket over her mouth.

Charlie squeezed her. "It's okay, sweetie. Take your time."

She inhaled and exhaled slowly.

"I shook his shoulders and yelled at him. *Myron, answer me. Do you hear me? Myron!* No response. Not even a groan when I slapped his cheek."

Marian wiped her eyes.

"I knew I had to get him completely out of the water and start CPR. I ducked under the water, shoved… my head between his legs, planted my feet on the bottom of the pool, and then stood up, pushing Myron's body out of the water onto the concrete."

Marian rubbed her lower back remembering how the muscles spasmed.

"I jumped out of the pool, tugged Myron on his side and slapped his back as hard as I could, hoping to clear any water from his mouth and lungs."

She grimaced.

"A fair amount came out. I pushed him onto his back, pinched his nose, closed my eyes, and pictured Charlie." Marian swallowed hard.

"I put my left hand on his chest to feel for the rise and fall of air making its way into his lungs. There wasn't any. I did chest compression, more breaths. I kept going until I got dizzy and exhausted."

Marian sighed.

"I yelled for help and shook him as hard as I could."

She dropped the blanket and held out her hands as if she were holding Myron's shoulders. "Come on. Wake up!"

Marian gazed at the coffee table.

"I looked at Myron's eyes. They were half-opened. I pressed my fingers on his neck and his wrist. No pulse. His skin was cold."

Marian leaned her head onto Charlie's shoulder. "I decided to give up and call 9-1-1. I remember standing over Myron's lifeless body and wondered if anyone would grieve for him."

Tears leaked from the corners of Marian's eyes. "Myron and I didn't like each other, but still."

Charlie pressed a tissue into Marian's clenched hand.

"Thank you." She blotted the corners of her eyes. "I kept thinking that somebody must have loved him, at least at one point in his life. I mean—"

Marian pressed the tissue to her nose then rested her hand on her flat belly. "You know. He used to be somebody's little boy. Somebody's baby."

Chapter 7

Chief Charlie McClung marched into the war room with Jack close on his heels. They had finished reviewing the autopsy report and were anxious to share the results with the team.

"Good morning, men. Most of you know Jack Jackson, associate medical examiner for the Georgia Bureau of Investigation."

Jack nodded and then distributed manila folders to the officers sitting at the long conference tables.

Thayer rearranged the crime scene photos on the eight-foot whiteboard in front of the room.

"We now know that Myron Herbert Wagstaff was murdered."

McClung wrote the word, Suspects, on the board then underlined it. "Wagstaff may have been murdered because of a blackmailing scheme."

He wrote, Dr. Arnold Carter under Suspects.

"Carter was seen running from the victim's backyard. Plus, he admitted to being blackmailed by Wagstaff. Myron tried to squeeze more money out of him. The good doctor claims he went to Wagstaff's house that morning to reason with him and that's when he found Myron.

In the pool. Dead. He guesses he was at Myron's house for two minutes, max."

McClung wrote, Shelby Culbertson below Carter's name.

"Ms. Culbertson is having an affair with the good doctor. We don't know if she's one of Myron's victims. Perhaps, she has secrets that she wants kept hidden. And there's the possibility of more people who may have been blackmailed."

Officer Marsh raised his hand. "Why are you certain it's murder?"

McClung pointed toward Jack.

"Open your folders. You'll find the autopsy report for Myron Herbert Wagstaff." Jack gave the officers a few seconds to flip through the file.

Jack cleared his throat. "As you can see from the first photo, there is visible bruising to both arms and in the second photo you'll see bruising on both sides of his body. Third photo, bruises on his chest and left shoulder."

McClung posted the photos on the whiteboard. "We believe someone sat on his chest, pinned down his arms with their knees, then pressed down on his left shoulder."

The men studied the enlarged photos.

"Myron also has bruises on his lips and abrasions on his tongue, the roof of his mouth, and in his throat. I also discovered several chipped teeth, as well as a contusion on the back of his head."

Jack handed five photos to McClung.

"This chip was found next near his body." Jack exhibited the last photo and pointed toward McClung. "Your intuition was correct. It's a chip from his tooth and these spots on the concrete are blood. The water washed it out, like the blood on Myron's clothes. His shirt lit up when I did the luminol test."

Officer Willard grunted. "Must've been a big guy to punch Wagstaff in the mouth hard enough to break his teeth."

Jack shook his head. "No. That's not what we think."

Officer Vincent Beckman smirked. "But it's obvious. Some guy punched him in the mouth. Wagstaff fell. Banged his head on the concrete, then the perp, let's say Carter, sat on him and popped Wagstaff in the mouth several times, then took off. Wagstaff's dazed and confused, stumbles, and falls into the pool and drowns."

Jack chuckled and wagged his long skinny finger. "McClung, should I tell them, or do you want to?"

"No, you're doing a fine job." McClung crossed his arms, anticipating his men's reactions.

Jack looked at Officer Beckman. "You got two things correct. Myron Wagstaff did fall, and he did drown. But he didn't drown in the swimming pool."

A rumble filled the room.

McClung enjoyed their looks of disbelief. He wanted his men to always think outside the box. And this case was a good one to get their little gray cells pumping.

"Ah, come on. How do you drown without water?" Officer Beckman mocked.

"A garden hose."

Beckman considered the hose theory. His eyes widened, then he snorted. "Ah, now, I see."

McClung rubbed his earlobe. "Explain it, Beckman."

"Myron was first punched in the mouth which broke his front teeth. He fell. The suspect sat on his chest and forced the hose down his throat. Which resulted in the bruised lips, the injuries in his mouth and throat." Officer Beckman grinned.

McClung paced in front of the room. "Sounds about right. We think the perpetrator rolled Myron into the pool, so we'd assume he'd fallen into the pool and drowned."

Officer Beckman held up his hand.

"Yes, Beckman." McClung stopped in front of him.

"So how do you know for sure Myron wasn't dead when he was rolled into the pool? Why are you convinced it was water from the hose that killed him?"

"Excellent question." Jack smiled. "Excellent question, indeed. Because I tested the water in his lungs and stomach. The chlorine levels were that of drinking water, not the levels you'd find in a swimming pool. And before you ask, I compared the water from Myron's pool to the water from his garden hose."

Beckman tipped his head side to side. "Okay, then. So, does Arnold Carter have busted knuckles?"

"No, but—." McClung pointed to Jack.

Jack added to his answer. "We're not certain Myron was clobbered by someone."

He indicated the picture of the patio furniture in disarray. "Myron may have tripped or been shoved."

Jack pointed to the garden hose. "Or got tangled in the hose. Then he fell and hit his head. Slamming the metal part of the hose with enough force against his mouth could have broken his teeth and bruised his lips."

Officer Beckman nodded. "How long had he been dead?"

"Since Myron was in the pool it's hard to use body temperature to determine the time of death."

McClung tapped the picture of the yardstick shoved into the mud. "According to the county extension office calculations of the water pressure, the length of the hose, and its diameter, the water was probably running for about fifteen minutes."

"So, if the good doctor is telling the truth about the time he arrived, then he's not the killer." Thayer interjected.

"That's correct. But I'm not taking him off the suspect list. Not yet." McClung bounced the dry erase marker on the palm of his hand as he remembered something. "I think we can add Myron's stepsister to the list."

He printed Sheila Gerber under Shelby Culbertson's name.

Thayer cleared his throat. "Why's that, boss?"

"Remember when we told her that Myron was dead, she said something like, '*now I can get my rightful inheritance*'?"

"Yeah. How did she know she'd get his money? Why not his kids?" Thayer tapped the board. "Maybe we should add his ex-wife's name?"

McClung pursed his lips. "Can't hurt." He wrote, Janie Dawson.

He searched the room and found who he was looking for, Jenny and Stewie.

"What have you two uncovered?" McClung asked his brilliant administrators.

Jenny glanced at Stewie.

"Go ahead."

Stewie picked up a stack of files and passed them out.

Jenny beamed as she rubbed her hands together. "Lots of stuff. We got warrants first thing this morning and boy we've been busy digging into Wagstaff's financials. We're still waiting for the phone records."

McClung grinned. "Go on, Jenny."

"Well, Myron didn't have a job. He had a savings, checking, and brokerage accounts. All of them quite substantial. He makes large monthly deposits. Cash. All under ten thousand dollars."

McClung pointed at Arnold Carter's name. "We're positive he was being blackmailed. Any of these people could have been victims. Who knows how many more we'll find?"

"That would explain the cash deposits." Jenny tapped her pen against her jaw. "I'd love to get a peek at his will."

"Oh, believe me, that's going to happen." McClung rested his fists on his belt as he stared at the board. "Okay, let's see where we are."

He jabbed another picture. "The only prints found on the tumbler and the whiskey bottle in Myron's kitchen belonged to him."

"Boss, I notice in one picture that the newspaper is leaning on the front door. Why wasn't it on his driveway or in the yard?" Officer Glen Henry spoke for the first time.

"Ah, good point, Henry." McClung pointed to another picture of a small landscaping advertisement stake near the mailbox. "Officer

Henry, track down the newspaper delivery person, the landscaper, and interview them."

Henry shot up his thumb.

Officer Beckman coughed. "What about me, Boss?"

"You go with Henry." McClung snapped his fingers. "Marian saw the curtains move from the house across the street. I want you and Henry to go over there and question everyone on that street."

"You got it, Boss."

"Marsh and Willard. I want you to get over to Wagstaff's house. Go through everything. There's got to be records of the blackmail somewhere. If you need help, let me know."

The two officers responded. "Sure thing, Boss."

"Thayer, you and I will question Sheila Gerber, Janie Dawson, Shelby Culbertson, and the Darlingtons."

McClung scanned the board. "Stewie, Jenny, get Sheila's timecards and find out if Janie's teaching summer school."

"That'll be easy to discover. Just a call to the school." Stewie scribbled on a legal pad.

"Let's hope she is. I'd rather not question her at home with her children there."

He examined the board again. "I think we've got it covered for now. You all have the autopsy report and the financials. Study them."

McClung stared at his officers. "I want detailed reports on my desk in the morning. If you uncover something that can't wait, call me."

"Stewie. Jenny. Keep digging into Wagstaff's background. Assemble dossiers on these folks too." He pointed to the names on the board.

"You all understand your assigned duties?"

Everyone responded. "Got it, Boss."

McClung extended his hand toward Jack Jackson. "Excellent work."

Jack pumped his hand. "Thank you, Boss." He smothered his laugh with his other hand, the lines at the corner of his eyes deepened.

"Boss, my eye. Get out of here." McClung laughed.

The officers filed out of the war room.

McClung stopped Stewie and Jenny. "Do you know a girl named Robyn Konopka?

"Nope." Jenny shook her head.

"Why do you ask?" Stewie scratched his bony elbow.

"Thayer and I ran into her at Carter's office yesterday. I got a strange feeling from the girl. She said she was at the Darlington Diner when she heard about Myron's murder. *Before* we knew he was murdered." McClung squeezed the back of his neck.

Jenny smooched up her lips. "Could just be gossip running wild."

"Yeah. It could be nothing at all. But still, if you have time, dig into her background."

Stewie gave him a two-finger salute. "Consider it done."

Chapter 8

Marian was dead-heading marigolds in the front yard.

A truck rumbled down the street and stopped.

She turned around to see who had parked near her house. Recognizing the lawn maintenance truck, she stood and walked toward the street.

A tall, sturdy man hopped out of the cab and stretched to his full height of six-foot-two. His wild sandy-colored hair waved in the summer breeze.

Marian waved. "Hey, Brian."

The man smiled, making the lines on his tanned face deeper. "Hello, Marian." He strolled toward her. "When did Joan move over here? Did she sell her house?"

"She decided to move after all that stuff happened before Thanksgiving. When the Paper Heart Stalker was terrorizing me." Without thinking, Marian pressed her hand on her stomach.

She had saved Charlie from the Paper Heart Stalker but falling from Joan's second-floor landing resulted in Marian losing the baby she didn't know she was carrying.

Brian frowned. "I was sorry to hear about all that mess. Really sorry for you, ma'am."

Marian jerked her hand away from her belly and massaged the palm of her right hand with her left thumb.

"Thank you." She murmured then faked a smile. "It'll be nice to have her across the street. I can spend more time with Trudy."

"Trudy?" Brian's weather-beaten face crunched together. "She's got a kid?"

"No. Trudy's a sweet little Siamese kitty that someone left on The Primrose's backdoor steps."

Brian grunted. "Well, as much as I'd like to chat with you all day, I don't get paid to do that. Gotta get this estimate done and a few more yards treated. Then my day's done." He bounced a well-used clipboard on his thick thigh. "See you around."

"Hey, did you hear what happened to Myron Wagstaff yesterday?"

"I did. Can't say I shed a tear for the ornery fellow." Brian scratched the back of his head. "I know that sounds bad, but I gotta speak the truth."

Marian chewed on her bottom lip. "Yeah, I get what you're saying. Myron and I weren't exactly what you'd call friends."

"That man was plain mean. I can't think of one good thing to say about him. He had…" Brian clamped his rough hand over his mouth as he shook his head. "I'm sorry. I need to get to work."

A sadness, a kind of hopelessness took hold of Brian as he walked with his head down and shoulders slacked.

Last May, right before she'd met Charlie, Brian Lane had knocked on her front door and introduced himself as her new lawn guy. His unruly hair reminded her of a lion's mane and his sad brown eyes didn't mirror the broad smile he wore. Brian wanted to know her preferences for hedge trimming, lawn cutting, and such.

The list was long, so she invited him in for iced tea and banana nut bread. Thirty minutes later, Brian thanked her for cake and tea then left with a manila folder just for her yard. With each of his visits, she learned something new about gardening. She considered Brian a friend and the best yard guy ever.

Marian sat on the front stoop fanning herself with a floppy straw hat as she watched Brian assess Joan's yard.

He walked around the house and then disappeared through the back gate.

Marian went inside her house, grabbed a bottle of water from the refrigerator, then boxed a few oatmeal raisins cookies for her favorite yard guy.

Marian walked out the front door and waited for Brian to reappear. She sat on a small curved stone bench under the shade of the Chinese Elm growing near the sidewalk.

Brian appeared on the other side of Joan Delaney's new home.

Marian rattled the white box over her head. "Hey, Brian! I have oatmeal raisin cookies for you." She called out in a sing-song voice.

He strolled across the street. "When I hear cookies, I'm like a sailor lured by a mermaid's melodious song."

A deep ragged laugh erupted from his barreled chest as Marian opened the box and waved it under his chin.

She patted the bench beside herself. "Please sit for a second and enjoy a cookie. Here's a bottle of water for you."

"I'm kinda smelly." He pulled a crumpled blue bandana from his back pocket and ran it over his face and the back of his neck.

Marian snorted. "I'm not exactly fresh as a daisy, myself."

Brian's knees popped as he eased down. Taking the water, he poured a small amount in one palm, then rubbed his hands together.

"There. That should be good enough." He selected a cookie, broke it in half and took a bite. "Mm-mm. Marian, you are definitely the queen of baked goods."

Brian winked at her.

Marian grinned as she dropped her head. From the corner of her eye, she watched Brian enjoy the rest of the cookie.

"Have you heard any rumors about Myron?"

Brian brushed the crumbs from his hands and lap. "People are saying things."

He sighed and crossed his arms. "All small towns are the same. There's the good guys and the bad guys. When a good guy dies, the whole town grieves, but when the bad ones die." He chuckled softly. "It's hallelujah and good riddance."

"Huh. I guess you're right." Marian straightened her spine. "So, you're from a small town?"

Brian bobbed his head. "Yes, ma'am. I've lived in a lot of small towns." He scratched the palm of his left hand. "I can't seem to settle down. Always searching."

"For what?"

He clicked his tongue. "Not sure. Peace maybe?"

"Is it here?" Marian searched his sad eyes.

Brian pursed his lips. "If everyone was like you, yeah."

"But there's bad people, like Myron? People I don't know?"

"In my line of work, I see a lot of things. Hear stuff." Brian pulled on his chin. "No disrespect, but you live a pretty sheltered life."

Marian considered his words. "Yes, I guess you're right but this past year—"

"None of that was your fault, Marian. You were a victim of bad people. People you didn't have any reason to think were wicked. Like the others, Myron's past finally caught up with him."

Marian's forehead creased. "Huh?"

"Evil deeds always catch up with you sooner or later Not you, Marian. Them. You're good people."

Evil deeds? Marian wondered what Brian knew about Myron.

Brian stood. "I need to hit the road. Sitting here eating cookies don't pay the bills, only deposits fat on my belly." He rubbed the slight bulge in his company issued long-sleeve cotton shirt.

Marian reached out. "Wait. Tell me about Myron's evil deeds."

Brian's face hardened, then he turned his head away as if he was looking far down the street.

After a heavy exhale, he looked at Marian with a sad smile. "Marian, I can't answer that question. Let's just say, I've been around all kinds of people. I know a bad seed when I see it."

Marian parted her mouth to say something, but there was a look in Brian's eyes that stopped her or maybe it was her imagination. Either way, she believed him. She knew Myron was deceitful.

"You're a fine lady. You shouldn't be worrying about such things." Brian dipped his head. "Have a good day."

He turned and walked away.

Chapter 9

McClung dreaded speaking with Sheila Gerber. As he and Thayer entered the hospital, he reminded himself that she felt the same way.

A year and a half ago, Sheila's husband celebrated too much after finding a well-paying job and was killed in a car accident. A job he wouldn't have needed if Myron hadn't cheated her out of a substantial inheritance. Since her husband's death, she'd been alone, dealing with her grief and anger.

McClung was responsible for part of her anger. He had questioned her as a murder suspect in the Paper Heart Stalker case since her husband had dated Marian. And now he was about to question Sheila as a suspect in Myron's murder.

Money was always a motive for death.

They walked into the hospital lab. McClung was relieved to see the waiting room empty.

Before McClung pressed the call button, the door leading to the inner sanctum of the lab opened. Sheila stood with her hand resting on the doorknob.

"What do you two want now?"

"Having a good day, are you?" McClung quipped.

Sheila huffed. "I'm going on break. Alone." She marched out of the room and down the hallway.

McClung strolled beside her with Thayer shadowing.

"I said I'm going on break."

She stopped short, her fists on her ample hips. "Why on earth do you want to speak with me? I already identified Myron. What else do you need from me?"

McClung shrugged. "Well, I have a question concerning Myron's will."

"What?" Sheila's eyes bugged out. She shook her head and continued toward the cafeteria.

"You think I killed Myron?"

Her pace quickened as her shoulders hunched up. "You're unbelievable." She hissed.

"Even if I had, it would've been justifiable. He was five years older than me. Myron was my stepbrother, but he was still my big brother. He was supposed to protect me. Instead, he tormented me to the point where my mother feared for my life. I was seven years old. Seven! And my mother hired a nanny to protect me from him."

McClung stepped in front of her.

She glared at him. "If I had wanted to him kill, I would have done it when his father died and he cheated me out of my inheritance."

Sheila sidestepped McClung and darted into the cafeteria.

McClung sidled up to her as she studied the few pastries that remained after the breakfast rush.

"Just answer this question and we'll be on our way."

Sheila pointed to the last caramel pecan-glazed cinnamon roll the size of a cat's head. "I'll have that."

She grumbled. "See what you've done? I overeat when I get upset."

After collecting the pastry, she continued down the line toward the coffee station. "Well, what's your question?"

"How do you know you're in Myron's will?" McClung considered getting a cup of coffee.

"Pfft. Easy. Janie, his ex-wife told me."

McClung paused to fill a medium-sized to-go cup with coffee. "Is that right? How does she know?"

"Technically, Chief McClung, that's two more questions." Sheila snapped a sippy lid on a large cup filled with coffee, light cream, and no sugar. She left McClung behind as she headed to the cashier.

McClung caught up with her. "I've got this." He handed the cashier a ten-dollar bill. "His, too." He pointed to Thayer's enormous cup of soda.

"Thanks, but it doesn't make up for you thinking that I killed my heartless stepbrother." Sheila tapped her toe as she waited.

McClung dropped the change into the tip jar.

"Since you paid for my food, I'll answer your questions." Sheila sat at one of the square four-top tables. "According to Janie, it was part of the divorce settlement. In addition to my inheritance, the kids get a hefty sum in a trust fund and her part isn't too shabby either."

Sheila ate a small chunk of the sweet roll. "Hmm, so good." She slid the small paper plate toward McClung and Thayer. "Have some."

They both waved it away.

She shrugged. "Back to your question. Janie told me that Myron bragged how he'd given me the shaft when his father died. She felt terrible about it. So, she made it part of the divorce decree that he'd leave me my rightful share."

McClung tapped the side of the thick paper cup with his index finger. "I thought they divorced ten years ago. What makes her think he didn't change his will?"

Sheila twisted her mouth as she stared at the plate. A sudden burst of air puffed from her lips. "I know his attorney. The family attorney. My attorney."

McClung waited for Sheila to look at him.

"Are you sure you don't want just a little taste?" She smiled sadly.

McClung shook his head. "So, the attorney-client privilege was stretched a bit."

"Yeah, I suppose you can call it that." Sheila sagged back onto the hard-plastic chair. "He felt bad about what happened. You know, my stepfather leaving everything to Myron."

"Did your attorney put a bug in Janie's ear about securing you a piece of the estate?" McClung studied her dark brown eyes.

Sheila leaned forward and held the warm cup of coffee between her hands. She nodded slowly.

"Yep. He made sure Myron didn't breach the divorce decree."

McClung scratched his cheek. "You know this is a motive for murdering Myron."

"Why?" A nervous laugh escaped Sheila's thin lips. "I mean why wait until now to kill him?"

McClung saw her eyes mist and a single tear trailed down the groove beside her nose. He handed her a tissue.

"Thanks." Sheila patted her face. "If I wanted to kill him, it would've been while my husband Larry was still alive."

Thayer tapped the Formica table with his empty cup. "That seems logical to me."

"Yeah, I agree." McClung pushed away from the table. He didn't want to rehash her husband's death. "I'll need your attorney's name."

"Schnarff, Mowinckel, and Tippler."

Thayer roared. "Are you serious?"

Sheila chuckled. "Yeah. I've gotten used to their names over the years. Davis Tippler handles all my legal stuff."

McClung scribbled down the names. "I'm sure it won't be hard to find them."

"You won't find them in the phonebook, for obvious reasons. I know Davis's number by heart." Sheila reached for McClung's pen and pad. "I'll write it down."

McClung sipped his coffee and wondered how many prank calls the attorneys received every year. "I understand why they're unlisted." He looked at Thayer holding back his laughter. "But how do they get clients?"

Sheila smirked. "They only handle clients with the right bank account, if you know what I mean. But Davis helps me. He's like the older brother I wish I had."

"Huh." McClung bobbed his head. He couldn't wait to learn what Stewie and Jenny unearthed in Myron's financials.

McClung retrieved his notebook and pen, then stood.

"Thanks. If you can think of anything or anyone who might be useful, let me know." He gave her a business card.

Sheila stuck it in her lab coat pocket. "Will do, and thanks again for paying for my snack."

McClung dipped his head and left with Thayer beside him.

As she watched them disappear around the corner, she shook her head. "Pfft! Men. I can live without the lot of them." Sheila gripped the plastic fork in her hand, then stabbed the sweet roll.

♦♦♦♦♦♦

"Hey, Peg ol girl, get out here. McClung and his sidekick just walked in." Frank Darlington yelled to his wife flipping burgers in the kitchen.

"I'll be right there, hun." Peggy hollered.

McClung shook Frank's hand.

Frank and Peggy had owed the diner for so long, no one could remember if there was ever a previous owner.

"Business looks good as usual." He straddled a padded swivel stool at the counter.

Frank trotted behind the counter. "Cup of joe or a diet Dr Pepper?"

McClung beamed. "A large Pepper."

"Got it. No ice, right?"

"Yes, sir."

"I'll take a large Coke, lots of ice." Thayer ordered.

Frank set the to-go cup with a straw next to McClung's fingers drumming on the laminate countertop. "What brings y'all in here today? Lunch or info?"

McClung sucked down a third of the soda as he looked at Thayer.

"Those hamburgers smell awfully good." Thayer sniffed the air.

"Both it is, Frank." McClung answered. "I'll have a cheeseburger, lettuce, and mustard with a side of fries."

"The same for me, except I want my burger fully dressed."

The kitchen door swung open. Peggy Darlington sashayed out with a plate in each hand.

"You boys are a pleasing sight to this old lady's eyes." Peggy winked at McClung and Thayer. "Frank, take these over to Sherry and Wes over yonder next to the side window. I've gotta say hey to these two."

McClung rose and returned Peggy Darlington's bear hug. Her hugs reminded him of his Ma's.

"Good to see you both." Peggy positioned herself between McClung and Thayer. "Now did I hear you tell Frank you're staying for lunch?

"Yes, the aroma of your hamburgers overpowered me." McClung rubbed his firm belly.

"Cheese, lettuce, and mustard, right?"

"Yes, ma'am."

Peggy poked Thayer's shoulder. "And you, son?"

"A hamburger with all the fixings and a plate of fries."

"Onions, too?"

"Yes, ma'am."

"Not seeing your sweetheart tonight, huh?"

Thayer blushed. "Uh, no."

Peggy grinned and slid one arm around Thayer's narrow shoulders. "I'm just teasing you. Any girl would want to kiss a handsome young man like yourself. Onion breath or not."

Thayer's cheeks flamed as he picked up his large Coke and drank.

"Two burgers and fries, coming right up." Peggy breezed into the kitchen.

Frank went around the counter and poured a mug of coffee, then pulled up a barstool and faced McClung and Thayer. "So, what kind of information are you looking for?"

"You heard about Myron Wagstaff."

"That I did." Frank gulped his coffee.

"Who told you about it?" McClung took a deep sip of his soda.

Frank narrowed his eyes as he cocked his head to one side. "Let me think who told me first."

He took their cups and topped them off as he thought. "I'd have to say, Robyn. Yeah, it was her, Robyn Konopka."

McClung and Thayer glanced at each other.

"Are you sure Frank?"

Frank drained his mug. "Yeah. She came in on Monday around ten-thirty, eleven o'clock."

Peggy set two burger plates in front of McClung and Thayer. "It was closer to eleven. We were just getting out the lunch menus."

McClung squirted mustard on the side of the plate, selected a fry, and dredged it through the mustard. "What did she say?"

Peggy picked up Frank's empty cup. "Mind getting me a cup?"

Frank slid off the stool. "Sure thing, hon."

"I was standing about there when Robyn came bouncing in." Peggy pointed toward the soda machine. "Frank, you were right here weren't you?"

"Yep, right here." Frank hopped up on the bar stool making his head almost even with his wife's.

"Robyn looked like the cat who'd eaten a prize canary. She plopped on that stool you're sitting on Thayer and said in a loud whisper. 'Did you hear Wagstaff was murdered?'"

McClung's second fry hung in the air. "She said *murdered?*"

Frank looked at his wife for confirmation. "Peg, she said murdered, right?"

"Yes, sir, she did."

McClung dropped a mustard-laden fry onto his plate. "That's interesting."

"Why's that?" Peggy and Frank asked as they leaned against the counter, their heads touching.

"Robyn didn't by chance mention where she picked up the news, did she?" McClung wiped his hands with a thick paper napkin. His appetite faded.

"As a matter of fact, I told her I didn't believe it." Peggy rolled her eyes. "She comes in with wild gossip every time she darkens the door. I don't pay no attention to half of what she says."

Frank tapped his temple. "I think the girl's got a screw loose, but she claimed to high heaven it was a bonafide fact. Myron was murdered.

Claimed she'd found out from a most reliable source, but she wouldn't say who."

McClung took a long sip, emptying his cup, then politely covered his mouth as he burped. How could Robyn know it was murder when he didn't know for sure until last night?

"Boss, it's impossible for her to have known." Thayer chewed a couple of fries.

McClung massaged his chin as he pondered the idea that Robyn Konopka was the killer. "I'm thinking the same thing. We'll just have to find out how she stumbled upon that tidbit of information."

♦♦♦♦♦♦

In a shady part of the town's square, McClung and Thayer found an unoccupied bench and sat down to let their lunch settle.

"Well, Thayer, how's that stomach feeling?"

Thayer leaned against the back of the wooden bench, stretched out his long legs, and cradled the back of his head in the palm of his hands.

"Okay. The Tums did the trick."

"Son, you're not a teenager anymore." McClung chuckled. "Chocolate milkshake mixed with a slab of cherry pie after a cheeseburger and a plate of fries don't make for good company."

Thayer groaned.

"How many large Cokes did you have?"

"I lost count after three." Thayer stood. "Maybe I'll feel better if we walk around the square."

McClung and Thayer headed past the old oaks and picturesque flowerbeds surrounding the square.

Thayer glanced at McClung. "Boss, are we going to bring Robyn Konopka in today?"

McClung rubbed his earlobe. "I was thinking about that."

He paused in front of their police cruiser and surveyed the nerve center of his small town. Everything was just as it should be. People shopping. Mothers with strollers trotting through the park. Couples sitting on benches leaning against each other and enjoying their time together.

McClung sighed as he thought of his wife. He daydreamed of sitting with Marian on the screened porch, sipping a cool beverage as they planned their vacation. Marian had a million ideas, all of them tempting.

"Boss."

McClung's solitude vanished. "Yeah?"

"What about the Konopka girl?"

"Let's head on over to Janie Dawson's school. Thank goodness for summer school. We'll talk about it on our way."

They got in the cruiser.

Thayer eased out of the parking space and crept around the crowded square, then headed to the expressway.

"We'll need to bring Robyn Konopka into the station for an interview. When we first saw her at Carter's office, I thought there was something more to the girl besides a shy maid." McClung stared straight ahead with an occasional glance at the billboards interrupting the scenery.

Thayer exited the expressway. "I remembered last night that Robyn and I were in high school together. She was a year or two behind me."

"Is that right? What was she like?"

"Ah, the typical cheerleader. Giggly, stuck up, and mean to anyone not in her inner circle."

McClung shifted in his seat to face Thayer. "A cheerleader you say. Popular, was she?"

"I guess. I didn't hang around her crowd." A smile toyed with Thayer's lips. "Believe it or not her people thought I was a nerd because I was in ROTC."

"I never would've guessed." McClung faked surprise.

Thayer turned into the school parking lot. "I wonder how she ended up being a maid."

"We'll soon find that out. Now, let's go find out if Sheila was telling the truth about Myron's will. May find out that Janie is a suspect."

Thayer parked the cruiser. "I don't think she will be, but I know the rule. Got to follow due diligence on every case."

"You're learning." McClung opened the solid glass door.

The cold air inside the elementary school was a refreshing relief from the hot, muggy June weather.

McClung shuddered. "For some reason, I have this feeling something bad's going to happen before this day is over."

Chapter 10

Penny was in deep discussion with someone on the telephone and didn't pay attention to McClung and Thayer as they entered the station.

McClung glanced at his watch. It was close to Penny's quitting time.

"Yes, Miss Johnson, I know rats are diseased ridden vermin, but you can't be shooting at them. You're going to end up hitting somebody. Maybe put out an eye or worse."

The receptionist groaned. "Yes, Miss Johnson, I know, but—."

They didn't wait around for the conclusion of Penny's conversation with the infamous Miss Judy Johnson, the Red Ryder BB gun-toting woman old enough to be Thayer's great grandmother.

They headed to McClung's office.

"Well, Boss, the day is over, and all is well." Thayer plopped down in the guest chair in front of McClung's desk.

McClung shook his finger. "Technically, the workday is over, but the day isn't."

The young sergeant snorted. "Yeah, well, we'll see."

"Don't mock your elders." McClung tapped his temple. "My Irish copper senses are telling me *beware*."

Thayer rubbed the back of his head. "You got me there. I'm a plain old American mutt."

A sigh eased through McClung's lips. "I was hoping Myron's ex-wife would shed some light on this case."

"Well, at least she confirmed everything Sheila told us so we can definitely rule her out as a suspect."

"Good point." McClung stared at the short stack of folders sitting on the middle of his desk. "Looks like the men have been busy. They've all turned in their reports."

"I'll stay and help you read through them."

McClung sat, slid a file toward Thayer and then opened the next one on the pile. He scanned the single sheet of paper. "Neither saw nor heard anything. Not at home."

"Yep, same here." Thayer picked up another report.

"Ah, this one states that no one was at home at the time of the occurrence but here's something interesting." McClung held out the file to Thayer.

The young officer smiled as he finished reading the statement. "Well, how about that? Robyn Konopka is the girl most likely behind the moving curtain. This lady suggests we talk to Robyn Konopka since she cleans most of the houses on the street."

McClung rubbed his chin. "Maybe she wasn't in the area during the time of the murder. But I wonder why she didn't say something when we ran into her at Dr. Carter's office? Think she's holding back something?"

"I'd say so. We know she lied to us. Frank and Peggy both said she's the one spreading the rumor."

McClung searched through the stack of folders. The last one was the one he was looking for, *Konopka, Robyn*. He opened it and found her address and phone number.

"Are we going to pick her up tonight?" Thayer laced his fingers together then bent them backward, every knuckle popped.

"Nope." McClung glanced at his watch. Penny's shift had ended. He picked up the telephone and dialed the night clerk. "Derek, how are you?"

"Fine. Why aren't you at home with your wife?"

The imposing deep voice of the former lineman made his question sound like a threat.

"Ah, Derek, don't you know I'd rather be in Marian's arms than sitting here chatting with you?"

"I hear that." Derek bellowed.

"Do me a solid. I want to get out of here before midnight. Contact Officer Crawford and have him pick up Robyn Konopka and bring her into the station." McClung gave him her home address.

"I'm calling him right now."

McClung hung up then ran his hands over his face and groaned. "Now I have to call Marian and tell her I won't be home in time for dinner."

"I'll get us some coffee."

McClung nodded as he dialed. "Hey, Puddin Pop."

"Hm, let me guess. You're going to be late." Marian laughed softly.

Charlie's shoulders sagged. Being at work for hours on end never bothered him before he'd met Marian.

"Yeah, I'm afraid so. What's for supper?"

"Nothing special. I figured there'd be late nights until Myron's killer was behind bars, so I made a chicken and wild rice casserole, but I wasn't going to put into the oven until you called."

"I'm sorry."

Marian shushed him. "Hey, I knew what I was getting into when I married a copper."

"I won't be too late."

"Dessert will be waiting for you."

"Hmm, maybe we'll start with dessert." Charlie grinned.

"Well, I'll be waiting with noth—." Marian was interrupted by the shrill sound of Charlie's second phone line.

Charlie growled. "Hang on to that thought."

He pressed the hold button, then answered the call. "McClung."

Derek's deep voice was disconcerting. "Sir, Officer Crawford is handling an incident at Judy Johnson's residence. He's called for back-up."

"Hold on, Derek. I'll be right back." McClung switched back to Marian. "Sweetie, I'm sorry, I gotta take this other call."

"Okay. Be careful, Charlie."

"I will. Love you."

"Love you, too. Bye."

Charlie hated the word *goodbye*. Instead he replied, "I'll see you soon." Then he clicked back to Derek.

"What's the situation?" McClung rose.

"Old lady Johnson's at it again. Shooting at everything that moves."

Thayer walked in with two mugs of coffee and saw McClung's stern face. He turned on his heels back to the break room to get to-go cups.

McClung caught up with Thayer.

"The Konpoka interview will have to wait. Miss Johnson is on the warpath."

Thayer handed McClung a large foam cup. "Who's pissed her off now?"

"The wind for all I know." McClung strode toward the back stairwell, burst through the door, and jogged down four flights of steps to the first floor.

Thayer's voice bounced off the concrete block walls. "She's a nut I tell you. A nut."

♦♦♦♦♦♦

McClung and Thayer snaked between the neighborhood gawkers and police cruisers, and finally parked in the middle of the street, two houses away from Judy Johnson's home.

The sun filtered through the arching branches of the ancient oaks sheltering the remodeled 1930s homes. The only house in the neighborhood in need of refurbishment was Judy Johnson's.

McClung listened to the chatter of her neighbors as he and Thayer picked their way through the crowd. It was clear from their comments that Miss Johnson was the scourge of the community.

"What's the situation, Crawford?" McClung yelled as he approached three of his men deep in conversation.

Officer Billy Crawford turned and pointed to his forehead. "This! Just look at what that crazy old bat did."

McClung pulled back his head at the sight of an angry red welt above Crawford's bushy left eyebrow. "Holy cow. She did that?"

"Yes. As soon as I got half up her driveway, she shot me with her BB gun."

"Why?"

"Because she's a lunatic, that's why." Crawford shook his fist at the old house obscured by English ivy and Wisteria vines.

McClung lowered Crawford's fist. "Crawford, that's not going to help. Tell me what's got her riled up."

Crawford rubbed his forehead. "Well, this kid and his mama were walking down the street. The kid picked a dandelion from the edge of her yard to give to his mama, and that crazy woman shoots the kid on the arm with a BB. Then when his mama yells at her, old lady Johnson shoots her twice on her chest."

"Sheesh, a little kid picks a weed, and that caused her to go off her rocker. That's what you're telling me." McClung's jaw clenched.

"That's right."

McClung crossed his arms and studied the Johnson property.

The flowers in the weed-filled beds were all low-maintenance perennials. Phlox, crinum, black-eyed Susan, and hibiscus were among the mishmash of plants.

Dandelions dotted the lawn. A crushed bloom lay on the sidewalk near the toe of McClung's boot.

A few strips of grass had been mowed recently. The house paint was in varying stages, brilliant white to dull and peeling.

Interesting, McClung thought.

Somebody had only been halfheartedly taking care of the property or maybe they'd been forced to abandon the tasks.

"Miss Johnson lives alone, right?" McClung strolled to the driveway.

"Yes. Her husband died long before I was born." Crawford rubbed the welt on his forehead.

McClung turned and surveyed the crowd gathered on the sidewalk across from the Johnson property.

A woman stood out from the mob. She wore a pink tank-top and sported two angry red welts on her chest, resembling the injury above Officer Crawford's eye. A boy around the age of five peeked around the woman's slim hips, his arms wrapped around her right leg.

"Is that the woman who called in the complaint?" McClung nodded toward the pair.

"Yes." Officer Crawford looked at his notes. "Cindi Knowles and her son, Dustin. They live two blocks down the street. Moved in the neighborhood about a month ago."

McClung approached the young woman.

"Hello, I'm Chief McClung. I apologize for what's happened to you and your son."

The woman sported a feeble smile. "It's not your fault. I'd been warned about her, but I never imagined she'd shoot a kid for picking a weed from her yard."

McClung looked at the shy boy. "Dustin. That's your name isn't it?"

The boy's eyes widened, and his small mouth parted as he nodded. "Am I in trouble for pickin the flower?" Dustin's eyes glazed.

"No, son. You did nothing wrong." McClung tussled the boy's long brown curly hair. "Where's your boo-boo?"

Dustin held out his right arm and pointed to the brilliant red lump on his skinny foreman. "Mommy kissed it and made it better."

Cindi Knowles crouched beside her son, hugged him, and then hefted Dustin up on her hip.

"You're a brave young boy." McClung learned from his years of walking the beat that simple things can make a child smile. He pulled an adhesive bandage from inside his jacket and gave it to Cindi Knowles. "I think Dustin may like this."

She looked at the design and giggled. "Look, Dustin."

"Wow, a zipper. Put it on me, mommy." He held up his thin arm.

"Wait until we get home. I need to put something on your arm. Okay?"

Dustin frowned. "I wanna go home."

Cindi looked at McClung. "May we leave? I don't want to press charges. She's old and apparently senile. Just make sure she understands she can't go around shooting little kids. If it happens again, I will press charges."

"Are you sure you don't want us to take her in?"

The young mother puckered her lips. "My knee-jerk reaction is to lock her up and throw away the key, but I think about my Nana. She has dementia."

Cindi paused. "Uh," her voice wavered, "Nana says things mean things. Hurtful stuff."

Her eyes filled with tears. "It's not her. I know my Nana loves me. So I understand that Miss Johnson may not be right." The young woman tapped her temple. "Maybe it's time for her family to put her somewhere."

McClung nodded. "I understand. Go on home. I'll make her understand that this can never happen again or else. We may contact you later if that's okay."

"Sure, it's fine. Thank you, Chief McClung." Cindi kissed Dustin's head. "Let's get home so we can put this neat bandage on your arm."

"Yay!" The skinny boy clapped his hands.

Cindi stared at McClung. "Make her understand if this happens again…" Her voice trembled. "Well, you know what to say to her."

"Yes, ma'am." McClung watched them wind their way through the thinning crowd. When the two disappeared from sight, he turned and walked toward his men.

Thayer approached him. "What's next?"

McClung rubbed the back of his head. "Well, I guess we need to go have a chat with Judy Johnson. Maybe she's settled down. She hasn't shot anyone since we've arrived."

"If we wait until it gets dark, she can't see well enough to hit us."

McClung grunted. "Don't tell me you're afraid of an eighty-year-old woman with a BB gun."

"She could hit one of us in the eye." Thayer rested his fists on his gun belt. "I don't know about you, Boss, but I don't have any spare eyes lying around."

"Then keep your head down or stay here. Doesn't bother me. It's not going to get dark for another hour or so, and I want to go home to my wife."

Thayer didn't budge.

"At least move the cruiser from the middle of the street."

"Right."

McClung strolled toward the dilapidated house and shouted. "Mrs. Johnson, this is Chief McClung. Don't shoot. I just want to talk with you. That's all."

The front porch lights flicked to life. The elderly woman stepped out onto the wide front porch with the Red Ryder BB gun cradled in her arms.

He held up his open hands shoulder high as he drew closer to the uneven walkway leading to the porch.

McClung was surprised.

Normally, Judy wore a bright housecoat or duster straight from the 1950s, sometimes belted, sometimes hanging loose. She favored orange and purple. Her feet were always clad in sensible flats.

McClung wondered if she made her own clothes.

Judging by the deep wrinkles and sagging skin, Judy Johnson appeared to be well into her eighties if not already into her nineties. But she always made up her face with bright pink rouge and deep red, almost brown lipstick. Her long, curved fingernails matched her pink cheeks. Judy's eyebrows were hidden by the bangs of a shoulder-length Canary yellow bob.

Today, she wore dirt-smeared, worn-denim overalls, and a dingy, tattered tee shirt underneath, and muddy sneakers.

McClung was curious why the change of outfits. She certainly hadn't been working in the front yard. So, what was she doing behind her house?

He stopped at the bottom step.

The furrow between her eyebrows made it impossible to see her beady eyes. Her thin lips were pursed as if she'd just sucked on a rather tart lemon.

"How are you doing tonight, Mrs. Johnson?"

The BB gun shifted. "You can put your hands down. I ain't going to shoot you."

"Thank you." McClung lowered his hands and shoved them in his pockets.

She sat in one of the two sun-dulled green, metal lawn chairs. "Sit."

McClung did as she commanded even though he knew his dress pants would be in need of a serious dry cleaning. "Ms. Johnson, why are you so upset that you'd shoot a five-year-old boy?"

"Pfft. Kids these days have no respect for other people's property. All I did was put the fear of God into that boy. I bet he won't be stealing no more." She stroked the wooden stock of the rifle.

McClung scratched the side of his neck. "Well, yeah, but it was just a dandelion. He was doing you a favor by pulling up the weed."

"That's how you see it. It's my yard, my weeds, and I didn't give that brat permission to step into my yard and pull weeds. I don't need no charity from him or nobody."

McClung pulled on his lower lip. "I understand. Well, why did you shoot my officer?"

Judy scowled. "That little bulldog of a man came barreling toward my house, his hand on his pistol grip, and murder in his eyes. I was in fear of my life."

He covered his smirk with his hand. Yeah, Crawford did resemble a bulldog but murder in his eyes?

Clearing his throat, McClung replied. "Really? I'll speak to Officer Crawford about his behavior."

"You best do that. I can't guarantee if there's a next time that I won't put out his murdering eyes."

McClung leaned toward Miss Johnson and rested his elbow on the chair arm. "Now, you don't want to seriously hurt anyone. We've had this discussion before. One day someone may press charges and then there'll be nothing I can do but arrest you. Do you understand?"

The old woman turned away from McClung and stared at a large clay pot with leggy petunias draped over its edges. Curled brown flower heads were scattered across the porch.

Something caught McClung's eye. Torn bits of paper. He bent forward and picked up the pieces. They were damp. He arranged the scraps on his lap. It was a business card for a landscaping company. The one Marian used.

"When did you get this card?"

She turned her head, halfway looked at McClung. "What card would that be? Lots of salesmen try to ply their wares to me. I shoo them all away. Confounded leeches. All they want is your money. The thieves."

"This one is from a reputable landscaping company."

Miss Johnson groaned and twisted around to face McClung. "Oh, really. Who?"

"Stellar Landscaping."

She rolled her eyes. "That blasted man shows up every now and then claiming he'll cut my yard for free." Judy scoffed. "Free my eye. There's always a catch. Bloodsucking leeches. The lot of them. Nothing but crooks."

"Did he try to cut your yard?" McClung pointed to strips of recently cut grass.

Judy cackled. "I had to shoot him in the butt a couple of times to get him to leave." Her bony hand flicked toward the less-dingy white paint on the house. "About a year ago, I caught the sucker trying to paint my house. I shot him then, too."

McClung didn't recall any complaints from the landscaping company about her. He'd have to check in the morning.

The sky was growing darker, and the crowd had gone. Only his men were left.

"Mrs. Johnson, one last question, and then I'll leave."

"Spit it out. My show is about to come on and my trigger finger is getting antsy."

"Why are your shoes and clothes so dirty?"

The cranky woman stood. "I told that man today that if I ever saw him again on my property, I'd kill him."

McClung shook his head as he stood. "You don't mean it, Mrs. Johnson."

She pointed a gnarled finger at him and held the BB gun against her narrow hip, the barrel pointed at McClung's feet.

"You listen here, mister. I mean what I say. Don't push your luck with me, sonny. I ain't a fearing of you." She marched to the front door and cracked it open. "I dug a grave for him and an extra one for whoever pisses me off next. Maybe you."

McClung's mouth tightened; his voice hardened. "I'll say this just once. You shot an innocent child and my deputy today. It's unjustifiable. If I hear of you shooting anybody else, I don't care what your reason is, I'll slap handcuffs on you myself and throw you behind bars for as long as the law will allow. Do you understand? I mean it. I will throw you in jail."

The older woman looked him over, then aimed the gun at his thighs. "I think I could shove you in it without too much trouble. Now git! If you got anything else to say to me, say it to my lawyers."

"I suggest you contact your lawyers. The boy's mother feels sorry for you. She's not pressing charges. But I can."

"Then do it." Mrs. Johnson growled. The front door banged against the inside wall as she mule-kicked it open, never taking her eyes away from McClung's face. She backed in, slammed the door, then flicked off the porch lights.

Chapter 11

Charlie washed the dishes as Marian sat at the kitchen table drinking coffee.

"So, Myron's ex-wife and stepsister are no longer suspects."

Charlie rinsed the bread pan. "Yeah, they both have solid alibis. Even though they have a reason to kill him, like inheriting loads of money, there's not enough evidence to press charges."

"I kind of know Robyn. She cleans Haven Place Day Center. Does an excellent job." Marian sipped the coffee as she thought of the special needs clients who attended the program, a big part of her world.

"That doesn't mean she leads a squeaky-clean life." Charlie scrubbed the casserole dish. "Right now, Robyn is high on the list of suspects."

Marian tilted her head from side to side. "I don't think you should completely ignore Carter or his girlfriend. And what about Mrs. Johnson? I mean, come on, she's digging graves." She rolled her eyes. "Who knows? Maybe her husband is buried back there."

Marian gasped. "Oh, that makes sense. It's the reason she doesn't want anyone around her house."

Charlie grinned. "She's ornery enough for that to be true, but I highly doubt she killed Myron. As far as I know, there's no history between the two of them."

Marian set down the empty cup and drummed her fingernails on the tile-topped kitchen table. "Yeah, I suppose you're right. He wasn't killed with a BB gun."

"I'm afraid when we start digging into Myron's blackmail schemes, we'll have more suspects than we can handle."

"Do you reckon that's how he made his living, blackmail?" Marian sauntered to the dishwasher and put the cup on the top rack.

"Done. Time for dessert."

"Again?" A wicked smile was plastered on Marian's face.

"Well, I was thinking about the mile-high apple pie warming in the oven." Charlie dried his hands then tossed the towel on the counter.

Marian strolled next to her husband and trailed her fingers over his chest. "I guess you're not a spring chicken anymore either." She laughed and darted way from Charlie's grasp.

He caught up with her in the master bedroom.

She was sitting on the edge of the bed. "What? No pie."

"Pie is no longer on my mind." Charlie stood in front of his wife. His fingertip traced her full lips.

"No? Well, I wondered what could be more tempting than a warm slab of apple pie with a scoop of vanilla bean ice cream on top." Marian murmured.

Charlie pulled off his tee shirt. "I'll just have to show you."

◆◆◆◆◆◆

Charlie was content with Marian snuggled close to him, her head on his bare shoulder. The bedroom was quiet except for the low hum from the ceiling fan. He considered himself the luckiest man in the universe.

Marian whispered. "Are you thinking about pie?"

"I am now." He kissed the top of her head. "After my stellar performance, that's what you're thinking about, pie?"

She laughed. "I was thinking how great you are and that got me thinking of what led to this."

"Pie." They said simultaneously.

Charlie playfully slapped her bottom. "Time for pie, my love."

She rolled out of bed, picked up her slippers, smacked them together, shook them, and then put them on.

"No bugs?"

"No bugs." This was one of Marian's many quirks. Ever since she saw a movie about a man dying after he shoved his feet into his shoes and a spider bit him, this had become her routine.

Charlie stepped into a pair of sweatpants. "I'll go serve up the pie. Meet you on the loveseat."

"Sounds like a plan. Be there in a second."

He removed the ice cream from the freezer first to let it soften a little while he made a pot of decaf. Once finished, he pulled the warm pie out of the oven.

As the knife sank into the flakey brown crust, the phone rang.

"Ah crikey!"

It was a quarter to nine and Charlie wanted pie.

Now.

With his wife.

He heard Marian answer the phone in the bedroom and wished for the caller to be Joan. Although if it was her best friend, he hoped they wouldn't talk all night.

The sound of her slippers scuffling down hallway made his shoulders sag.

It was probably for him.

Probably the station.

Probably a problem only he could handle.

Triple crikey.

Charlie hoped when she entered the kitchen, she'd say it was only a sales call. But as soon as he saw her face, he knew his prayer was too late.

"No pie for me?"

Marian shook her head. "It's Derek. Mrs. Johnson is dead."

♦♦♦♦♦♦

McClung found Thayer waiting for him on Judy Johnson's front porch. "What do we have here?"

"The neighbor to the left called it in. The ambulance should arrive soon. I asked the paramedics to wait on the street just in case we determine it's murder. Didn't want them messing up any evidence."

Thayer scratched his cheek. "Although, Sam Goldstein just left. I let him take a couple pictures of the body. We were really careful not to mess up anything. He was dressed in a tuxedo. The mayor is having a fancy party and Sam's covering it. That's why he didn't stick around."

"That's fine. Show me where she is."

Thayer relaxed as he led McClung to the side of the house toward the backyard enclosed by a dilapidated eight-foot wooden fence.

McClung and Thayer stepped beyond the warped gate.

Judy Johnson was propped up in a metal lawn chair matching the ones on the front porch, dressed in the same dirty overalls and tee shirt. Her head tilted backward, mouth open, a fine thread of dried blood ran from her nose. The once bright, angry eyes were cloudy as they stared at the twinkling stars.

"I wonder what happened." McClung slipped on a pair of latex gloves.

Thayer's flashlight illuminated her neck as McClung examined the wrinkled skin for wounds and bruises.

None visible.

McClung studied her head. "No visible injuries." He walked around her body. "Nothing unusual. Maybe natural causes? We're going to need Jack to establish the cause of death."

The floodlights mounted at the back corners of the house cast bizarre shadows. McClung noticed that the condition of the backyard was the exact opposite from the front. From what he could see through the trees, a thick layer of pine straw covered the ground, not a weed in sight.

A mass of heirloom roses filled the immaculate flowerbeds against the dingy house. McClung clicked on his penlight and checked the roses. His mother had these same roses, Cecile Brunner, in her rose garden.

"Let's search the yard for the two graves Judy Johnson claimed she dug earlier in the day. I'll take the right side. You go left. And be careful. There may be booby traps. No telling what she's capable of."

The young sergeant nodded.

After an exhaustive search of the backyard, the only thing they found was a freshly turned vegetable garden with stakes sporting the empty seed packets like little shrunken heads.

McClung and Thayer returned to the front yard.

Two emergency techs jumped out of the ambulance parked at the end of the driveway.

"Are you ready for us to remove the body?" Leanna Wallace asked. The striking young girl, the first female paramedic in Lyman County, had the rear doors open and one hand on the gurney.

McClung looked at Thayer. "Where's the coroner?"

Thayer flopped his head backward. "Ah, you're going to love this. He said, and I quote, 'If the chief is there, he'll know if she's dead and if it's a suspicious death. If he wants me there, I quit'. End of quote."

McClung grunted. "Call him and give him the good news. I'll gladly turn in his resignation for him. No need for him to put himself out." He shook his head. "The coroner is a waste of the taxpayer's money."

"He's right, Boss. You know dead and if it's suspicious. The coroner's useless. The man's a tailor for Pete's sake."

Leanna walked up to Thayer. "Hey. Are we good to go?"

Thayer blushed. "Uh."

McClung smiled. *There's something going on between them.*

He answered for Thayer. "Yeah. Be careful. Try not to disturb anything. I have a gut feeling she didn't die of natural causes."

"So, take her to Gibb's Funeral Home and tell them to hold for an autopsy?" Leanna glanced at Thayer.

Thayer cleared his throat and tugged at his collar.

McClung nodded and held his amusement as he witnessed young love blossom. "Thayer, show her where the body is."

"Yes, Boss."

Leanna motioned for her partner to join her. They walked to the backyard with Thayer strolling beside Leanna.

McClung looked toward the house left of Judy Johnson's. He needed to interview them.

All the houses in the neighborhood had their porch lights on. Most of the houses had floodlights on each corner as well.

The neighbor to the left stepped outside with his wife and stood on the front porch, then waved at McClung.

McClung and the neighbors met halfway.

The man extended his hand. "Hi. I'm Stephen Atkins and this is my wife, Rainne."

McClung shook the stocky man's hand and nodded to Rainne who kept her crossed arms pressed against her full bosom.

"I understand you were the one who called the department."

"My wife did."

McClung shifted his attention to Rainne dressed in a tie-dyed tee-shirt with a long flowing skirt skimming the tops of her bare feet. She tucked her long mousy brown hair behind her ears adorned with multiple pierced earrings.

The woman stared at him.

"Well, what did you see that made you call this in?" McClung had the feeling Rainne didn't like cops. Maybe it had something to do with the skunky, burnt rope scent being carried with the night's breeze.

"That old lady dead?"

"Yes."

"Awesome."

Stephen elbowed her.

Rainne scowled at her husband. "What? The cow had it coming."

McClung arched his left eyebrow. "What do you mean?"

"That mean old hag was constantly shooting at the squirrels in my yard, not just in her yard. My yard. My squirrels."

"Technically, they were on her fence." Stephen corrected his wife.

Rainne dropped her arms with her fists landing on her narrow hips. "How dare you take her side?"

Stephen took two steps away from his wife.

She snarled at her husband then looked at McClung. "That woman was the menace of the street. A menace to anything that moved or crossed her path." Rainne shot her arm toward her own house. "You should examine the dings in our siding and the chipped glass in our windows."

McClung ran his hand over his mouth. "Look, I know your neighbor's history. You don't have to worry about her anymore. Just tell me what caused you to call in."

"Fine. I want to get back inside, anyway." Rainne crossed her arms. "I heard the old bat yelling which isn't unusual. She hollers at everything. But I thought I heard another voice in her backyard, so I looked out of the upstairs bedroom window."

McClung turned at the sound of the paramedics wheeling the gurney to the ambulance.

Thayer was chatting with Leanna as they walked toward the street.

McClung hated to interrupt his sergeant's budding romance, but he needed Thayer to hear what Rainne was saying.

He whistled.

Thayer's head snapped toward him.

"I got a witness here."

Thayer trotted over.

"This is Sergeant Thayer. These are the Atkins."

"Sir. Ma'am." Thayer shook hands with Stephen then removed his notepad from his front pocket.

McClung looked at Rainne. "Please continue."

"As I was saying, I looked out the upstairs bedroom window. It was already getting dark. I could see Mrs. Johnson sitting on the patio holding that old BB gun on her lap. She was arguing with someone. Whoever it was stood out of sight, but I could see a shadow on the patio."

Thayer glanced at the ambulance as it passed by. "Was it a man or a woman with her?"

"Weren't you listening to me? I said I couldn't see them."

McClung thought Rainne was just as crabby as Mrs. Johnson. "Did the other voice sound male or female?"

She gawked at McClung. "I don't know."

"Did you understand anything she said, even if it was one or two words?"

"Again, no." Rainne shook her head and mumbled. "Men. Pfft. Never listen."

McClung considered taking the Atkins into the station to just to piss her off. But it would be a waste of his time and he wanted to go home to his wife. And pie.

"What else did you see?" McClung continued.

"The next time I looked, she was still sitting in the chair with her head flopped backward. I watched her for a few minutes. She didn't move a muscle. It was unnatural. So, I raised the window and yelled at her. When she didn't shoot at me, I knew something was bad wrong."

"Why did you yell at her? I thought you didn't care for her."

Rainne rolled her eyes. "I don't care for her. Gah, I'm not heartless."

Thayer opened his mouth but locked eyes with his chief.

McClung tapped his chin with his index finger.

Thayer decided not to comment on Rainne's last remark.

"Is there anything else you can add? Maybe a car in front of her house?" McClung rubbed his temple.

"Again, I was looking out of the back, not the front window." Rainne hit her forehead with the palm of her hand. "Would you leave us alone if I just admitted that I killed the old biddy?"

Stephen gasped. "Shut up, Rainne. Stop being such a—."

"Such a what, Stephen? Such a what?"

Her husband clamped his mouth closed as he stepped closer toward McClung.

Thayer looked at his boss.

McClung dipped his head.

"You have the right to remain silent." Thayer slid the notepad in his shirt pocket, reached for his handcuffs while he continued giving Rainne her Miranda rights.

"Wait, a minute! What's he doing?"

"You've given us cause to arrest you. Did you kill Judy Johnson?" McClung moved closer to Rainne.

She stumbled backward, and her eyes became owl-like as her red tongue darted across her dry, thin lips. "Uh, no, sir. I didn't kill her. I told you everything I know. Can I please go back inside?"

McClung crossed his arms and stared at her for a few seconds. "I don't know. You seem to have hated Judy Johnson enough to kill her. Are you sure you're not making up the backyard scenario to cover up your involvement in her death?"

"Honest, sir, I'm not lying. I didn't kill her. I swear I didn't." She reached for her husband. "Stephen, tell them I didn't kill her."

He tossed his head side to side. "No, sir, she didn't. Rainne was with me. I swear." Stephen crossed his heart then held up his open hand. "I'm telling you the whole truth and nothing but the truth."

Stephen held his wife tight as she pressed against him.

McClung removed a card from his inside suit pocket. "Call me if you remember anything else. Anything."

The couple bobbed their heads. "May we leave?"

"Have a good night." McClung motioned to Thayer that it was time to leave.

As they approached the cruiser, McClung noticed a woman across the street standing under her front porch light.

"Yoo-hoo, officers." She waved a knotted hand. "I need to speak with you."

They strolled toward her.

"Yes, ma'am, what can we do for you?" A warm feeling spread throughout McClung's body as she gripped his hand.

"Oh, I remember you. You two were here earlier today." A pair of hexagon eyeglasses framed her light green eyes.

"That we were." McClung motioned to her bronze-colored frames. "I like those. Nice."

She blushed. "Thank you. My granddaughter talked me into getting these the other week. The sweet child said I needed to be *cooler*. Whatever that means."

Thayer chuckled. "Those are cool frames, ma'am."

"Thank you." She patted Thayer's foreman. "Judy Johnson is dead, isn't she?"

"Yes, she is." McClung murmured.

"Please come inside. I think I may be able to help you gentleman." The silver-haired lady motioned for them to follow.

McClung and Thayer trailed behind her into a living room with butter yellow walls and a pale blue chintz sofa and loveseat.

She sat down in a navy-blue recliner. "Please have a seat," she said. Leaning forward, she reached for a silver pot setting at the end of the coffee table and then poured coffee into three china cups. "Don't worry, it's decaf."

"Thank you." They each took a cup from the tray.

"Here is cream and sugar if you like."

She raised a glass dome from a cake stand. "You must have a slice of my sour cream pound cake, the best in the state I'm told."

Not wanting to offend her by refusing, McClung held up his thumb and index finger a half-inch apart. "Just a thin slice."

"The same for me, ma'am."

The slices were three inches thick. "Now eat up."

After the first bite, McClung was happy for the three-inch slice. "Ma'am, don't tell my wife this, but I have to agree this is the best in the state."

Thayer's head bobbed as he shoveled another large chunk into his bulging cheeks.

"I guess I should introduce myself. My name is Lula Belle Darby." With her crooked index finger, she warned them. "Don't be callin me Mrs. Darby. Call me Lula Belle."

"Thank you, Lula Belle. You may call me Charlie."

"Call me Ben." Thayer set his crumb-free plate on the coffee table.

Lula Belle placed another thick slice of cake on Thayer's plate. "Here you go, Ben." She smiled with a soft sigh.

"My family was one of the first to move into this neighborhood back in 1938."

"You've seen a lot of changes in Lyman County." McClung had a good feeling about Lula Belle.

"Yes. Yes, I have." She glanced at the mantle clock on the side table next to her recliner. "Mercy, it's getting late. Let me say what I've got to say so you boys can get on home."

McClung set his empty plate away from Lula Belle's quick knife. "All right." He pulled his notepad from inside his suit coat pocket.

"I've known Judy since she moved in a year after I did. Her husband had just died. So, she was alone. I tried my best to befriend her. She'd have none of it." Lula Belle tossed up her hands in defeat.

"Why do you suppose?" McClung hoped to get a glimpse of what was inside Judy Johnson's head.

Lula Belle smirked. "I wish I knew. But a year ago, Judy's niece started visiting her at least once a month."

"Do you know her name?"

"Shelby Hornbuckle. Judy's not very nice to her." Lula Belle tapped the earpiece to her glasses. "I see everything. I'm part of the neighborhood watch. Daytime only. Been so for years."

McClung grinned. "Is that right? What did you see today?"

121

"The nice yardman, Brian, is very persistent about keeping Judy's grass cut. I don't need a yardman. Between my sons and grandsons, they do everything for me." Lula Belle beamed.

"That's wonderful your family looks after you. Did the yard guy come by this week?" McClung remembered the two strips of cut grass.

"Yes, he did, two days ago. Judy ran him off with her BB gun. As she was shooting, she screamed just like she always did that she didn't need no charity and she would have him arrested for trespassing. Called poor Brian every name in the book. Last week, she threw a rock at him as he walked away. It hit him so hard on the back, he stumbled. Oh, that Judy Johnson is one foulmouthed, mean woman."

"Brian Lane is the yard man?"

"Yes, do you know him?"

"I know him by sight only, but my wife speaks highly of him."

Lula Belle hunched her shoulders. "But poor Brian keeps coming back. Every now and then he gets the yard cut and weeded when Judy's gone to get groceries. He's even managed to plant some nice flowers around the front of her house."

McClung rubbed his chin. "Why do you suppose Brian keeps coming back?"

"I asked him that one day." The old lady grinned. "Bless his sweet heart. He said he just liked doing good and that maybe one day Judy would be nicer if someone showed her a little kindness."

Thayer grunted. "Doesn't appear to have worked."

"Sadly, Ben, you're right, but I don't think Brian will ever give up. He has a kind soul."

McClung wondered if the niece and Brian had more in common. "Tell me more about the niece."

"Not much to say except she's pleasant. Nothing like her aunt. Real good manners, too. I met her the first time she visited Judy. Poor girl was sitting in her cute little convertible crying."

McClung and Thayer glanced at each other.

"I felt sorry for her sitting there all alone. So, I went over and asked if I could help."

Lula Belle refilled their cups.

"She said no, but the next time the niece visited she showed up at my front door wanting to talk about her Aunt Judy."

McClung sipped his coffee. "What did she want to know?"

"In a nutshell? To understand why Judy was so cantankerous. I couldn't help her. Only the good Lord knows." Lula Belle clicked her tongue. "I don't know why she's so faithful to her aunt."

Thayer stacked his clean plate on top of McClung's. "Did you witness Mrs. Johnson shoot the little boy late this afternoon?"

Lula Belle shook her head. "No, only the aftermath. I was watching the news. It's the first time Judy's shot a child. Anything that encroaches on her property is fair game. Animals and adults, but never a child. No. Never a child."

"Did you see anyone visit after the police left?" Thayer drained his cup.

"No, I'm sorry to say I was watching my shows." Lula Belle ran her hands over her thin arms. "Do you think someone murdered Judy?"

McClung rubbed the side of his neck. "We're not sure."

"Well, it wouldn't surprise me. But I did see that little convertible Shelby drives race down the road before y'all arrived tonight. I can't say for sure if she'd been visiting Judy. Shelby passes this way on her way to visit her doctor friend."

"Arnold Carter?" McClung sat up.

Lula Belle pointed her finger. "That's the one."

McClung replaced his notepad into his coat pocket. "Thank you, Lula Belle, you've been most helpful. The cake and coffee were a nice treat. Thank you, again."

He pulled a business card from his front coat pocket. "If you think of anything else, please call me."

Lula Belle read the card. "McClung, that's Irish isn't it?"

"Yes, ma'am. Full-blooded but born in America."

McClung stood. "We'll be leaving now. Thank you again for your hospitality."

"Now you boys must take home a nice slice of cake. Just wait right here." She trotted off and returned shortly with a roll of aluminum foil, then placed two huge chunks of cake on two pieces of foil, wrapping them neatly.

"You're too kind." McClung knew Marian would enjoy talking with Lula Belle. "I believe you and my wife would hit it off. Would you mind if she called on you?"

The old woman's face brightened. "Oh, I'd fancy a visit."

She sat and scribbled her phone number on a yellow sticky note. "Here you go. I'm here all time. I love to entertain."

McClung and Thayer headed for the front door with Lula Belle close behind.

"Thanks for the cake. It's been a pleasure." McClung held out his hand.

Lula Belle's hands enclosed his. "The pleasure was all mine." She patted his shoulder. "All mine."

As the door shut behind them, a landscaping truck glided down the road.

Chapter 12

Marian pressed her eye to the peephole in the front door then swung open the door.

"Morning, Marian." The young sergeant stood at attention and waited for an invitation to enter.

"Well, go into the kitchen. Don't act like a stranger."

He followed the aroma of coffee and cinnamon blueberry pancakes.

Charlie looked over his shoulder as he flipped the last of the fifteen pancakes onto a platter. "Hey, Thayer. Pour yourself some coffee and have a seat at the table."

"Morning, Boss." Thayer filled a mug with coffee and sat in front of a plate. His stomach growled.

Marian set a warm syrup dispenser in the middle of the table. "Be careful. Don't touch the glass. It's hot."

"Stop fussing and sit down, sweetie. We have everything we need." With one hand, Charlie set the platter of stacked pancakes on the table while the other hand pulled out a chair for his wife.

After grace, the two men waited for Marian to serve herself. She slapped three pancakes on her plate.

"The rest are yours, boys."

From a platter piled with bacon, she snatched two pieces of bacon while they battled for the remaining twelve pancakes.

Once they finished eating and after another pot of coffee was made, they pushed the sticky plates to the side and discussed their plan of attack.

Marian relaxed and enjoyed listening to her husband.

"We'll interview Robyn Konopka and the neighbor across from Myron Wagstaff. What's her name, again?" McClung looked at Thayer.

He shrugged. "I don't remember. Her file is on my desk."

"Her name is Jennifer Sutherland, no wait, she remarried. It's Leeson now." Marian piped in.

"Thank you." McClung scribbled the name on his notepad. "You don't by any chance have her number, do you?"

Marian shot up. "Let me get the neighborhood directory." She ran into the living room, pulled it from the sofa table drawer and then jogged back. "Here you go."

"We should make a copy of that, don't you think, Boss?"

"You're a smart man." McClung flipped through the pages. "I'll call her to set up a time for an interview."

Thayer shifted his focus toward Marian. "Isn't your yard guy with Stellar Landscaping?"

Marian narrowed her eyes. "Yes. You think Brian is involved?"

"Judy Johnson hit him with a rock last week." Thayer topped off his coffee.

Marian pulled back her head. "Why?"

"Because he was cutting her grass." McClung frowned. "We saw a truck with the Stellar logo drive by the Johnson house last night."

"Brian isn't their only employee." Marian sniped.

McClung rubbed his eye. He knew how much his wife enjoyed talking plants with Brian. And she was right. They didn't see who was driving the truck and had no valid reason to pull the truck over.

"We have to investigate every clue and suspect."

Marian stacked the plates and utensils. "I understand." She put the dishes in the sink.

McClung glanced at Thayer and motioned toward the front door.

"Boss, it's getting late. I'll wait in the car, and call Stewie to check if Shelby Culbertson and Shelby Hornbuckle are the same."

"Let me get you a to-go cup for your coffee." Marian reached inside the pantry for a disposable hot cup.

Thayer held his full mug and the thick paper cup over the sink as he transferred the coffee.

Charlie didn't move until he heard the front door close. He went over to Marian, never taking his eyes off her.

She focused on rinsing the dishes.

As he stood behind her, Charlie thought she made everything she wore alluring.

Her aerobic pants accentuated the curves of her body as the pale pink tee shirt skimmed the top of her hips. Charlie slid his hands down her bare arms and held her forearms.

She froze.

He kissed the top of her ear, then her cheek.

Marian eased her head to the right as he kissed her neck. Chills danced over her arms.

"You know I love you." He breathed into her tiny ear.

Releasing Marian's arms as she reached for the dishtowel, Charlie spun her around and held her firm shoulders. "I'll never do anything to intentionally upset you."

Marian bit her bottom lip and nodded.

"I realize you like Brian. We're doing our jobs. That's all."

She wrapped her arms around his waist and rested her head on his chest. "I know, it's just that he's so kind. I can't imagine him killing somebody."

"Look, why don't you bake something and then call Lula Belle to see if she's up for a visit. You'll love her."

"She does sound nice. I need a motherly friend." Marian leaned away and looked at her husband. "She'll never take Ma's place, but it'd be nice to have someone like her close by."

Charlie squeezed her. "Let me take you for Chinese tonight."

"Consider it a date written in ink. No way out." She wiggled out of his grasp. "Do you want me to meet you there?"

He watched as she pulled flour and sugar from the pantry. "Nope. It'll be a proper date. I'll come home and change clothes then escort you to the restaurant like a true lady should be."

"Oo, my knight in shining armor. I like that." She batted her eyelashes at Charlie.

He gathered her into his arms and kissed her.

"Whoa. You better go to work now or else." Her eyebrows danced up and down. "Thayer is probably imagining all kinds of naughty things about us as it is." Marian giggled.

Charlie leered at her. "Yeah, you'll get a proper snog tonight. See you later."

"Later."

He winked then headed for the front door.

◆◆◆◆◆◆

Thayer grinned as he pulled out of McClung's driveway. "Where to Boss?"

"The station. We need to bring the squad up to date." McClung noticed his sergeant's smirk. "What's that about?" He pointed to Thayer's face.

"Nothing. I'm hoping one day I'll have a marriage like yours."

"Patience, my son. Patience." McClung gazed out the passenger's window. "Like my granny used to say, 'you'll know her when you find her'."

Thayer shot out onto the main road. "Yeah, I believe I will."

McClung said nothing. He guessed Thayer was thinking of Leanna Wallace.

"Let's change the subject. If we find out Judy Johnson was murdered, do you think they were killed by the same person?"

Thayer picked up the to-go cup and sipped. "I believe the two murders are unrelated. I'm leaning toward Shelby Culbertson killing her aunt." He ran his tongue around his front teeth. "I have no clue about Wagstaff. Maybe the good doctor is lying, and he did it."

"Possibly." McClung's index finger tapped his thigh as he considered a handful of scenarios. "Are you certain Shelby Culbertson and Shelby Hornbuckle are the same person?"

"Absolutely. They have to be. I mean, how many Shelbys drive a convertible and are fooling around with Carter?"

"I agree."

The radio crackled.

"McClung, go ahead."

"Sir, there's been a break-in at the Wagstaff property."

Thayer looked at his boss then twirled his finger in the air.

McClung nodded. "Turn around."

"Headed there now. Who called it in?"

"Jennifer Leeson. Wagstaff's neighbor across the street. Officer Marsh is at the scene."

"Copy that." McClung replaced the radio receiver. "This case keeps getting more interesting."

♦♦♦♦♦♦

McClung and Thayer parked in front of Myron Wagstaff's house. Officer Marsh was across the street, standing in the neighbor's driveway and speaking with a redheaded woman. A German Shepard sat by her left foot.

"Good morning." McClung extended his hand. "I'm Chief McClung and this is Sergeant Thayer."

"I'm Jennifer Suth… I mean Leeson. I just got married two months back." The redhead chuckled. "Not such a good morning for me."

McClung glanced at Officer Marsh. "Fill me in."

"Okay, Boss."

"I can tell you myself, Chief McClung."

McClung smiled at Jennifer. "Thank you."

"All right, I'll just start at the beginning then. Well, Luther here 'bout scared the bejeebies out of me barkin his fool head off as he stared out the window toward the murder house."

Jennifer Leeson shuddered. "I'm alone here with Luther. My husband works on an oil rig out in the Gulf. He's on the rig for two weeks and home for two weeks, but it pays darn good."

"Yes, ma'am I bet it does." McClung peeped over his shoulder at Myron's house. "Luther was barking at someone?"

"Oh, right." Jennifer giggled again. "I get off track sometimes. Let's see." She bit her thumb as she thought.

"Luther started barking and scratching at the front window there." She pointed to a bottom floor window. "He was staring at Myron's house. I was afraid it was his ghost prowling around."

"Why do you say that?"

"I saw a light flickering around upstairs. They say murdered people refuse to believe they're dead and won't leave, that's why they haunt." Her eyes grew big.

McClung blinked a few times. "What time did you see the lights?"

She bit the inside of her cheek and stared at the sky. "Well, it was right about five o'clock. I wasn't going to call thinking y'all might think I'm crazy. That's why I waited to call. I keep thinking about it and thought what if it's a thief and not a ghost? Then what?"

"You did the right thing calling us."

The German Shepherd whined.

"Does Luther bite?"

"No, sir. Let him smell your hand first."

"Hey, buddy." McClung held out his hand. Luther sniffed then gave Charlie's hand a sloppy lick.

"Good boy." McClung squatted and scratched the dog's ear. "I wish you could talk, Luther." He continued to pet Luther as he looked at the redheaded woman.

"Did you see anyone leave the house?"

Jennifer shook her head. "No, I called the cops mainly because I saw a shadow pass in front of the upstairs window. I don't think ghosts cast a shadow. Do they? No, they don't. So, I figured I'd better play it safe and call you guys."

McClung gave her one of his cards. "Thank you. You've been very helpful. If you remember anything else, please call me."

"Yes, sir, I'll definitely do that." Jennifer held up the card. "Marian's your wife, right?"

"Yes, ma'am." McClung smiled.

"Tell her, I said *hey*. She's so nice."

"Thank you. I'll tell her."

Jennifer hunched her shoulders, grinned, and waved goodbye. "Come boy, let's go get you a snackie."

McClung turned away then stopped. Trying to keep up with Jennifer's rattling on made him forget to question her about Robyn.

"I need to ask you a few questions concerning your maid, Robyn Konopka."

"Oh, she's great. Robyn's been cleaning my house for a couple of years now. Is Marian thinking of hiring her?"

"No. Was she here the day Myron was killed?"

"What? Uh, let me think." Jennifer stuck the tip of her thumb between her teeth. She snapped her fingers. "Got it. That was Monday. No. She only comes on Friday."

McClung tugged his earlobe. "Were you home at the time?"

"No, Luther and I were out all day, at the children's hospital. He loves kids."

"Does Robyn have a key to your house? Did you notice anything out of place when you got home? Anything unusual?"

Jennifer drew her brows together. "No. Why are you asking me these questions? Are you trying to tell me someone was inside my house when Myron was killed?"

"Well, it appears so. A witness saw a man run from Myron's backyard and saw someone close the curtains in one of the upstairs windows. When the officers knocked on your front door that morning, no one answered."

Jennifer Leeson gasped. "It must've been her. Robyn does have a key to my house. Why was she here that day?"

Luther stared at Jennifer and whined.

"It's okay, honey bunny. Mama's okay." Jennifer stroked Luther's head.

McClung tried to ease Jennifer's mind. "It's possible the air conditioner kicked on and ruffled the curtains. There wasn't a car in the driveway."

The redhead's nostrils flared. "Robyn parks in the garage so her car won't get hot sitting in the sun. I'm going to have a good talk with her. She's got some explaining to do."

McClung shook his head. "No, I'd rather you not. We need to question her about the day of the murder. We want to catch her off guard."

"I'll do whatever you think is best."

"Thank you. I want to make sure I understand. No one else has access to your house. Only you and Robyn."

She started to nod then shook her head. "Well, my husband does, of course, but he's not due home for another week. So that makes three people."

"If you have time, I'd like to ask you a few questions about Myron."

"Sure, Luther and I can do walkies later. I can't tell you much. I avoided him like the plague."

Thayer and Marsh did little to subdue their laughter.

Jennifer looked past McClung. "Y'all know what I'm talking about, don't you?"

McClung looked his at men.

One glance at their boss's Medusa stare sent Thayer and Marsh's amusement to a screeching halt.

The chief turned his attention to Jennifer. "As you were saying."

"Yeah, uh, well, Myron, for some reason, didn't like me." Jennifer shot up a finger. "But he did like Robyn. A lot. I'd see her over there quite often. Maybe he was a neat freak. It's gotta be that. I can't see Robyn having an affair with him." She wrinkled her nose.

"Interesting. Does Robyn have a boyfriend?"

Jennifer shrugged. "I don't know. All we ever talk about is cleaning."

"All right. How did you come about hiring Robyn? Does she work for many people in the neighborhood?"

She stroked Luther's head as she thought. "Come to think of it, I got a welcome basket from the Homeowners Association when I moved in. Robyn's business card was in there. I don't know everyone in the subdivision. It's huge you know, but those I know who use a maid, use Robyn."

"Do you know Arnold Carter?"

"Ick. I see him at the HOA meetings. He thinks he's God's gift to women, hits on any female, no matter their age. I think he's slimy. A pervert if you ask me." Jennifer giggled. "You are asking me, aren't you?" She giggled again. "Oh, I've seen him at Myron's place a couple of times, usually late in the day. Never stays long. Just a few minutes."

McClung was ready to wrap it up, but Jennifer was giving him a few interesting tidbits.

"Are you acquainted with Judy Johnson or Shelby Culbertson?"

"Nope."

McClung retrieved his notepad from his pants pocket and made a few notes.

"Can you think of anyone who'd want to kill Myron?"

Her eyes widened. "So, it is true. He was murdered."

"Yes, ma'am."

Jennifer scratched her freckled nose. "Well, I don't know of anyone who hasn't had a run-in with him at one time or another. You've seen Myron driving his golf cart around the neighborhood handing out citations for the tiniest violation of the HOA covenants. He reminded me of a pompous king inspecting his kingdom, looking down his nose at everyone. Anyone who ticked him off paid a price. If he could have, I believe he'd throw them in a dungeon."

McClung heard Thayer mumble to Marsh. "It must be good to be king."

Jennifer giggled and glanced behind McClung. "That's it on the nose. I think he honestly believed he was our king." She crossed her arms. "But the most recent run-in was the paper guy. He loathes Myron."

Thayer coughed. "Remember the newspaper propped against the door?"

"Yes, I do. Why did the delivery man dislike him?"

Her head rolled back along with her eyes. "This happened about a week ago."

Luther whined.

"Go sit on the porch, boy. There's water waiting for you." Jennifer dropped the leash.

Luther trotted to the front door, lapped the water, and then sat at attention; eyes trained on his master.

"I'm impressed with Luther."

"He's a great dog. Anyway, the paper guy isn't exactly a—." Jennifer snapped her fingers. "Oh, what's that award a baseball pitcher wins."

"A Cy Young." McClung answered.

"Yeah, that's it. The poor old man would sometimes hit the driveway. Sometimes the yard or bushes. It's like lookin for Easter eggs some days."

McClung stifled a laugh.

"Late one morning last week, Monday, I heard Myron yelling at the top of his lungs at the paper guy. Myron's practically lying on top of the car hood."

Jennifer held her arms wide open with her legs splayed out to imitate his pose.

"Then Myron walks to the driver's side window, reaches in, grabs the old man's shirt and yanks him around."

She demonstrated by grabbing an imaginary person and shoving them back and forth.

"Myron threatened to sue him, have him fired, public humiliation, whatever it took to get good service. He screamed something about having the goods on him, then demanded that his paper be waiting for him at his door every morning."

Marsh punched Thayer. "It's a wonder the guy didn't run over Myron."

"The poor guy was mortified. All the neighbors gawking, me included, obviously." Jennifer smirked. "If it hadn't been for Brian, I think Myron would have pulled the paper guy out of the car and stomped on him."

"Brian, the landscaper? What did he do?" McClung was intrigued. Brian's name was popping up as much Robyn and Shelby.

"You know him?"

McClung nodded.

"Then you know he's a big guy. A giant compared to Myron. Anyway, Brian was cutting Myron's yard. When he sees Myron assaulting the paper guy, Brian calmly walked over. Tapped Myron on the back."

Marsh scoffed. "I'd love to have seen that."

McClung held up his hand to quiet the young officer.

"Oh, oh you'll love what happened next." Jennifer's mouth opens wide in a silent laugh. "Myron whipped around. Seething. Snarled at Brian, '*What do you want, you big dumb ox? Get back to work*'. Then Myron turned back to the paper guy, but Brian snatched Myron's right arm before he could reach inside the car."

McClung stopped her. "You said Myron called Brian a big dumb ox?"

"Yes, sir."

"Go on." McClung supposed Myron must have been drunk or temporarily insane to go up against Brian.

"Like I was saying, Brian grabbed Myron's arm and flung him around. Myron jerked his arm free then pulled it back like he's going to punch him. Then all Brian said was, '*Mister Wagstaff, that's enough*'. The tone of Brian's voice plus whatever Myron saw on Brian's face made him think twice."

A sly grin pulled on McClung's lips as he visualized the scene. "What happened next?"

"Well, Myron squinted his beady little eyes, then spat on the ground, stomped up his driveway, into his house and slammed the front door." Jennifer snorted.

"And Brian?"

"He finished cutting Myron's yard."

"That's it?"

"Yep." She continued. "I don't understand what power Myron has to get people to bend to his will. But from that day on the paper guy leaves his car on the street, walks up Myron's driveway and places the paper at the door. I can see the paper guy's lips moving when he returns to his car. I assume he's cussing Myron. I would if it were me. Oh, and his hands are balled tight, too."

Thayer muttered. "Myron's a nut."

McClung sighed. "Okay. That's all the questions I have for now. Thanks again for your help."

Jennifer flicked his business card on the side of her hand. "Will you tell me what excuse Robyn offers for being in my house when she wasn't supposed to be?"

"Yes, I can certainly do that."

"Boy, I thought she was trustworthy. Never had any complaints." Jennifer groaned. "I don't want to find another maid."

McClung shifted his weight. "Well, maybe she has a good reason. You never know."

"I hope so. I'll be waiting for your call." She waved, then joined Luther sitting on the front porch.

McClung and the officers crossed the street to check out Myron's house.

After inspecting the locks on the front door and windows, they headed toward the side gate.

No fresh footprints on the once sloppy wet ground that had now been baked solid by the Georgia sun.

Once they passed through the gate, they checked the backside of the house for open or broken windows.

None.

The sliding glass door was shut.

McClung slid on a pair of latex gloves before pulling on the metal door handle.

The door glided open.

Not good. McClung jerked his head toward Marsh.

"Boss, I swear this house was locked up tight when we left."

McClung believed his officer and turned his attention to the floor inside of the house.

No footprints on the tiles.

The snapping sound of latex echoed in the empty house as Thayer and Marsh put on their gloves then followed McClung.

They inspected each room. Nothing appeared out of place.

Next, they climbed the steps.

The first room they entered was the one in which Jennifer Leeson saw the light.

Myron's office.

McClung went behind Myron's expansive antique oak desk. The scarred top made him wonder if the desk once belonged to Myron's father.

The Criminal Search Team had purposely left each drawer slightly open so there would be no confusion as to which drawers had been searched. Now, they were closed. Someone had been looking for something. McClung worried that his CSI team missed something critical to the case. Had the intruder found it?

He shook his head. Impossible. The team was top-notch.

When they searched Myron's house, the only financial items found were the HOA records, his personal account, and a binder of numbers and initials.

CSI had removed all of it and then put it into evidence after Jack Jackson ruled Myron's death a homicide. Stewie and Jenny were working on deciphering the odd binder.

"Boss, Marsh and I will split up and examine the other rooms."

McClung waved them away. Even though he knew the drawers were empty, he examined each one. No clues. Nothing.

Something about the desk gnawed at him. What was it? A memory stuck in his brain he couldn't quite grasp.

He squeezed his eyes closed as he massaged his temples.

"Ah, nothing." McClung exhaled as he realized he'd been holding his breath.

"Got nothing, Boss. Everything looks in order." Thayer stood in the doorway.

McClung patted the desktop. "Let's go. Make sure every door and window is locked. Now that we know this is a crime scene, put a seal on every window and all the doors including the interior ones.

He stared at the desk then shut the door. What was it about the desk that bothered him?

Chapter 13

When they got back to the station, they found Shelby Culbertson sitting in the front lobby, reading a dated *People* magazine with Lady Diana on the cover.

"Well, hello, boys." Shelby purred as she arched her back, tilted her head to one side and leered.

McClung was glad she was here. Now they wouldn't have to track her down for an interview.

"Ms. Culbertson, what brings you to the station?"

She stood and smoothed down her black pencil skirt. A red, off-the-shoulders, spandex shirt with quarter-length sleeves, bare legs, and a pair of black leather strappy wedges completed her outfit.

"I'm here about my aunt. I went by her house and a neighbor told me she died last night. Why wasn't I informed?" She shimmied toward them.

McClung now had confirmation that Shelby Culbertson and Shelby Hornbuckle were the same person.

"Judy Johnson is your aunt?"

"Yes."

"I'm sorry for your loss."

Shelby pressed her lips together. "Don't be. She was a rather difficult person."

McClung turned away thinking it would be rude to agree with her. He waved at the receptionist. "Good morning Penny. How's it going?"

"Morning. So far so good."

"Do me a solid and sign in Ms. Culbertson and get her a visitor's badge."

Penny pulled out a form and a badge. "Consider it done." She looked around McClung. "Miss, do you mind filling out this form? I'll give you a badge and then you may follow Chief McClung."

Once completed, McClung lead Shelby to one of the interview rooms. Thayer stopped by the break room for water.

McClung seated Shelby then left her alone as he waited in the hallway for Thayer to arrive.

"I got three bottles." Thayer held out one for his boss.

"Thanks."

They entered the room leaving the door open.

Shelby looked around the vanilla room. "This place could use a woman's touch starting with these uncomfortable chairs."

"No funds in the budget for frilly things." McClung said flatly as he removed a notepad from his suit coat pocket.

Thayer slid a bottle toward Shelby.

"Thank you, darling." She flashed her perfect teeth as she reached for it.

Thayer ignored the comment.

"So you are Judy Johnson's niece."

Shelby chuckled. "My, nothing gets passed you, huh?"

McClung scratched a few words on the pad. "Yes, ma'am. I've been told I'm a genius."

Staring at McClung's expressionless face, Shelby scoffed, opened the water, and sipped. "Well, handsome genius, can you tell me where Aunt Judy's body is."

"My name is Chief McClung, but you may call me McClung. Your aunt's body is at the funeral home waiting on an autopsy."

She pulled her head back in surprise. "Really, an autopsy. Why? She's old and grumpy and probably nastied away."

"Judy Johnson was seen arguing with someone before she died. We're considering her death suspicious, so an autopsy is required."

The crease between her eyes deepened as she chewed her bottom lip. "When will I get the death certificate?"

"Really, that's all you got to say about your dead aunt?" Thayer leaned forward. "Are you expecting a big inheritance? Is that why you killed her?"

The water bottle in her hand hit the floor. Shelby's mouth dropped open and her painted eyes grew wide.

"What? Killed?" Shelby shook her head. "No. No. No. I didn't kill my Aunt Judy."

Her upper body rested on the table as if she was going to do a pushup. "I swear I had nothing to do with it."

McClung loved Thayer's bad cop. He stood and picked up the bottle, happy to see the cap was still secured to the lipstick-stained rim.

After setting the bottle beside Shelby's hand, McClung returned to his chair. "Drink some water. Take a minute to calm down."

She pushed away from the table. "Calm down? After being accused of murder, you're telling me to calm down?"

"I'm not accusing you of murder. I have questions. That's all." McClung murmured.

Shelby seized the bottle then pointed it at Thayer. "He did."

Thayer shrugged.

Twisting off the cap, she drank deeply. "Do you have anything else stronger?"

"A Coke or Dr Pepper?"

She gawked at McClung. "That's what you consider stronger, a Coke?" Shelby crossed her arms, plopped backward and mumbled. "Genius, my eye."

They sat in silence for a moment.

McClung tapped his pen on the notepad. "Is your maiden name Hornbuckle?"

Shelby chuckled. "You've been talking to Lula Belle. Don't deny it, because she's the only person in this town I've told. That lady doesn't miss a thing." She buried her tongue behind her bottom lip, then shook her head. "Am I under arrest?"

"No, but—."

"But nothing." Shelby stood. "I'm tired and I want to leave."

Thayer jumped up and barred the open door with his body.

Shelby adjusted the off-the-shoulder sleeves over her shoulders. Her fists rested on her hips. "I don't mind wrestling my way out."

McClung stayed seated. "Please, sit down, I only have a few more questions. I don't want to arrest you to get my answers."

Her head whipped around. "Arrest me? You said you didn't think I killed Aunt Judy."

"No, I said I wasn't accusing you of murder. But now? Eh?" McClung looked at her with a smug grin.

Shelby stamped her foot and then marched to her chair and sat. "Fine. What are your stupid questions?"

"Thayer, for formality's sake, will you do the honors?"

"You have the right to remain silent."

"Wait, a minute. I thought you said I wasn't under arrest." Shelby glared at McClung as she drummed her long, hot-pink nails on the table.

McClung shifted. "Well, since you don't have an attorney present and you are cooperating, we have to Mirandize you, or you may sign a form waiving your rights."

"Which is quicker?"

"About the same."

"I'll sign the form. Reading me my rights for some reason makes me feel like I've done something wrong. I'm not the criminal kind."

McClung tipped his head at Thayer.

Thayer slipped out of the room. In a matter of seconds, he returned with the form.

Shelby signed the form without reading it. "There, are we all happy now?" She smiled sweetly and fluttered her eyelashes then gave them the stink eye.

McClung placed his notepad on top of the paper, then cleared his throat.

"Is Hornbuckle your maiden name?"

"No, one of my married names. Johnson is my maiden name."

McClung considered her answer. "Judy's husband was your father's brother?

Shelby laughed. "No, she was my father's sister. Aunt Judy was never married. Engaged but never married. That story she tells of a dead husband is a big fat lie."

McClung cocked his head and raised his eyebrows. "Will you please elaborate?"

"Yeah, it's a good one. I'll have that Coke now. Diet. Over a few cubes of ice. Not a lot. Just four or five cubes." Shelby looked at Thayer. "Make that two cans of Diet Coke. Please." She said with a tight grin.

Thayer and McClung stood.

"We'll be right back."

She looked at her gem-studded wristwatch. "Do hurry. I have a very important doctor's appointment, and I don't want to be late." Shelby's wiggled her eyebrows.

McClung closed the door without a remark.

"You stay here. I'll get the soda. Need anything?" McClung put his hands behind his back, interlaced his fingers, and then lifted his arms. A couple of joints popped as he stretched his shoulders and back.

"No." Thayer held up a full bottle of water.

McClung trotted along the hallway and considered buying a small refrigerator for the observation room and stocking it with drinks.

Quickly returning with the two Diet Cokes and a plastic cup with no ice, McClung took a deep breath before entering the interview room.

"Here you go."

"Thank you, but where's the ice?"

"We're out. Now tell us about the lie."

Shelby rolled her eyes. "Yeah, right." She took a sip. "Mm, nothing beats a Diet Coke. Well, except Diet Coke and Jack, that's one of my fav—"

Thayer cut her off. "Can you please get on with it?"

"My, looks like sonny boy got up on the wrong side of his crib."

McClung tapped his watch. "I thought you had an important rendezvous."

Shelby sat upright. "According to my parents, Judy was engaged to be married to this really rich guy. I don't remember his name. My dear old aunt played it smart." She tapped her temple.

"Aunt Judy was a wise old bird. She had the fiancé do a will and change his beneficiaries before they got hitched."

McClung grunted. "Meaning she'd get everything when he died."

"Yeah." Shelby burped behind her hand. "Evidently, my aunt was quite a catch in her younger years. She had tons of suitors buzzing around her. This man, the richest one, was crazy about her. Professed his undying love to her."

"Let me guess. She said prove it and he made her his sole heir."

Shelby clicked her tongue. "Bingo. Then the rich guy ups and dies before they even completed their wedding plans. Aunt Judy was a rich lady just like that." She snapped her fingers. "Still is."

"Heart attack?" McClung scoffed.

"That's what it was ruled, a heart attack, but my father's theory was Aunt Judy had something to do with it. He said she only wanted his money, not him."

"Huh, is that a fact?" McClung sat back and tugged his earlobe. "And you don't recall the fiancé's name?"

Shelby shook her head. "No, that was a long time ago. My parents are dead and I'm an only child." She gulped the soda.

"Any other family members you could ask?"

She threw up her hands. "I'm it. The last of the Johnsons. That's the only reason Aunt Judy put me in her will."

McClung made a note. "Who is your attorney?"

Shelby coughed then planted her feet on the floor. "Why? Do I need to call them?"

"There's no reason." McClung noticed she said *them*. "It wouldn't be Schnarff, Mowinckel, and Tippler by any chance, would it."

Diet Coke leaked out from Shelby's mouth as she continued to cough.

McClung reached under the table for a cube of tissues then slid it to Shelby.

She yanked a handful from the box and mopped her chin. "What? Are you a mind reader, too?"

McClung blinked a few times. "You're the sole beneficiary of your aunt's estate, aren't you?"

Shelby's cheeks flamed. "Who told you I was?"

"Your Aunt Judy doesn't seem the philanthropist type or the type who would want the government to get her money. Since you're the end of the Johnson line that only leaves you." McClung stabbed the air with his pen toward her.

She popped open the second can of Diet Coke. "Schnarff, Mowinckel, and Tippler are odd names don't you think?"

Thayer grunted. "Sound like made up names."

Shelby laughed. "Yeah, something the Three Stooges would use. Anyway, their office contacted me a year ago to verify I was still alive and kicking and to tell me dear Aunt Judy was looking for me."

"Your aunt wanted you to visit her?" McClung leaned backed and crossed his arms.

"Un-huh." Shelby yawned. "I'm not sure why. All she ever did when I'd stop by was boss me around and complain about everything and everybody."

Thayer crossed his arms. "Then why did you keep going back?"

"Pfft, the money." She smiled and sipped the Diet Coke. "Well, now and then she'd relive the past. About trouble she and my father would get into as kids."

Shelby sighed and stared beyond McClung's head. Shaking her head, she focused on him. "So, when can I get the death certificate?"

"As soon as the autopsy is completed and a cause of death is established. Probably within the next few days." McClung hoped it would be quick. He wanted this case over sooner rather than later.

She smirked. "You mean if Aunt Judy was murdered, you're going to arrest me?"

"It depends. You were seen in her neighborhood about the time she died. Visiting her?"

"Certainly not." Shelby shuddered. "Once a month is enough."

McClung glared at her. "Why did you drive by your aunt's house?"

"The neighborhood has nice scenery, well, except for Aunt Judy's place. Stingy old bat wouldn't pay for any improvements. Sheesh! That poor yardman took a beating from her. The poor guy only wanted to be nice and help her." Shelby snorted. "Crazy old woman. Psychotic, paranoid, ungrateful, mean, and hateful. That's what she was."

"You're avoiding the question." McClung growled.

She narrowed her eyes. "I was on my way to meet someone."

"Arnold Carter?"

"He's not the only man in my stable."

"Who then?"

"Why is the man's name so important?"

Thayer stabbed the table with his index finger. "Aunt Judy. Dead. Possible murder. You need an alibi."

Shelby turned sideways, slung her arm across the back of the chair, and crossed her legs. The top leg swung in overdrive as her mouth pinched closed.

"Waiting for a name." McClung grumbled.

The swinging leg froze midair, then she stamped her foot on the floor. "Fine! Brian. Brian Lane. There, are you happy?"

McClung took a few seconds to process the name. "The yard guy?"

"Yes." She leered and slid around in the chair, then rested her elbow on the table as she supported her chin between her thumb and curled index finger. "I can see you're stunned at my choice of men."

Shelby leaned back and smoothed out the tight skirt. "As the saying goes, you can't judge a book by its cover. The same goes for men and their pants."

McClung remained silent.

Shelby stood. "Are we almost finished here?" She tapped her wristwatch. "My appointment, remember?"

"For now. I'll contact you when the autopsy is completed."

McClung and Thayer stood then walked Shelby to the lobby.

"Don't leave town." McClung gave her a business card.

She tucked it inside her bra. As she patted it, Shelby bit her bottom lip and grinned. "I'll keep it close to my heart."

She sashayed to the front door, stopped, looked over her shoulder, then blew McClung and Thayer a kiss. Shoving the door open with her hip, Shelby faded into the bright sunlight.

Chapter 14

McClung had just left a call back number on Robyn's pager when Thayer poked his head into the office. A generous grin was plastered on his face

"Boss, I found Brian Lane. I called Stellar Landscaping."

McClung shot up a thumb. "Great job." He stood and slipped on his suit coat. "I hope it's somewhere close."

"You're not going to believe it. The square."

"Perfect, we can grab lunch once we're finished with Brian."

"I'm all in for that. Did you track down Robyn?"

A heavy sigh escaped McClung's mouth. "I left her another page. Jenny gave me Robyn's unlisted home number. No answer. No answering machine."

"Why is she avoiding us?"

"Good question."

They jogged down the back stairwell, and he instructed Penny to forward Robyn's call.

As they headed to the square, they passed Judy's house.

The grass was trim, and the flower beds had fresh mulch.

McClung and Thayer looked at each and said, "Brian."

The police cruiser entered the busy town square.

"Isn't that a Stellar truck?" McClung pointed at the street full of lunch goers.

The young sergeant saw the tail end of the truck as it turned on one of the side streets.

"Do you want me to chase him?" Thayer poised his index finger under the siren switch.

"No, too dangerous." McClung's stomach growled. "We know how to find him."

People jaywalked as they headed to the restaurants and shops. Lunchtime on the square was always a game of Dodge Cars and Frogger.

"Look!" McClung pointed at a car backing out.

"On it." Thayer flipped on the turn signal and waited as traffic went around the patrol car.

They walked half a block to the Darlington Diner.

McClung clutched Thayer's arm.

"Isn't that Robyn going in?" McClung tipped his head a mere fraction toward the woman entering the diner.

"That's her all right."

"How fortuitous." McClung released his grip and strode to the restaurant.

Robyn sat at the far end of the counter close to the kitchen door. She was wearing no makeup. Her long brown hair was pulled into a tight ponytail. She wore a pair of Capri jeans, light blue, short-sleeved tee shirt with a dark blue bib apron, and a pair of tattered sneakers. She could be considered a natural beauty, and more than likely, stunning with a makeover.

The little bell above the door rang.

She turned toward the sound and quickly covered her pale face with the menu.

Too late.

They saw her.

McClung and Thayer sat on either side of her.

Robyn couldn't escape and pretended to be unaware as she studied the menu six inches from her nose.

McClung drummed the countertop with his open hands. "What looks good on the menu, Robyn?"

"Mind if I borrow yours?" Thayer reached for the plastic menu in Robyn's hands.

"Oh, officers, I didn't notice you." Eyes forward, Robyn tossed the menu on the counter in front of Thayer.

"Thank you." He straightened it then rested his elbow on it. Thayer's fingertips supported his head as he stared at her.

Robyn stuck her hands between her knees, leaned forward with her back rounded as she concentrated on several permanent water rings on the faded countertop.

"You haven't returned my pages. You must be in high demand, Robyn." McClung caught Frank's eye and mouthed, *come back later*.

The diner's owner gave a two-finger salute and turned around to wait on two customers seated at the opposite end of the long counter.

Robyn said nothing.

"Too tired to answer, huh?" McClung tapped her shoulder with his menu.

"Yeah."

"Say, why don't you let me buy your lunch? We can chat here and you won't have to come into the station."

Her head jerked toward McClung. "Chat about what?"

McClung raised his eyebrows. "Lunch?"

Robyn returned her focus to the water rings. "Sure. Not gonna pass up a free lunch." She yanked the menu out from under Thayer's elbow.

The kitchen door burst open.

Peggy carried a large tray loaded with plates of burgers, sandwiches, and fries.

"McClung. Thayer. Well, I must be living right. Seeing y'all two days in a row." She looked for her husband. "Frank, get over here."

Frank turned in two lunch orders, then filled one large foam cup with Dr Pepper, no ice, and then another one with lots of ice and Coke.

With the drinks in hand, he followed his wife's voice, and set the drinks in front of McClung and Thayer. "Here you go."

Frank looked at his wife. "You want me to serve them burgers? That tray looks kinda heavy."

"Nah, I got it. I'll be back." Peggy took off as if she were carrying an empty tray.

Frank shook his head and laughed. "That wife of mine is one strong woman. Stronger than me to tell you the truth."

McClung compared Frank's thin five-foot, three-inch frame to Peggy's Amazonian five-foot, six-inch frame. "Yeah, Frank, I'm afraid you might be right. No offense intended."

Frank snickered. "I can't be offended by the truth, now can I?"

Robyn slid off the barstool.

Thayer jumped in front of her. "Now where are you going?"

She hopped up on the barstool.

McClung watched Robyn's jaw clench several times.

"Frank, get Robyn whatever she wants and put it on my tab."

The older man glanced between McClung, Robyn, Thayer, and back to McClung. "Got it. Robyn, want your usual chef salad?"

She sat upright, pressed her hands on the counter and drummed her fingers. "Frank, I'm feeling mighty hungry today. I want a steak, medium-well, with fries and gravy, and a large Sprite."

"All right. What about y'all?"

Thayer rubbed his flat belly. "I'll have the same as yesterday. Cheeseburger fully dressed and fries. Nope. Make that onion rings instead of fries."

McClung scratched his chin as he read the menu. "Got any specials today?"

Frank shot up two bony fingers. "Grilled BLT with fries and a grilled peanut butter and jelly with a fruit cup."

"Ah, grilled peanut butter and jelly sounds interesting. Give me that."

"You got it." Frank pushed through the kitchen door.

Robyn glared at McClung. "Are you going to interrogate me now or after I eat?"

"No interrogation. Just a few questions." McClung ripped the paper wrapper from the straw. "But if you would prefer, you can answer the questions down at the station after we eat."

"I bet it's just a few." She mumbled as she waited for her order.

Without a sound, Frank stood behind Robyn. "Here's the Sprite, hun." He reached between her and Thayer and set down a large Sprite.

"Thank you, Frank." She sipped the drink. "What's your first question?"

McClung removed his notepad. "What were you doing at Jennifer Leeson's house the morning Myron Wagstaff was killed?"

"I was looking for an earring I'd lost. Next question."

"Did you find it?"

"No. Next question."

McClung wanted more details but short and to the point was better than nothing. "Did you see anything or hear anything unusual while you were at Jennifer Leeson's home?"

"No."

"Really? Did you hear or see Arnold Carter speeding away from Myron's house?"

"Nope."

McClung bounced his pen on the notepad. "A witness said she saw the upstairs' curtain move as he sped away. You can think about the question before you answer."

She scowled at McClung. "I didn't look out the window. I was searching for my earring. The curtain must have moved as I was feeling the carpet for it."

"Did you see Myron that morning?"

"No." Robyn finished the soda, held up the cup, and then rattled the ice to get Frank's attention.

Frank held up a finger as he took a customer's order. "Be right there."

"Were you and Myron having an affair?"

Robyn laughed. "Well, that's the funniest thing I've heard in a week. Do you honestly believe I'd be attracted to a man like him? Gah, what a stupid question." She grunted.

McClung couldn't imagine Myron and Robyn as a couple. But then again, tastes varied. He moved on to another question. "Why did you visit him so often?"

Peggy appeared with three plates. "Here you go, darlings."

"Robyn, would you like some steak sauce?" Peggy asked as she picked up McClung's half-full cup.

"No, ma'am. The gravy is all I need." Robyn inhaled the aroma of the grilled steak. "Mm, smells divine."

"All righty then, anyone else need a refill?" Peggy held out her hand.

Thayer nodded, his cheeks bulging, as he pushed his empty cup toward Peggy.

Robyn ran three fries through the thick white gray and delicately put them into her mouth.

McClung watched Robyn as she dodged the question. After she swallowed, he asked again. "Why were you at Myron's so often?"

She patted her lips with a thick paper napkin. "That's a rather personal question."

"No, it isn't since we're considering you a possible murder suspect."

161

Robyn held her knife and fork poised over the perfectly cooked steak. "Excuse me. You think I killed Myron?"

McClung chewed off a bite of his thick sandwich.

Peggy returned just in time with his Dr Pepper. "What do you think of the grilled peanut butter sandwich?"

After he washed down the gooey bite, McClung smiled. "It's an epicurean taste sensation, Peggy."

She beamed and gave Thayer his Coke. "Can I get y'all anything else?"

"Nope, we're okay." McClung answered for everyone.

"Yell at Frank if y'all need anything." Peggy dashed into the kitchen.

Robyn set aside her silverware as she turned to face McClung. "You answer my question. Do you think I killed Myron?"

"Yes. You see, what I don't understand is how you knew Myron was murdered before anyone else. How do you explain that if you had nothing to do with his murder?" McClung waited for her reaction.

Robyn's eyes froze wide open, and she pulled in her lips. She blinked several times, inhaled, held her breath, and then suddenly exhaled.

"Frank." Robyn shouted. "Will you please get me a to-go box?"

"Answer the question, Robyn. How did you know Myron was murdered?" McClung stood.

Thayer followed his boss's lead.

Frank set a box in front of Robyn but looked at McClung. "Is everything okay?"

McClung shook his head ever so slightly.

"I'm late for my next appointment. That's all." Robyn moved her uneaten food into the box.

Frank rubbed his wrinkled cheek and walked away.

Thayer leaned toward Robyn's ear. "Answer the Chief's question."

She ignored him and picked up the box, then looped the purse strap over her shoulder.

"Robyn, please don't make a scene."

She stared into McClung's chest. "Am I under arrest?"

"That's up to you."

Thayer jiggled the handcuffs hanging from his duty belt.

Robyn's eyes shifted around the restaurant. A few heads turned toward their direction. "Fine. You win. You go out first, then I'll follow." Robyn sat and waited.

Thayer walked to the front of the restaurant and stood beside the door.

McClung motioned to Frank. "Can we get a couple of to-go boxes and lids for our drinks?"

Frank boxed Thayer and McClung's lunches and refilled their cups.

"Thanks, Frank." McClung laid a twenty and a ten on the counter. "For your favorite charity." He winked and headed toward the door.

Robyn followed McClung out of the restaurant. She grumbled. "It's about time. I've got houses to clean."

Once outside, Robyn stood her ground. "I'm not going to the station to answer your questions. You can grill me just as well sitting over there."

McClung followed the direction of her finger to a park bench tucked under the shade of an enormous oak tree in the square.

"Fine with me. You first." McClung waited for Robyn to take the first step. He and Thayer trailed behind.

She sat in the center of the bench, opened the to-go box, selected two fries buried in gravy, and ate them.

McClung and Thayer sat either side of her.

"For the third time. How did you know Myron had been murdered before the autopsy was completed?" McClung opened his to-go box, plucked a red grape from the fruit cup, and popped it into his mouth.

She shrugged.

"That's not an answer."

Robyn closed the foam box.

"Fine. I looked out the window. A few times. I saw the paper guy knock on Myron's door. He started cursing as soon as Myron opened it. Myron jerked him inside. After a few minutes, the paper guy stormed out of the house, and got in his car. He sat there for a second and then went to Myron's front door and propped the newspaper against it."

Interesting, McClung thought.

"Which window did you see all of this?"

"Downstairs living room window."

"You looked more than once. Who else did you see?"

"I heard a car right after the paper guy left. I didn't look because I was walking up the stairs. I don't know if the car parked or turned around in the cul-de-sac."

McClung knew Robyn had seen Marian. "I know you looked out the upstairs window."

"Yeah. I guess it was about twenty or thirty minutes later, I heard someone pounding on Myron's front door. So, I looked out. It was Arnold Carter. When Myron didn't answer, he went through the gate leading to the swimming pool." Robyn's cheeks developed a pink tinge.

"And then what?"

Robyn opened the box and removed a fry. She bit it in half. "I don't know. After a few minutes he came running through the gate, jumped into his car and hightailed it. That's when I noticed your wife and I ducked out of sight."

"Why didn't you want Marian to see you?"

"Because I wasn't supposed to be in Missus Leeson's house. That's why I didn't answer the door when the cops came over."

McClung squinted. "I don't think you were only looking for your earring. If, in fact, you were looking for it at all. You could have called Missus Leeson about the earring. What were you really doing?"

Robyn tossed the other half of the fry to a pigeon strutting in the grass. Leaning forward, she braced her elbows on her knees and stared at the bird as it pecked the fry to pieces.

McClung looked at his watch. "I thought you had houses to clean."

Her head sagged as she pushed away from her knees. Falling back onto the bench, Robyn's eyes focused on the sky filtering through the thick tree canopy.

"I knew that Jennifer Leeson wouldn't be home until after six o'clock. She has all the movie channels, and a TV mounted on the wall at the foot of the tub. A jetted tub. I like to use it and watch a movie."

Robyn sat upright and glared at McClung. "Jennifer will fire me when she finds out. But I always clean the tub and I bring my own towels. Still. She'll fire me. I know it."

"Were you there to look for your earring or strictly the tub?"

"Both. I didn't find the earring."

McClung scratched the back of his head. Why did he feel sorry for Robyn? If Jennifer Leeson found out the whole truth, Robyn would probably lose all of her customers.

"Robyn, will you promise me you'll stop taking advantage of your customers' amenities and only clean their homes?"

Her head whipped toward McClung. "Yes, promise. Cross my heart." She used a finger to draw an *X* on her chest.

"Then I'll tell Jennifer Leeson you were looking for a lost earring. And there's one other thing."

"Anything. I can't lose my business. Cleaning houses is the only job I've ever had. Please, I'll do whatever it takes to keep my business."

"Why did you spend so much time with Myron?"

Her cheeks flamed. "Uh." She covered face with her hands.

McClung heard a muffled *gah*.

Robyn's hands fell. She clutched her thighs and gritted her teeth, then inhaled deeply and sighed. "This so embarrassing. I don't know why but..."

McClung rubbed the space between his nose and upper lip. He held his breath as he waited for Robyn's revelation.

She stared at McClung. "I liked spending time with him. There I said it."

Thayer snickered.

"Shut up." Robyn growled at Thayer then turned toward McClung. "You're his boss. Tell him to go over there." She pointed across the street.

McClung stood and clamped a hand on the young sergeant's shoulder.

"Give us a minute. Wait for me in the cruiser and while you're there call in to the station and tell Penny we'll be there in a few minutes."

"Yes, Boss." Thayer did his best to stifle his laughter as he walked away.

Robyn sat with her arms crossed. She glanced sideways at McClung. "We weren't having an affair. Nothing like that." The back of her hand ran under her nose. "I don't understand it either but Myron and I clicked. Nothing sexual. Friends only. We'd sit around. Drink and talk. That's all."

An image darted through McClung's brain as he stood in front of her. *Beauty and the Beast.*

"What did y'all talk about?"

Robyn's lips bunched. "Just stuff. Politics. Movies. Celebrities. Ordinary people."

"People from Lyman County?"

"Yeah."

"I see." McClung sniffed. "Was Myron using you for his blackmail scheme?"

"What? Blackmail?" She shook her head. "No. No way. He'd never do anything like that."

McClung didn't believe Robyn.

"Are you sure about that? You never said anything embarrassing about your clients?"

"No, sir. Nu-huh. Never. Never."

McClung sat beside her. "Look at me."

Robyn obeyed.

"How did you know Myron was murdered?"

Her eyes darted over his face. "Because that's how Myron said he'd die. Somebody would kill him."

Chapter 15

"Boss, do you buy Robyn's story?"

"Mm." McClung squinted. "Bits and pieces. Being inside Jennifer Leeson's house. The jetted tub."

"What's your theory?" Thayer asked as they drove back to the station.

"I think Robyn was already at Myron's house when the paper guy banged on his door. How else did she hear him swearing?"

Thayer stopped at a four-way stop. "Bionic hearing?"

"Funny but no. The houses are too far apart. If Robyn was inside the Leeson's house, she could hear traffic and yelling but not actual words."

McClung glanced at Thayer. "Trust me. I live in that subdivision. Even when the neighborhood kids are playing in the yard across the street and we're inside the house, we can't understand their squawking."

Thayer's lead foot pressed the gas pedal.

McClung pointed to the posted speed limit, 35.

The sergeant frowned and eased off the gas.

"Back to my theory, I believe Robyn saw the killer. Waited until she felt safe, then went to Jennifer Leeson's to calm down and plan her next move."

"Why not call us?" Thayer peeked at the speedometer.

"Good question, but I definitely think she's the one who supplied Myron with the incriminating information for his blackmailing scheme."

Thayer slowed as they approached Judy Johnson's house.

Sitting in the driveway was a Corvette convertible with the top down.

Shelby Culbertson's car.

"Stop. Let's see what she's doing."

Thayer parked in front of the house.

They walked toward the front door and noticed it was cracked open.

McClung knocked on the sun-bleached door. "Hello. Ms. Culbertson. It's Chief McClung. Everything okay? May we enter?"

"Be there in a jiffy." Shelby's voice echoed from the back of the house.

She entered the foyer with a camera in her hand. "My. My. Why are y'all on my porch?"

It intrigued McClung that Shelby already claimed her aunt's house as her own. "We saw your car. Making sure all is good."

She pinched up her face as she lifted her shoulders. "Right as rain I suppose. Just taking a few photos."

McClung put his right foot on the threshold. "May I?"

"Sure."

170

He and Thayer followed her into the living room. Thick plastic covered the sofa and love seat. The furniture was dust free. Floral Tiffany lamps sat on the end tables. Antiques graced the room.

"I guess you don't know anything about antiques do you?" Shelby looked McClung over. "Nah, of course not. You're a man."

"Actually, my knowledge of antiques is extensive. My family has been in the business since the turn of the century."

"Gawd. A genius, a mind reader, and an antiquarian all wrapped up in one handsome cop. My, I envy your wife."

McClung cleared his throat. "Yep, that's me."

He picked up a lamp and examined the brass base. It had a nice patina and was stamped with the correct Tiffany mark. There was a turn-paddle knob socket for the on-off switch. A good sign.

Next, he placed his hand on the shade, put his ear close to the glass and knocked it. It rattled. Another good sign.

"This one is a genuine Tiffany."

Shelby clapped her hands. "Oh, goody." She took a few photos of the lamps from different angles. "I'm taking inventory of the house."

"We'd prefer you leave the house untouched until the cause of death is determined."

"I'm not taking anything. Yet." She picked up the lamp. "Can you hold it up? I gotta get a shot of the maker's mark."

McClung obliged. "But you may destroy evidence." He gently replaced the lamp.

Shelby groaned and rolled her eyes. "Fine. I'll leave."

"Why are you doing an inventory?"

Wagging a perfectly manicured index finger at him, she looked at McClung in disbelief. "Soon everyone will know she's dead and one of the no-account bums in Lyman County just might loot all this stuff."

"Makes sense. But Lyman County doesn't have that many no-account bums." Thayer guided her to the front door.

"Thank you, sweetie. But I'd have to say you're wrong there. You just had a murder. That makes for at least one no account." Shelby rubbed his firm bicep. "Nice."

"Yep, you got me there, ma'am."

"Don't call me that. I'm not that old."

"Yes, Ms. Culbertson."

Shelby groaned.

As they stepped outside McClung asked, "Did you dust the furniture today?"

Shelby locked the door and dropped the key into her deep cleavage. "Pfft. I don't clean. I pay someone. I think Aunt Judy had a woman come by every other week to do the hard stuff, like cleaning the oven and scrubbing floors. Jobs like that. Aunt Judy dusted every day. Hated dust with a passion."

McClung strolled beside Shelby toward the Corvette.

"What's the cleaning woman's name?"

Shelby picked up the scarf lying on the passenger seat, wrapped it over her head, and tied it under her chin, Jackie Kennedy-style.

"I don't know, gotcha, canape?" She snapped her fingers. "No, it's Kopna."

McClung smiled at Shelby's disastrous pronunciation of Robyn's last name. "Do you mean Konopka?"

"Yeah, that's it and she has a bird's name, Sparrow, maybe?"

"Robyn?"

"Gosh, you're good at this." She beamed. "I told you it's a bird's name."

"Does she have a key to Judy's house?"

Shelby laughed. "Hah! I had to beg the old biddy for this one." She patted her ample bosom. "Aunt Judy gave me the key under strict orders I never use it unless she was dead."

"So, now you're the only one with a key?"

"The attorneys may have one. You'll need to ask them." Her hand rested on the car door. "Am I free to go?"

McClung gave a thumb's up. "You're free. Drive safely."

Thayer opened Shelby's car door.

"My, my. Cute, young, and a gentleman." She clutched the steering wheel. "Ta, ta, gentlemen."

The two police officers watched her back the Corvette out of the driveway.

Shelby honked and waved then buzzed down the street.

McClung and Thayer looked at each other and said, "Robyn."

♦♦♦♦♦♦

McClung pointed. "Are my eyes deceiving me or is that a Stellar Landscaping trunk in one of our visitor's spots?

"Got to be Brian's truck." Thayer wrote the tag number on his palm.

McClung pulled open the heavy front door of the precinct. "We'll know in a second."

A man stood when they entered the lobby.

McClung recognized the tall, lean man with hair resembling a lion's mane.

Brian Lane.

The weathered man extended his hand. "I understand you're looking for me."

McClung clasped his rough and calloused hand. "Good to see you, Mr. Lane. We have a few questions for you, if you have the time."

"My time is yours."

Once Brian had his visitor's badge, the three men entered the heart of the building.

McClung walked beside Brian as Thayer trailed behind.

They entered interview room two.

"Mr. Lane, would you like some water or a soda?"

He waved away the offer. "Please call me Brian, if you don't mind."

"Not at all." McClung sat across from him. "I don't believe you've met Sergeant Thayer."

Brian dipped his head as he eyed the young officer. "Seen him around. A pleasure to meet you."

Thayer stood up halfway and shook Brian's hand. "Sir."

McClung removed his notepad from his inside coat pocket. "Let's get started."

"Okay."

"First of all, you're aware that Myron Wagstaff was murdered Monday morning and Judy Johnson was found dead Tuesday night." McClung waited for Brian's reaction.

A sadness swept over the landscaper's face. "Yes, I heard about them."

"I understand you and Judy Johnson had a confrontation Tuesday afternoon."

Brian leaned forward and put his forearms on the table. "I don't want to speak ill of the dead, but she's one stubborn lady. Her yard is an eyesore. I can't stand a messy yard, you know."

McClung matched Brian's posture. "I can understand that. Tell me what happened."

"I try to keep up her yard. No charge. She doesn't get it. The Golden Rule that is. I don't see why she refuses to let me help her."

The furrow between Brian's bushy eyebrows deepened. "Here lately, she's been more violent than ever."

"How's that?" McClung wasn't aware of anything outside the usual shenanigans.

Brian pushed away from the table. "I've been finding dead birds and squirrels in her yard. Occasionally, I can rescue an injured animal and save it." He examined the cuts and bruises on his hands. "Good people are exposed to Judy's foul language and violence. I don't like seeing the innocent get hurt."

"Do you mean the little boy, Dustin?"

He nodded. "It's not the first time she's shot at a kid. Never hit one before. Birds, squirrels, cats, and dogs are bad enough but kids? Pfft." Brian's jaws bulged a few times.

"Why did you keep going back knowing she'd shoot you?"

He looked at McClung and smirked. "I don't know. I'd hoped that she'd eventually have a change of heart."

Brian slung his left arm over the back of the chair. "I guess now she's getting her just rewards."

McClung wondered what Stewie and Jenny would find out about Brian. He moved from Judy Johnson to Myron.

"What did you think of Myron Wagstaff?"

Brian studied the corner of the ceiling. "Myron was a mean man. A bully. A certified bully." His hands dropped between his knees. "Myron may not have shot anyone, but his words… Myron's words stung worse than a paper cut doused with lemon juice."

Thayer shuddered.

"That man knew just the right insults to make a grown man cry." Brian sat back and crossed his arms.

"What did Myron say to you?"

Brian grinned lopsidedly. "Oh, Myron tried to humiliate me." He slid the chair closer to the table and tapped his wide chest. "But I've got thick skin. I know who I am. And that made Myron furious because he couldn't figure out which of my buttons to push."

"But you've witnessed Myron mock and ridicule others?"

"Yes, sir. His neighbors."

"Tell me about Myron's confrontation with the paper guy."

Brian frowned. "You heard about that."

"Yes."

"Not much to tell. Myron was unusually cranky that day. Criticized everything I did. But all I said was, 'Yes, sir. Whatever you say, sir.'" Brian laughed. "That's the best way to get his goat."

"I understand you went after Myron."

"Yeah. Yeah, I did. I mean a man can only take so much." Brian ran his hand over his weathered face. "Like I said before, I don't like seeing the innocent get hurt. You've seen the newspaperman. Haven't you?"

McClung pictured the frail man. Marian said he was sixty-five, but he appeared to be ninety. His fingers crooked. That's why his aim was off. And he wore thick glasses.

"Yes, I have."

Brian threw up his right hand. "Then you know the poor guy can't defend himself. So when Myron reached through the driver's side window and jerked the old man around, that was all I could take. I did what you would've done. I stopped Myron."

McClung arched one eyebrow. "You're probably right."

"Of course, you would've. You're a policeman. Serve and protect." Brian grinned. "And you probably want to know where I was when Myron took his last breath on Earth, don't you?"

"That would be helpful." McClung's pen was poised over the notepad.

"What time did he die?"

"Around eight-thirty, give or take a few minutes, Monday morning."

Brian's tongue ran over his bottom lip as he thought. "Ah, Monday, I was in your subdivision. I start in the back and work my way forward. I don't do every house in the subdivision. Some homeowners do their own yards. Some use other landscapers."

He shook his head. "I have too many to get to in one day. A few customers are particular about which day of the week I tend to their yards. Time, too."

"So, it's possible you could have been at Myron's house."

"I reckon anything is possible, but I wasn't. You can call my supervisor at Stellar to verify the houses I serviced that day."

McClung sighed heavily and wondered how he could solve Myron's murder without any witnesses. The only witness was Robyn, and she claimed she didn't see anything.

He switched paths.

"Have you ever seen a woman named Robyn Konopka at Myron's house?"

"The woman that cleans houses? Brown hair. Brown eyes. About your age." Brian pointed to Thayer.

"Yes, that's the one."

"Mmm hmm."

"How often?"

Brian scratched the stubble on his chin. "A fair amount. When the weather's good and warm, I'd see her around Myron's pool. Other times, I'd see her either driving her car into or out of Myron's garage."

He laughed as he moved his scratching to the back of his head. "I can't figure out women. But they say opposites attract. I reckon that's true with them two."

Brian pointed his finger at McClung. "Now you and your wife. A match made in heaven. Yes, sir. Made in heaven."

McClung nodded. "I feel most fortunate she agreed to marry me. Every morning I thank God she didn't leave me in the middle of the night."

Brian chuckled. "That's a good one." His smile faded. "I guess it's tough being married to a policeman."

"I try to be the best husband I can. Marian is my priority."

"That's good." Brian nodded. "If the offer is still good, I'd like that water."

Thayer jumped up, then darted out the door and returned a few seconds later with three bottles of water.

Brian took one. "Thank you, son."

McClung waited for Brian to swallow. "How did you know Judy Johnson died last night?"

Brian's top lip twitched imperceptibly as he stared at McClung. "Heard people talking about it. Around town."

"Where were you last night?"

"I was discussing business with Shelby Culbertson."

Shelby was telling the truth sort of, McClung thought. "She implied it was something else?"

A sound of amusement slipped from Brian's jagged grin. "Now that's a real good one."

"Why's that?" McClung said flatly.

Brian's grin vanished, leaving only the snarl. "Ms. Culbertson isn't my type. What's your next question?"

"What time did you meet her?"

"I don't know the exact time. No watch." He held up his bare tanned wrists.

"Stellar Landscaping leaves me a message every day about any new jobs or cancelations. They left a message saying Shelby Culbertson needed an estimate and that I needed to call her and set up an appointment. So, I did."

McClung tilted his head. "I'm confused. You said a few of your clients were fussy about the time you tended to their yard. So how do you know you're on time?"

Brian clicked his tongue. "Well, I have an alarm clock that gets me up in the morning. Five o'clock. I hit the road when the sun pops up over the horizon by one hand."

"What do you mean *by one hand?*" Thayer's forehead wrinkled.

Brian chuckled. "Chief, should I explain?"

"No. I know what you mean." McClung scratched his eyebrow. "One hand equals one hour. You tell time by the number of hands between the horizon and the bottom of the sun."

"Yep. Impressive." Brian grinned. "Sunrise is roughly six-thirty. Now, do you understand, sergeant?"

Thayer smirked. "Yeah, you leave for work at seven-thirty, but what do you do when it's raining, or cloudy?

Brian reached into his hip pocket and dangled a watch from a chain. "I use this."

McClung laughed. "That makes sense. Where did you meet Ms. Culbertson?"

"When I got in touch with her, she wanted to meet me in the square. Then she asked how fast I could get there. I said if she didn't mind my work grime, I'd be there in ten minutes. I rent a house outside of town."

McClung was getting frustrated. "Can you guess?"

"It was getting dark." Brian picked at his thumbnail. "Eight. Eight-thirty, I suppose."

"And you were where before that?"

"Taking care of a client's dogs. They're out of town."

"Can anyone verify that?"

"Nope. Like I said, they're out of town."

"What's their name and address?"

"Bill Toomey lives on two acres out on Highway 350. Roscoe and Rita are German Shepherd mix. Fine dogs."

McClung studied Brian as he drained his water bottle. Hard to pin down this guy. "What did Shelby need?"

"You won't believe this. Judy Johnson is Ms. Culbertson's aunt. Did you know that?"

"Yes."

"Of course, you do." Brian grunted. "Anyway, Ms. Culbertson was embarrassed by her aunt's overgrown yard. That's what the meeting was about. She wanted an estimate for cutting her aunt's front yard. Weekly."

Brian tapped his index finger on the table. "And pull weeds. Keep the place spit-spot is what she said."

Thayer snorted. "What did you do to Ms. Culbertson for her to send you on a weekly suicide mission?"

"You got that right." Brian dipped his head toward the two remaining water bottles. "Do you mind if I have another one?"

McClung handed him a bottle.

"Mighty kind of you." He drank a fourth of the bottle. "Well, I said I didn't mind keeping up the yard. On my time. I could bail out and not finish the job if Ms. Judy got too belligerent."

"Shelby Culbertson would pay you?"

"Yes, but I told her I didn't relish the idea of dodging bullets, even if they are BBs. They can put out a man's eye you know."

"I'm confused. Why would Shelby pay you for something you were doing for free?"

"She wanted me to keep up the yard no matter how abusive her aunt got. Get the job done every week regardless of injury. Ms. Culbertson said she had standards."

The wrinkle between McClung's brows deepened.

Brian gave a heavy sigh.

"Y'all don't get it. It's not all about the abuse or the money. It's the Golden Rule. Ms. Judy was cantankerous with the entire world. She needed to get right in here." Brian tapped his forehead. "And here." He patted his chest.

McClung drummed his fingers on the table. "Let's see if I understand. You were trying to teach her a lesson, love your enemy and bless those who curse you, hoping to make her a nicer person."

"Yep."

"What about Myron?"

Brian finished the second bottle of water then crushed it. "Myron was beyond redemption."

"And Ms. Judy wasn't?" McClung gave Brian the last bottle of water.

He poured water into his mouth then lifted his left shoulder and let it drop. "She closed that door when she shot that kid."

Chapter 16

"What do you think?" McClung sat at his desk staring out the window; Thayer sat on the opposite side.

Thayer leaned back in his chair and gazed at the acoustic ceiling tiles. "Everyone's guilty." He dropped his chin to his chest. "Maybe this is a *Murder on the Orient Express* deal. They all killed Myron."

"So, you're saying throw them all in jail, Robyn, Brian, Shelby, and Carter."

"Yeah."

The telephone rang.

"McClung." His sour expression perked up. "Jack, what's going on?"

Thayer stood and whispered, "Should I leave?"

McClung motioned Thayer to sit. "Are you kidding, Jack? Hang on, Thayer's here. I'm putting you on speakerphone, he's got to hear this."

"I finished Judy Johnson's autopsy. She was most definitely murdered," Jack reported.

Thayer's mouth dropped open. "How?"

Jack cleared his throat. "It's the first time I've seen someone killed in this manner. The killer shoved the BB gun up her nose and pulled the trigger. The pellets entered her brain, which caused swelling and bleeding. She was more than likely unconscious immediately and died shortly thereafter."

"What made you look for a BB pellet in her brain?" McClung squeezed the bridge of his nose.

"There was a fine line of blood originating from her left nostril. I examined the inside of her nose and discovered a few deep abrasions, which led to a hole in the thin bone that separates the nasal passages from the brain. Next, I checked out the brain and found bleeding, swelling, and the pellets. Three of them to be precise."

Thayer grimaced and covered his nose with his hands.

"Did you find any evidence on the BB gun?"

Jack sighed. "Not much. It appears to have been wiped clean. I found a tiny amount of blood and tissue on the end of the barrel. The specimens matched Judy Johnson's blood type."

"No fingerprints. Huh. Well, that means it wasn't suicide by a Daisy Red Ryder." McClung ran his hand over his head. "We now have two murders."

"Unfortunately, you're right about that. I wish I could tell you the same person committed both murders. The only common factor is bruising on the torso. Judy had bruising on the right side just above her breast and bruising on the left thigh."

"My theory is since we found the victim sitting, the killer pressed their knee on her leg and a hand on her chest to hold her down as they shoved the gun up her nose. What do you think, Jack?"

"Considering the placement of the bruises, sounds right."

McClung looked at Thayer. "What's your opinion?"

Thayer stood and acted out the scenario. "It's a good theory."

"Got anything else, Jack?" McClung poised a finger over the *end call* button.

"Take me off the speakerphone. No offense, Thayer."

"None taken. Boss, I'm getting coffee. You want a cup?"

"If you don't mind, will you start a pot in the war room and ask Jenny and Stewie to meet us there?"

Thayer closed the office door.

McClung picked up the receiver. "What's going on?"

"What I'm about to say is just between us. Got it. And whatever you do, don't tell Marian."

"You got it." McClung's heart skipped a beat, afraid Jack was going to end things with his wife's best friend, Joan.

"Ah, man. I've got it bad I tell you. Bad."

McClung's mouth felt like cotton. "Are you sick? Dying? Just spit it out."

"I'm in love with Joan. Madly in love. I can't get Joan out of my head. Being away from her is torture."

McClung's elbow banged on the desk as he rested his forehead in his palm. He chuckled. "Well, that's great. All kinds of horrible things were running around my brain. But this? This is wonderful news."

"It's incredible. I mean the first time I laid eyes on her I knew she was the one."

McClung smiled. "Yeah, the same for me when I saw Marian. My granny always said when I met the right girl, I'd know. She kept telling me not to settle but wait for the one you're meant to be with. I didn't think it'd ever happen. Patience isn't an easy virtue."

Jack said nothing.

"Are you there?"

"I don't know if Joan feels the same. Has Marian said anything?"

McClung snickered. "We sound like a couple of high schoolers."

"I'm sorry. You've got two murders to solve. I'm faxing the report to you now."

"Don't apologize. Look, according to Marian, Joan is crazy about you. So, don't worry about it." McClung stood. "Thanks for getting Judy Johnson's autopsy done so fast."

"No sweat. Talk to you later."

"Probably sooner than later." McClung's fax machine kicked on. "The autopsy report is coming through now."

"Good and remember."

"Yeah, yeah, yeah. Mum's the word."

The aroma of coffee wafted out of the war room. Good coffee, not the jet-black stuff Stewie made. McClung was surprised Stewie's coffee didn't crawl out of the pot and into the cup on its own.

McClung entered the room.

Jenny, Stewie, and Thayer stood around the breakroom. A box of Krispy Kreme donuts sat on the table.

"Looks like the party started without me." McClung glanced into the open box. Six out of twelve donuts remained. "Let's get down to business. Jenny and Stewie, tell me what you've found."

Stewie's hollow cheeks were bulging and his lips were glossy with donut glaze. He nudged Jenny with his elbow.

"I'll start with the easy ones." Jenny opened the first manila folder. "Robyn Konopka is basically blemish free, only one parking ticket. Her cleaning business, which is quite profitable, has all the proper permits and licenses. Taxes filed every quarter and on time."

McClung wrote Robyn's name on the whiteboard. "Let's see how these people are connected."

Thayer spoke as he wiped his hands with a paper napkin. "Myron, Wagstaff, Carter and Judy should go under Robyn's name." He looked at Jenny. "Does she have an attorney?"

"Good question." McClung waited for Jenny's response.

She reopened the folder and ran her finger over the papers. "Here it is. Schnarff, Mowinckel, and Tippler."

"Why hadn't I heard of these attorneys before this week? Had you?" McClung pointed to Stewie and Jenny.

"Nope. I've never needed one but with names like that I'm surprised I haven't heard of them."

Stewie swallowed. "I'm with Jenny."

"As far as we know, everyone except Brian Lane and Arnold Carter uses them." McClung wrote the initials S.M.T. under Robyn's name.

"No, Carter uses them, too." Stewie licked his sticky fingers. "Jenny, make sure I'm correct."

She opened a thick folder and scanned the documents. "Yep."

McClung wrote Arnold Carter on the board, then listed Myron, Robyn, Shelby, and SMT under his name. "Did you find out anything else about the good doctor?"

Jenny shook her head. "Not really. The good doctor withdrew one thousand dollars the Friday after Thanksgiving and then the second Friday of each month since."

"We can't trace the money to Myron." Stewie added.

"What about the weird ledger with letters and numbers? Have you deciphered it?" McClung scribbled *$1,000* beside Dr. Carter's name with an arrow connecting it to Myron's.

"We think it's a list of your neighborhood's residents, covenants they've violated, and fines they paid."

"Why's that?"

Stewie elbowed Jenny.

"Oh, um, because we found the initials *MFS* with the word *resolved* next to them. We are guessing it stands for Marian Frances Selby."

"Good guess." McClung nodded.

"Last year, after mid-September, the initials changed to *MFSM*, Marian Frances Selby McClung. And no other entry had the word *resolved* written next to it."

McClung laughed. "I can assure you that Marian never gave a dime to Myron Herbert Wagstaff."

Stewie added. "To verify our hypothesis, we got a copy of your subdivision's directory and covenants. The letters match residents' names. The numbers match the covenants' codes and associated fines."

"So, the ledger doesn't prove blackmail. But we know for a fact Myron was blackmailing Arnold Carter." McClung bounced the dry erase marker on the palm of his hand. "Do Schnarff, Mowinckel, and Tippler also handle Myron's money?"

"Could be. They're certified financial planners as well." Stewie strolled toward the donuts. "We found their address, phone number, and licenses. That's it."

Stewie selected two donuts, and sauntered back to his spot, giving Jenny one.

"Boss, there's really nothing interesting in anyone's dossier. Rather boring people. Well, except for Shelby Culbertson. She's changed husbands four times. The last one dumped her for a younger model. She dumped the previous three for younger and richer ones."

Jenny evened up the edges of the manila folders, then slid them toward McClung. "Maybe you'll see something we didn't."

"I hope so." McClung turned and scribbled the other four names on the whiteboard, Myron, Brian, Shelby, and Judy, and listed their connections. "These people are connected. What is the common thread?"

Jenny screwed up her face. "They really don't have just one common denominator."

"But," McClung touched Robyn's name, "She seems to know each of them, even Brian."

"How's that?" Thayer squinted at the names.

"Remember Brian said he saw her at Myron's." McClung shrugged. "Maybe they've had words and Brian failed to mention it."

"You think Robyn killed Myron and Judy?" Jenny tore off a chunk of her donut and held it to her lips, anticipating McClung's answer.

"Why not?"

Still holding the donut, Jenny pushed out her lips. "What's Robyn's motive?"

McClung wrote the word *Money* and circled it.

"Nope. I'm not liking that theory." Jenny popped the donut chunk into her mouth.

"And why is that?" McClung rubbed his hands together.

She washed down the pastry with a swig of coffee, then wiped her mouth with a napkin. "Why would Robyn do it for money?"

"Someone paid her to kill them." McClung crossed his arms.

Jenny shook her head. "Nope. I think it's Shelby. She'll inherit the house and stuff. Myron was siphoning money from the good doctor. Money that could have been hers if she conned Arnold Carter into marrying her."

"Maybe the lawyers were siphoning money from the victims' accounts and they found out about it. Had to kill them to shut them up."

Thayer looked at McClung. "A trip to the attorneys, Dewie, Cheatem, and Howe?"

McClung snorted as he picked up the dossiers. "I like those names better."

Chapter 17

Thayer and McClung drove slowly down the road in search of the law offices of Schnarff, Mowinckel, and Tippler.

McClung pointed at two large stacked-stone pillars each topped with a reclining lion. "There."

A neatly clipped, twenty-foot boxwood hedge surrounded the estate and an open ornate iron gate welcomed those who dared to enter.

Thayer turned in between the pillars. "I've seen these lions all my life. Just assumed old rich people lived here."

"Never curious enough to sneak inside?"

"Nope. I figured a place like this probably had mean guard dogs."

The long driveway circled in front of a white antebellum mansion with Ionic columns. Landscaping was low-key and trimmed.

A small parking area spurred off the circular drive.

McClung and Thayer exited the police cruiser and strolled toward the front porch spanning the front of the house.

They surveyed the expansive lawn as they stood on the brick steps.

"It sure is quiet."

"Uh-huh." McClung glanced at Thayer. "I wonder who does the landscaping."

Thayer tilted his head. "You don't think it's Brian Lane, do you?"

"One way to find out."

Thayer pushed open the double doors.

Brilliant sunlight spilled from the doors and eight-foot windows flooding the foyer. A rich red Persian rug muffled their footsteps.

A woman sitting behind an antique desk greeted them.

"Good afternoon. Do you have an appointment?" The attractive middle-aged woman smiled. Bright red lipstick framed her perfectly straight capped teeth.

Her massive desk sat front and center of a marble staircase. At the top of the steps, the handrails curved right and left, leading to hallways stretching along the sides of the house. Between the banisters stretched a thick, twisted red velvet rope. A sign dangled from its middle. It read, *Private*.

As McClung approached the receptionist to present his credentials, he noticed the sunlight highlighting strands of silver in her hair. "No, ma'am. We are investigating the murders of two of your clients, Myron Wagstaff and Judy Johnson."

Her eyes widened. "Judy Johnson was murdered?"

"Yes, ma'am. The autopsy report arrived a few hours ago."

She removed her reading glasses. "Oh, dear. We were informed about the brutal and untimely death of Myron Wagstaff, but not Ms. Johnson." Her words faded, then she sniffed and coughed, regaining her composure. "She was nearing ninety, and we thought she had died peacefully gazing at the stars."

McClung cocked his head. "Who told you that?"

"Shelby Culbertson."

"Hmm." McClung wondered how Shelby knew she was found outside with her dead eyes looking upward. "May we speak with Mr. Tippler? Ms. Johnson mentioned he handled all her affairs."

"Yes, that's true. Let me ring him to see if he's available."

"Thank you."

McClung and Thayer stepped away from the large desk to give the receptionist the illusion of privacy.

She picked up the phone and pressed the button for Mr. Tippler. Turning her back toward them and covering her mouth made it impossible for them to hear the conversation. She put down the receiver and escorted them to a waiting area.

"You may select a book to read as you wait." Her hand waved over the floor-to-ceiling bookshelves complete with a library ladder.

Next, she pointed out the coffee and water. "Is there anything else you require?"

"No, ma'am. Thank you."

She gave a faint smile as she nodded and left the room.

"Sheesh. How long will the wait be if we need a book to read?" Thayer stepped on the ladder then glided across the bookcase. "Smooth as silk."

"Who knows with lawyers?" McClung studied the spines, expecting to see law books. Instead, there were leather-bound classics and current hardbacks; fiction and non-fiction.

He tapped a hardback. "Marian just finished reading this one."

Thayer read the spine. "*Rutland Place* by Anne Perry. Was it good?"

"Hard to say. She loves everything by Anne Perry."

Thayer removed the book.

"Excuse me. Mr. Tippler will see you now."

Rolling his eyes, Thayer shoved the book back on the shelf.

McClung admired the antiques as he walked down the hallway.

Entering Tippler's office, the receptionist introduced them.

"Gentlemen, please come in and have a seat."

The attorney smiled generously as he stood and walked around the desk to shake their hands.

McClung hesitated, expecting to see a stooped, frail old man with liver spots covering his hands.

Tippler was five-foot-eight and had bright hazel eyes and black hair with graying temples. Fit and trim. Maybe sixty.

"Do you care for anything to drink?" Tippler motioned them to sit.

McClung chose the chair closest to the door.

"No, thank you. We won't take too much of your time."

"Thank you, Ms. Bailey." Davis Tippler dismissed the receptionist. She nodded and disappeared.

Tippler returned to his thick padded chair. His smile vanished. "Ms. Bailey informed me about Judy Johnson." He shook his head. "First, Myron Wagstaff, now this. Terrible news."

"Murder is always dreadful news." McClung sat erect in the comfortable Churchill side chair.

Tippler nodded as he nestled into the leather chair, his hands hanging over on the chair arms. "What may I do for you?"

"Ms. Johnson said you handled her affairs."

"That's correct. As my father did before me."

McClung imperceptibly tipped his head at Thayer.

Thayer removed a pad and pen from his shirt pocket, prepared to take notes.

"Did you handle her finances as well?"

Tippler flipped his right hand. "Some. She handled the day-to-day things, like paying her bills. I did all the investing, reconciling her accounts, yearly taxes, and her legal items."

"What about Myron Wagstaff?"

"Now with Myron, I handled anything legal, paid his bills, and filed his taxes. He made his own investments."

"I see. So, you did their wills."

"Yes."

McClung leaned back. "Sheila Gerber said she's expecting a sizable inheritance. Myron's ex confirmed it."

Tippler rested his chin on his fingertips and nodded. "Ms. Dawson will get the bulk of Myron's estate and trust funds are in place for each of his two children. Sheila will get her due share."

"I understand this was part of their divorce agreement."

"Yes, my father was a major influence in Sheila getting her stolen inheritance back."

"Stolen?" McClung perked up.

Tippler rolled his chair forward, resting his elbows on the desk. Smirking, he tilted his head side to side. "I can say this because Myron is dead and everything is public record."

He looked at the leather desk blotter, then back at McClung. "Myron was greedy. Toward the end of his father's life, Myron manipulated him. His father's cognitive abilities were diminishing, and Myron took advantage of it. You get where this is going."

"Yes. So, why did Myron agree to the terms of the divorce decree?"

"My father told Myron that he couldn't take the money with him. He had three choices, give his money to charity, the government, or his family. Naturally, he chose his family. Myron was far from charitable and hated the government."

McClung raised an eyebrow. "Shelby assumes Judy Johnson's estate is all hers."

"She is the sole surviving heir." Tippler held up two fingers wiggling them. "Judy and Myron. Two of a kind."

"Enough said." McClung paused, then spoke. "Please satisfy my curiosity. How do clients find your firm? There's no signage, and you're not listed in the Yellow Pages."

Tippler smiled and leaned back, resting his left elbow on the cushioned chair arm.

"Our grandfathers were men of wealth, position, and levelheadedness. This business was like a hobby to them, something to keep them busy while making more money. They were attorneys as well as financial advisors. People in their circle trusted them. Clients came by word of mouth. One can say, we inherited their clients."

McClung stared at Davis Tippler. "Interesting. I understand Ms. Johnson came by her wealth through her fiancée. So, his family were clients?"

"No. Herbert Wagstaff referred her to us and before you ask, I don't know their relationship. That's none of our concern."

"Any rumors or gossip to hint at their relationship?" McClung held his breath, hoping for a clue.

"Our business is facts and figures, not hearsay and scandal."

"Speaking of scandal, do you think Myron was profiting from scandal?"

Tippler's stillness and unblinking eyes gave him away.

McClung grinned. "So, you believe he was."

The attorney clasped his hands together. "I can't answer that question."

Thayer chimed in. "Can't or won't?"

Tippler shifted his attention to the young officer. "I can't answer the question if I don't know the truth. Like I said, we are attorneys and financial planners, not rumormongers."

McClung stood, planted his hands on the desktop and leaned forward. "Off the record, what do you suspect?"

Tippler looked at McClung and pointed to his posture. "You don't have to do that. There's nothing to hide. Please sit."

McClung pushed away from the desk but didn't resume his seat, instead, he strolled around Tippler's modest-sized office. "You have a number of priceless antiques."

He ran his hand along the side of a library bookcase. "Solid oak." McClung studied the pudgy cherubs on the upright pilasters. "Hand-carved. Late nineteenth century. French. Am I correct?"

"Spot on." Tippler walked over and stood beside McClung. "Your knowledge of antiques is remarkable."

"My family has owned an antique store for three generations. I worked in the store every summer and most weekends. That is until I became a police officer."

Tippler's lips parted. "Wait a minute. Your accent. Are you from Virginia? Mercy City to be exact?"

"Yes, born and bred. I moved to Lyman County a year ago."

Tippler opened one of the glass-paneled doors and removed an ornate dance card. "I believe this came from your family's shop."

McClung studied the enameled pansy adorning the mother-of-pearl cover. French. Early to mid-1800s. Ladies of wealth used the notebook to record the names of the men they intended to dance with at balls, it still had its original paper and pen.

"Since there's only one antique shop in Mercy City, I'm sure it did but I'll check with my Aunt Ella to be sure. Either way, the quality of the chasing and engraving is exquisite."

"Does she wear a hat?"

"Aunt Ella is never without a hat."

Tippler smiled. "Charming lady. Just charming. I love that quaint shop. I must visit it again, soon."

"Thanks. I'll tell her. How did you end up at my family's shop?"

Tippler replaced the valuable antique and returned to his chair. McClung followed.

"I was in D.C. on business. A friend referred me. Huh, guess we have a connection, Chief McClung."

"It appears we do." McClung relaxed.

Tippler placed his hands on top of his desk, fingers splayed. "What I'm going to say is off the record and I expect utmost confidence. My opinion only. Understand?"

McClung's heartbeat skipped. "Understood."

Thayer closed his notepad and pushed it into his pocket.

"My opinion? Myron Wagstaff was a psychopath. As far as Judy Johnson, she was just plain mean." Tippler held up a hand. "Now and then, she showed a sliver of goodwill."

"Why do you think Myron was a psychopath?" McClung licked his lips, hoping this would be the break in Wagstaff's murder and possibly Miss Johnson's.

Tippler coughed. "To be honest, the guy gave me the creeps. Myron never made an appointment. He'd show up and expected to be seen right away. Made threats to take his business elsewhere."

"If he was that big of a nuisance why didn't you ask him to leave? Myron's that valuable?"

"Yes. Quite valuable. The thing is, we have no clue where he got his money and Myron had a lot. Like I said, he made his own investments,

I would have advised him if he had asked. My recommendations are good but wouldn't result in the return Myron achieved."

Tippler sat back and pushed his lips out. "When I asked him about it, he snickered and said, 'You don't need to know where the bodies are buried'."

McClung wondered if Myron literally buried bodies. "What did he mean?"

"Again, off the record." Tippler leaned forward. "My father told me tales of Myron's youth. Myron left dead birds in his stepsister's bedroom, under pillows, in her coat pockets. He was cruel even with his own parents. His mother died at an early age. Understand this is strictly hearsay."

McClung and Thayer nodded.

"Rumor is Myron's mother was terrified of her own son."

Tippler threw up his hands. "Sheila's mother wanted Myron committed but old Herbert would have none of it. To protect Sheila, her mother hired a constant companion. The companion was a tough old bird. Your question about bodies, who knows?"

"I see." McClung rubbed his earlobe. "Did it surprise you when Myron married Janie Dawson?"

"Pfft. Shocked. We all were. Janie was too young. All she wanted was a stable life and children. We were impressed the marriage lasted as long as it did. Two, three years I think."

Tippler slid back his chair and opened a short cabinet behind him. "Water anyone?"

"I never would've figured that to be a mini frig." Thayer gawked.

"Our handyman is a genius. Water?" Tippler held up a bottle.

"No, thanks."

Tippler opened the bottle and poured water into a crystal glass. "Once again, this is off the record."

McClung nodded.

"If I had to guess where some of Myron's money came from, I'd say blackmail."

"Why's that?"

Tippler sipped the water. "We've noticed a pattern, a correlation of withdrawals and deposits between a few of our clients and Myron's accounts."

"You'd be correct. We know for a fact that Dr. Arnold Carter was one of Myron's victims. Who are the ones you suspect?"

Tippler shook his head and chuckled. "That I cannot say."

McClung shrugged. "Didn't hurt to ask." He inhaled and then asked, "Do you suspect Judy Johnson or Robyn Konopka are his victims?"

"As far as Judy goes, I don't know anything about her involvement with Myron, if any. All I can say about Robyn is Myron asked us to handle the legal work for her business. Licenses, insurance, limited liability company setup, things like that. Make her legit."

McClung bit the inside corner of his mouth. "Would you say it's out of character for Myron to ask you to help Robyn?"

"Oh, yes. Definitely. Even more shocking, he paid all the fees." Tippler shook his head and chuckled. "That made me wonder if there was a relationship between the two."

McClung needed to press Robyn about her involvement with Myron. Maybe she failed to reveal all the facts when she made her statement.

"Uh-huh. Can you think of anyone who'd want either of them dead?"

"Myron had far too many enemies to name just one person. Your guess is as good as mine with Ms. Johnson."

"What about the niece, Shelby Culbertson?"

Tippler squeezed the back of his neck. "I don't know her well enough to say if she's capable of murder. She'll be rich. Not as rich as Myron's beneficiaries but she'll be comfortable."

Thayer held up a hand. "Will Ms. Culbertson use your services now?"

"We hope so."

McClung stood. "Well, that's it for now. If you remember anything that may help, we'd appreciate it." He placed his card on Tippler's desk.

The attorney picked up the card. "Definitely will. Let me walk out with you."

Their footsteps clicked on the old wood floors as they walked down the hallway to the open foyer.

McClung stopped at the receptionist's desk.

"Thank you, Ms. Bailey." McClung tipped his head toward the staircase. "What's up there?"

She glanced at Tippler.

"Our offices are downstairs." Tippler pointed up the stairwell. "Upstairs is for out-of-town clients, private dinner parties, or a place to sleep when we need to pull an all-nighter."

McClung nodded. "Do you live here in Lyman County?"

"No. In Atlanta with our families."

"I see." McClung looked around. "The house is beautiful, and the landscaping is impressive."

McClung walked to the front door then turned toward Tippler. "Speaking of landscaping, who does yours?"

Tippler looked at Ms. Bailey.

"Stellar Landscaping."

"Hmm, Brian Lane by chance?" McClung approached her desk.

"Oh, dear. A whole crew comes every Friday. I take them refreshments, but I don't know their names. If you describe him, I may recognize him."

McClung held up his hand at head level. "He's this tall, tanned, and wild brownish-blonde hair. Soft-spoken gentleman."

Ms. Bailey perked up. "Looks like a lion's mane."

"That's right."

"I believe he's the crew chief. Sometimes he brings me flowers." She grinned and pointed to a vase of flowers sitting on a side table next to the door. "Such a nice guy."

Chapter 18

"Well, Thayer, what do you think?" McClung asked as they pulled out of the driveway.

"We got to speak with Robyn again."

"Yep. She's holding back. We have to figure out the real connection between her and Myron."

"What about Brian Lane? He's everywhere."

McClung drummed his fingers on his thigh. "This is getting complicated."

Thayer approached the stop sign at the town square entrance.

"Look." McClung pointed toward a man and a woman standing on the sidewalk surrounding the square.

"Well, I'll be. Robyn and Brian."

"Don't move. Let's watch."

Brian appeared to be listening, his thick arms crossed over his chest.

Robyn was doing all the talking. Her hands were on her hips as she leaned in toward Brian, then she stabbed her finger onto Brian's wide chest.

"Uh-oh. Talk about poking a hornet's nest. She's got spunk." Thayer leaned his head out the driver's side window. "Augh. I can't hear what she's saying."

"Move forward. Let's find out."

Brian Lane's arms burst apart, his fists fell by his side. His mouth opened then clamped shut, and he turned away from Robyn. In four long strides, he jumped into his truck, leaving behind a red-faced Robyn.

The truck shot backward.

Robyn stared after Brian, her lips tight as she grumbled to herself.

Thayer pulled into the vacant spot.

McClung hopped out of the cruiser. "Robyn, what's going on here?"

Robyn flinched, then clutched her chest. "Ah! You scared me." She snarled. "What do you want?"

"You and Brian were having words. He didn't look very happy." McClung stepped toward Robyn.

"Gah!" She stormed away.

Thayer jumped in front of her. "Whoa, now."

Robyn inhaled deeply and held it as she glared at Thayer.

McClung waited for her to exhale.

"What? What do you want?" Robyn's fingers curled into tight fists.

"Take it easy." McClung held up his hands. "We thought you needed help."

Robyn's eyes shifted between Thayer and McClung; she shook her head. "No. I'm fine." She smirked. "It's comforting to know we have officers willing to aide a damsel in distress."

"Did Brian offend you? You look pretty upset." McClung didn't budge.

"No. I'm fine." She sidestepped Thayer.

"Now hold on, Robyn." McClung blocked her departure. "You need to come to the station."

"Why? I haven't done nothing wrong." Robyn turned and walked away.

McClung's eyes rolled. "Come on." He punched Thayer's shoulder and then caught up with her.

"Robyn, it's not up for discussion. Come with us. Now."

Tears pooled in the corners of Robyn's big brown eyes as she looked at McClung. "Why? I haven't done anything." Robyn sniffed and wiped a single tear.

McClung wasn't buying the woe-is-me act, but being a gentleman, he gave her a tissue. "We have more questions. You'll have to come with us to the station."

Robyn pressed the tissue to the corner of her eyes. "Fine." She cleared her throat and looked at McClung. "You're not putting me in the back of your car. I can't have people thinking I'm being arrested. I'm driving my own car to the station."

"Sure. We'll follow you."

Robyn got into her Datsun and they waited for her to back out.

"What's taking her so long?" Thayer's thumbs tapped the steering wheel.

McClung hoped she'd drive to the station and not make a run for it. He wasn't in the mood for a car chase, and he didn't relish throwing Robyn in jail.

The Datsun's backup lights came to life. "About time." Thayer grumbled.

♦♦♦♦♦♦

Robyn Konopka sat in interview room one, running her fingers through her long ponytail as she chewed gum and blew ginormous pink bubbles.

McClung and Thayer watched her from the observation room.

"She doesn't look nervous at all, rather relaxed I'd say." Thayer drank from a sweaty water bottle.

"Makes me think she's either innocent as a baby bird or a sociopath." McClung sighed.

Thayer walked in the interview room holding two bottles of water, setting them on the table.

"Thanks." Robyn snared one, twisted off the cap and drank half the bottle. "Ah, that hit the spot. Can we get started? I've got one more house to clean before I go home to cook grandmother's dinner."

She propped her elbows on the table then rested her chin in her open hands.

McClung raised an eyebrow. "All right. Tell us your real relationship with Myron."

"We were, I'd guess you'd say, friends. Next question."

"How close of friends?"

Robyn pushed away from the table and crossed her arms. "Just friends. No extra benefits if that's what you're trying to get at."

"Myron paid for your legal expenses to start your business. I'd say it's more than just friends."

A small pink bubble protruded from her lips, then it popped. "I paid him back."

McClung watched her jaw as she chewed, mesmerized at how fast and hard Robyn worked the gum.

"According to witnesses, you spent a lot of time at his house."

Robyn shrugged. "A lot or a little depends on one's perception of time."

"What was your disagreement with Brian Lane about?"

"Landscaping." Robyn finished the bottle of water.

McClung's neck tightened. "Please elaborate on what you mean by landscaping."

"He hasn't tended to Myron's yard."

Thayer grunted. "So. What concern is it of yours? The man is dead. What? Did you inherit his house?"

McClung added. "I'm not buying your story, Robyn. Why were you arguing with Brian? The truth this time."

Robyn tapped the empty bottle on her chin and stared at McClung.

"We can wait all day, but I thought you were in a hurry."

She set the bottle on the table, stood, then leaned forward. "Am I under arrest?"

"No. Not yet." McClung mirrored her stance, their noses six inches apart.

Robyn walked toward the door with Thayer close behind.

"Ms. Konopka, don't leave town."

She turned the doorknob and looked over her shoulder at McClung. "I'll think about it."

Thayer held the door, refusing to let her leave.

"Thayer, let her go." McClung walked toward the door, his eyes narrowed.

She winked at him as she blew a small bubble and sashayed out of the room.

McClung and Thayer trailed Robyn, making sure she left the building without any side trips. After seeing her exit the front door, McClung headed to Stewie and Jenny's office.

Thayer matched McClung's long strides.

◆◆◆◆◆◆

Jenny's desk was just plain chaos. Dust-free family photos sat on an eye-level side shelf, segregating them from the clutter. McClung was amazed she never lost anything, always extracting the correct file from the messy piles.

Organized chaos covered Stewie's desk. A rearview mirror mounted on the corner of his monitor alerted him when someone entered the room.

"Tell me you've found something, anything to shed light on this case."

Stewie whipped around. "Sorry, Boss, we've searched. Nothing new." He puffed his cheeks.

"Well, there is something peculiar about Brian Lane. He doesn't stay in one place for very long." Jenny collected five sheets of paper from under a pile and gave them to McClung.

He studied the list of landscaping and handyman companies where Brian had worked for the past twenty years.

"Hm. Never more than… what… a year in each city?" McClung handed a page to Thayer.

Jenny bobbed her head. "Some for only a few months. He's worked in all twelve southeastern states."

"Maybe he has a wandering spirit." Thayer scanned the papers as McClung passed them, one by one.

"Possibly." McClung took the pages from Thayer. "There are a few breaks here and there in Brian's work history. I wonder why?"

Stewie shrugged. "Extended vacation. Visiting family. Couldn't find work."

McClung bobbed his head side to side. "Yeah. We should speak with Brian again." He snapped his fingers. "I just remembered something. Sheila Gerber had a companion when she was a kid living at home with Myron. I want the companion's name. Maybe she knows who'd want Myron dead."

"On it, Boss. It should be easy enough to find out. One call to Sheila should do it." Stewie dropped onto his chair.

McClung and Thayer waited.

Stewie's fingers zoomed over the keyboard. The information he needed popped up on the monitor. He put the telephone on speaker then dialed the hospital.

"Lyman County Medical Center. How may I direct your call?"

"I need to speak with Sheila Gerber in the lab."

"Hold please."

Elevator music entertained them as they waited for someone to answer.

Jenny swayed to *Don't Cry for Me Argentina.* "I love this song."

"Lab, Jonathan speaking. What can I do you for?"

"Sheila Gerber, please."

Jonathan clicked his tongue. "Oh, no can do. Sheila took a half-day for a dentist appointment or something. She'll be in at seven tomorrow morning. I can help you."

"No, thank you. I need Sheila Gerber. I'll call her in the morning."

"Well, suture yourself." Jonathan chuckled then hung up.

Chapter 19

Charlie and Marian snuggled on the loveseat as they watched the Atlanta Braves.

"I didn't visit Lula Belle today."

The television held Charlie's attention until the batter popped out. "Yeah, why is that?"

"She had a hairdresser's appointment. I'm going over there tomorrow for tea."

"That's nice." Charlie focused on the game.

"I took dinner to Billy Crawford's family."

"Yeah? Any news on the uncle?"

"He's going to be okay."

"That's good."

Marian waited for a commercial break. "I don't want to bring it up."

"But you are." Charlie cut off his wife as he kissed the top of her head. "You want to know how the Wagstaff case is going, don't you?"

Marian sat up and studied his face. No emotional tell. Safe to proceed? Probably. "Well, yeah. You haven't mentioned it once since you've been home."

"Not much to report. Seems all our leads run into never-ending rabbit holes or smash into brick walls, but we think it's all about blackmail."

Charlie stood and paced in front of the television, the baseball game forgotten. "Have you ever heard of the law office of Schnarff, Mowinckel, and Tippler?"

Marian laughed. "No."

"They're attorneys who only have clients they choose, like Myron Wagstaff, Judy Johnson, and Robyn Konopka." He flicked up a finger for each name.

Marian scratched the back of her neck. "Surely, they have more than three nasty clients. The rest of their clientele can't be as bad as those three."

He shook his index finger. "Yeah, but Tippler handles all three of them. Maybe he lied? Trying to steer us away from himself. Maybe he is the center of the blackmailing scheme. Maybe he knows all their nasty secrets."

"That sounds plausible. Each attorney with their own little corral of scoundrels."

"Sounds good. I like that idea." Charlie nodded. "Not only are they attorneys but get this, Certified Financial Planners."

"Now that is convenient. How long have they been in business?" Marian stood and stretched, a few joints popped.

"Their grandfathers started the business as a hobby."

Marian chuckled. "A hobby. Well, it must be a lucrative one."

"Yeah, you should see their office or rather mansion. You've probably seen it. The property with the hedge fence and the stone lions at the end of the driveway."

"Yes. I thought a hermit lived there. No one I know knows a thing about the place, but then again, the few people I do hang with don't associate with the ultra-rich except Joan, but she's never mentioned them."

Charlie looked at his watch. "Too late to call Thayer."

"Hmm." Marian yawned.

"Am I boring you?"

"No. Long day in the yard. I'm not a spring chicken anymore. Remember?"

Charlie's arms wrapped around her. "Oh, I don't need reminding."

Marian pushed against his chest. "What do you mean by that?"

He laughed and threw up his forearm for protection. "Now hold on. Just teasing you, sweetums. You'll always be my blushing bride. Besides, you're the one who married a haggard old rooster."

"You're not haggard. You're practically perfect in every way."

Charlie gasped. "Practically. Practically. Why aren't I perfect in every way?"

"You're still old." Marian ran to the bedroom.

"I'll show you old." Charlie chased her.

Squeals bounced off the trey ceiling as he captured her.

Marian's lips skimmed Charlie's ear as she whispered. "I don't call this old."

Charlie nibbled her neck. "No, what do you call it?"

215

"Expertise."

"Yeah."

"Yeah. Show me your well-crafted skills." Marian sighed.

Charlie leered. "As you wish."

♦♦♦♦♦♦

Hushed voices from the kitchen woke Marian. Darkness shrouded the bedroom. Her arm slid across the bed in search of Charlie, finding cold sheets instead of his warm body. *5:30 AM* glowed from the bedside clock.

The aroma of coffee infiltrated the room. She tiptoed to the door and listened. It was Charlie's voice, the other one was Thayer's.

Marian threw on a robe and fast-walked to the kitchen.

Charlie and Thayer sat at the kitchen table.

Thayer hopped up as she entered the room.

"Morning, Marian."

"Why didn't you invite me to your party?" Marian replied.

Charlie met his wife halfway and gave her a peck on her cheek. "I thought you needed the sleep."

"I can take a nap later. What do y'all want for breakfast?"

Thayer opened his mouth, but Charlie answered.

"No need to make us breakfast."

"Don't be daft. I'm fixing myself some eggs and bacon."

"Eggs sound good to me." Thayer mumbled.

Marian grabbed a pound of bacon and a carton of eggs from the refrigerator. "Charlie?"

"Fine, but I'll help you." He snatched a loaf of wheat bread from the pantry. "Thayer, you like your toast with lots of butter, right?"

"Yes, Boss." Thayer leaned against the countertop. "What can I do to help?"

"Set the table. You know where the plates are." Marian cracked eight eggs into a bowl. "I hope scrambled is okay."

"Yes, ma'am."

"I'm going to guess y'all were discussing the attorneys." The eggs sizzled as Marian poured them into the buttered pan.

"Spot on, my dear." Charlie peeled six slices of bacon from the thick slab and placed them on a bed of paper towels.

"Our theory is it may be a pyramid blackmailing scheme." Thayer added as he placed each utensil a quarter inch apart.

"Really?" Marian swirled the eggs around the pan. "You believe the attorneys are at the top and their clients make up the base."

"Exactly." Charlie poured a cup of coffee.

"Huh." Marian's top lip hunched up as she lowered the flame under the eggs. "Does Brian have enough assets to interest the attorneys? Him being a lowly worker bee for a landscaping company."

Four pieces of golden-brown bread jumped from the toaster.

Butter melted over the hot bread as Charlie slathered on a thick layer. "I studied on that fact. Stewie and Jenny will delve into Brian's finances today. But…" He pointed the dull knife at Marian. "Brian has the perfect job to dig up dirt on his wealthier clients."

Marian snorted. "Love the pun."

"Yeah, I thought it was a good one."

"Brian may get a cut of the blackmail." Thayer side stepped Marian as she carried the skillet full of eggs to the breakfast table.

"I understand, but if Brian is part of the blackmail scheme, what's he got to do with the murders?" Marian scooped the eggs onto the plates, giving the men twice as much as herself. "Or are the two crimes unrelated?"

Charlie twisted his mouth as he set down the platter of buttered toast and crispy bacon. "You've got a point."

"Just an observation." Marian sat. "Let's eat before the eggs get cold and no police talk while we eat."

"Yes, ma'am." Thayer sat and waited for the blessing.

Charlie grinned and kissed the top of his wife's head before he took his seat. "Yes, dear."

◆◆◆◆◆◆

Charlie and Thayer cleaned the kitchen while Marian sat on the screened-in porch with the *Lyman Daily Newspaper* and a cup of coffee.

"Hey, Charlie." Marian rushed into the kitchen. "Myron's funeral is today. It's a private graveside service." The corners of her mouth turned down as her shoulders sagged. "Family only."

"Where?" Charlie turned on the dishwasher.

"It doesn't say, but I know where the Wagstaffs are buried. Joan and I toured the oldest graveyard in Lyman County, and we ran across the

Wagstaff's mausoleum, like in Dark Shadows. He's got to be buried there with the rest of his ancestors."

Charlie pulled on his bottom lip to keep from laughing. Marian was a diehard fan of the 1960s gothic soap opera. She refused to call it a soap opera even though that's what it was. He had agreed to watch a few episodes where the vampire, Barnabas Collins appeared, but he just didn't get it.

"Thayer, polish up your shoes. We're going to a funeral. I want to know who is considered family and who wants to see Myron entombed."

Chapter 20

Thayer parked the cruiser at the caretaker's house and walked down the serene winding road to the Wagstaff's plot.

Pristine tombstones mingled with dingy ancient stones. Some were elaborate with carvings of flowers, birds, and sweet words of remembrance. Statues of angels, Christ, or the Virgin Mary guarded a few. Others were plain with just a name and dates.

Century-old trees sheltered sections of the well-maintained graveyard with shade and comfort. Colorful flowers planted around the tree trunks enhanced the warmth of sunlight filtering through the thick canopy.

McClung and Thayer slowed their pace as they neared a wide-open space dotted with graves. On the side of the road, five cars were parked behind a black hearse. Not one living soul in sight.

McClung pointed to a plain stone building surrounded by headstones and vaulted graves. A spiked wrought-iron fence enclosed the large plot.

"I wonder how many Wagstaffs are buried there." Thayer whispered.

McClung looked for cover to get a better view inside the mausoleum. If they walked to the backside of the building and the family came out before they made it then they'd be in plain view. He didn't want to ruffle anyone's dander.

"Looks like we're stuck here."

"Yeah." Thayer handed McClung a pair of binoculars as they stepped behind a wide tree trunk.

He scanned the area and spied a truck parked in the distance. "I think it's a Stellar Landscaping truck. Can you read the writing?"

McClung pointed to the spot and gave the binoculars to Thayer.

"Yep. You're right." He passed them back to McClung. "Do you want me to check it out?"

"No. I need your eyes on that." He pointed to the mausoleum.

McClung focused on the building. Deeply etched into the mottled stone plaque above the open double doors was a single word, *Wagstaff*.

Thayer mopped his face with a stark white handkerchief. "It must feel like an oven inside that thing. How many people do you think are in there?"

"Only five cars. Can't be too many. I wish I could hear what they're saying."

"Step back." McClung pulled Thayer behind the tree trunk. "They're coming out."

McClung squatted and peeked around the tree. He counted eight people, recognizing three. Myron's ex-wife, Janie, Sheila Gerber, Myron's stepsister, and Davis Tippler.

Through the binoculars, McClung stared at the mourners. "One man is obviously the minister. Tippler is standing between two men. Nice suits. My guess is they're Schnarff and Mowinckel."

"Thayer is that…"

The young sergeant looked through the binoculars. "Robyn Konopka? She's not family, is she?"

"If she is, it's news to me. That older woman next to Robyn must be her grandmother." McClung clicked his tongue. "Looks like another chat with Robyn."

"We need to get back to the cruiser before they do." McClung pointed his head toward the group of grievers. "I don't want Robyn to know we've spotted her."

They trotted through the wooded cemetery back to the caretaker's house.

Gravel spewed from the rear tires of the cruiser as it shot out of the parking lot and sped down the road. There were plenty of hiding spots on the quiet road as they waited for Robyn's Datsun to pass.

After its taillights disappeared around the bend, they followed the dingy car several miles to her home.

Robyn's car glided into a two-car garage.

Once the garage door shut, Thayer parked in the driveway and started to get out of the cruiser.

"Hang on. Let them get settled first."

After about ten minutes, Thayer asked, "How much longer?"

"Now."

They walked to the front door of an upscale duplex with exquisite landscaping.

"Do you reckon Brian does their lawn?" Thayer stood beside his boss on Robyn's front stoop.

"We'll soon find out." McClung scoffed at the brass plate under the doorbell. *Press for Attention*. "Let's get their attention, shall we?"

He pressed a ceramic button encased in a brass disc.

The white sheers covering the sidelight moved. Robyn's eyes appeared.

McClung heard a painful groan.

Robyn opened the door a mere three inches. "I'm getting fed up with your harassment. What do you want now?"

"We need to speak with you and your grandmother."

"Grandmother? Why?"

Cool air escaped from the cracked door, a small but welcomed respite from the hot humid air. "We won't take long. Please, may we come in?"

Robyn gritted her teeth. "Or what? Haul us in for questioning?"

McClung shrugged.

"Fine." She pulled open the door. "Follow me."

They walked behind her down the hallway highlighted by shiny terrazzo flooring.

Robyn stopped inside a doorway. "Grandmother, there are two police officers here to see us."

"Have them come in."

Robyn escorted them into the stark white room.

"Gentlemen, please have a seat," her grandmother said as she motioned them toward a white damask loveseat.

"Thank you. We'll only be a few minutes." McClung held out his card.

She read it then stared at him. "Your name. Irish?"

"Yes, ma'am." McClung returned her glare. "This is Sergeant Thayer."

"I don't like people looking down on me. Please sit."

McClung hesitated then sat on the edge of the plush cushion. Thayer mirrored him.

"Thank you." She looked at her granddaughter. "Robyn, be a dear and bring coffee and cake."

Robyn nodded and obeyed the command.

"Now, Chief McClung, let me introduce myself since my granddaughter forgot her manners." The charcoal gray suit she wore accentuated her slim figure, a somber contrast against the white wingback chair. A diamond brooch was pinned above her heart.

"My name is Rose Emerson. What may I help you with today?"

McClung shifted closer to the edge. "I need to know your relationship to Myron Wagstaff."

"Why do you ask?"

"His graveside funeral was for family only."

She sneered. "Apparently, you were there. Am I to assume you are family?"

McClung's right eye twitched. "I'm investigating Myron's murder. What is your relationship to the Wagstaff family?"

Rose's dark brown eyes narrowed. "I've known the family for a number of years. My late husband and I were friends with Herbert Wagstaff, Myron's father."

"Then you've known Myron most of his life."

Robyn announced her entrance with the sound of rattling dishes.

"Do be careful, my dear." Rose sat to attention as her granddaughter set the silver coffee service on a side table without a sound.

"Shall I pour, grandmother?"

Rose looked at McClung and Thayer. "Will you be staying for coffee?"

"Yes. I have a few more questions." McClung noticed a wee falter in Rose's plastered smile.

"Very well, then. Cream? Sugar?"

"I'll take mine black,"

Thayer shook his head. "None for me. Thank you."

"Perhaps some lemonade or sparkling water for you, Sergeant?" Rose offered.

"Plain water will do, if it's not any trouble."

"No trouble at all." Rose glanced at Robyn.

The young girl turned on her heels and scurried out of the room.

Rose stood. "I'll pour. A slice of amaretto almond pound cake for either of you gentlemen?"

Both men replied no.

"Tsk. You don't know what you are missing. Not only is my granddaughter a topnotch maid, but an outstanding pastry chef as well. Simply marvelous."

Rose gave McClung an ivory-colored cup and saucer with a ridged border and a thin inner pink band with blue flowers.

"Beautiful china."

"A wedding present from Herbert Wagstaff."

McClung lifted the cup, very nice aroma, then sipped. "It's Lenox, correct? The pattern is Priscilla?"

Rose's left eyebrow arched. "I'm impressed."

"Why is that?"

"Tut!" Rose's eyes rolled. "You're a policeman. How should I say this? People in your profession aren't generally considered — well-rounded."

Thayer huffed.

McClung bobbed his head. "I can understand how the — ill-informed can arrive at such an erroneous conclusion." He set the expensive china on the coffee table with a definite rattle.

Rose's cheeks flushed scarlet red as her nostrils flared.

Robyn entered the room, defusing the rising tension. "Here's your water." The glass came within an inch of Thayer's temple.

The Sergeant reared back, took the glass, and stared at the suspiciously cloudy water then handed it back. "I've changed my mind."

"Wise." Robyn murmured as she retrieved the glass and returned it to the kitchen.

"Chief McClung, please get on with your questions. This day has been exhausting. I need to rest."

"Very well. Have you lived in Lyman County all your life?"

"Most of it. When I was five years old, my parents moved here from Atlanta to get away from the city noise."

Robyn reappeared and stood inside the doorway, eyes fixed on Rose.

"Did you meet your husband here?"

Rose tapped her empty cup.

Robyn hustled with a refill.

"Thank you, my dear." Rose sniffed. "I don't see how that's relative to Myron's murder investigation."

McClung nodded. "All right. Did you work outside the house?"

Her eyes narrowed. "I was a teacher in a private school until my daughter, Shirley, was born. After her second birthday, I returned." Rose set her cup on the table beside her chair. "Chief McClung, I'm quite tired."

McClung stood and looked down his nose at Rose. "You've known Myron all his life."

"Yes." Rose cleared her throat then sipped the coffee and glared at McClung over the rim of the cup.

"So, you know about Myron's persecution of his stepsister, Sheila."

Rose smiled but McClung saw the evil lurking behind her eyes.

"Who said that?"

"Sheila Gerber."

"You shouldn't listen to inaccurate memories of a depressed child."

McClung stepped closer to Rose.

"Who said Sheila was depressed?"

No response from Rose.

McClung pressed on. "Is it true he liked to torment Sheila by leaving dead birds under her pillow?"

Rose glanced at Robyn who stood with her mouth open and her eyebrows hunched together.

"My granddaughter is right. You are harassing us."

Rose stood, eye level with McClung, neither one retreated.

"Robyn, please escort these men out the front door."

"Yes, ma'am."

McClung held out his hand. "Now wait a second. Why won't you answer the question?"

"It is clear you already know the answer."

McClung ran his hand over the back of his head. "All I need is a yes or a no to dispel the rumors."

"Secrets should stay buried. If uncovered, they can cost you dearly." Rose leaned toward McClung, her nose just shy of his. "If you have any pertinent questions, I advise you to contact my attorney, Lester Schnarff."

Rose walked out of the room. McClung and Thayer followed her into the hallway.

"One more question. Do you know Brian Lane?"

Her footsteps faltered. Rose huffed. "I believe I made myself clear. Good day, gentlemen." She disappeared down the corridor.

Chapter 21

McClung bounced the end of an ink pen on his desk, flipping it over and over. "So, Thayer, we agree that Robyn and her grandmother are squirreling away something we need to know."

"Yep. I think dear old grandmother is in the thick of this thing."

"Mhm." McClung stood and collected the dossiers off his desk. "I'm not so sure about Robyn anymore. It's obvious her grandmother has total control over her."

"War room?"

McClung walked out of his office. "Yeah, I need space to spread out. I have this nagging feeling we are just one piece of the puzzle away from solving this crime and I'm afraid Rose has it tucked in her pocket."

"Are you thinking we should visit Schnarff's office?"

"Nah. The whole client-attorney privilege thing." McClung waved his hand. "We won't get anywhere."

He detoured toward Stewie and Jenny's office.

"Where's Stewie?"

"Boy's room." Jenny rubbed her hands together. "I got a copy of Brian Lane's birth certificate but not the official one. He was adopted at birth, so there's not much information."

"Interesting." McClung passed the document to Thayer.

"Brian was born in Atlanta?"

"Look at the adoption records. You can see there's not much here. An older couple in Tennessee adopted him."

McClung studied the forms. "Brian is the same age as Myron." He rubbed his earlobe. "I wonder if there's a connection."

Jenny shook her head. "I know what you're gonna ask. I haven't discovered who Brian's mother was."

"Agh! My brain is throbbing." McClung squeezed his face between his hands. "Forget the war room, Thayer."

Jenny rattled a bottle of aspirin. "Need these?"

McClung waved them away as he glanced at his watch. "Almost five o'clock. The old gray cells are useless. Let's go home."

"We don't mind staying late." Jenny crossed her arms.

"Speak for yourself. I've got plans." Stewie strolled to his desk and shut down his computer.

"No. Y'all go home or whatever." McClung tapped his temple. "My brain needs to recharge. See you guys in the morning."

◆◆◆◆◆◆

Marian hugged Charlie as soon as he entered the kitchen. "Oh, boy, have I got some juicy gossip for you.

He kissed her forehead. "Can it wait? My head is spinning."

Marian twisted her lips to one side. "Sure. No problem but my gut says this is good stuff. You need it."

"Yeah?" Charlie poured a cup of coffee. "And where did you get this valuable information?"

Marian retrieved two filet mignon steaks she had marinating in the refrigerator. "Today, I had a very interesting gab session with Lula Belle Darby."

"Hey, I thought we were going for Chinese?"

"I changed my mind after visiting with Lula Belle. What I have to reveal is best done at home. In private." Marian stood on her tiptoes and kissed his cheek. "We can go tomorrow."

"Is that right?" Charlie leaned against the counter.

Her hands rested on her husband's shoulders. "Yeah. If you're hungry, we can eat the salads before I cook the steaks."

"Let's do that. You can give me a replay of your day."

Marian grinned. "Dining room or kitchen table?"

"Kitchen table." Charlie opened a drawer and pulled out napkins and placemats.

"I love Lula Belle. Such a delight. She's lived in Lyman County since 1938." Marian set the salad bowls on the table. "I can't believe I haven't met her before now."

Charlie wondered how long it'd be before Marian got around to the juicy bits of their conversation.

"Anyway, Lula Belle said she remembers when Herbert Wagstaff got married and when Myron was born." Marian opened a bottle of Riesling. "Do you want a glass?"

"Sure. Please tell me she was invited to the wedding."

"Lula Belle played the piano at the church where they married. She said she remembers it like it was yesterday."

Marian jumped up. "Oh, I have rolls warming in the oven."

Charlie poured honey-mustard dressing on his salad, waiting patiently for his wife to continue the story.

"Like I was saying, she remembers everything. Such a charming lady. Anyway, Robyn's grandmother was a bridesmaid. Rose Emerson is the grandmother's name, and she had one daughter, Shirley, who had one daughter, Robyn."

"Fascinating. Does Lula Belle know Rose Emerson by chance?"

Marian bobbed her head and licked a smear of ranch dressing from her bottom lip.

"Well, what did she say about her? I think Rose holds the key to this investigation, but I can't get anything out of her."

"Oh, you will love this." Marian's eyes widened. "Judy and Rose were best buddies at one point. Lula Belle said they were two peas in a pod, mean as yellow jackets. And get this, they didn't like Elsie, Myron's mother."

"Why?"

Marian collected the empty salad bowls. "Sit over here while I cook the steaks." She pointed to the breakfast bar.

"No, you sit and talk. I'll cook and listen."

"Deal." She hopped up on the high barstool. "Apparently, Rose wanted Herbert, but he was only interested in Elsie."

"Jealousy? Really?"

"Yup." Marian slid off the chair. "Want another glass of wine?"

"Not now." He flipped the steaks. "What else are we having?"

She pointed to the lower oven. "Baked potatoes. If you like, I can throw frozen limas or green beans in the microwave."

"Depends on dessert?"

"Chocolate Kahlua cake."

"Pass on the beans. Did Lula Belle say anything else?"

"Guess who was Sheila's nanny?"

Charlie whipped toward Marian. "Judy?"

"No. Rose."

His breath caught in his throat. "Wait, a minute. Yeah. Yeah. Now it makes sense." Charlie pulled Marian into his arms. "I need to give you a raise."

She grinned. "I was counting on that. But let's eat first and no more job talk until after dessert."

◆◆◆◆◆◆

Charlie sat on the sofa, feet on the coffee table, his hands clasped behind his head as he stared at a cobweb in the crevice of the high-pitched ceiling.

He knew Marian hadn't noticed it or she would have had scaffolding put up to wipe it away.

Definitely not going to point it out.

She went to bed early leaving him to sort out everything he'd gleaned from her visit with Lula Belle Darby. The silence made Charlie's thoughts bounce around his brain like a pinball machine.

Lula Belle's eye-openers turned the direction of the investigation. First thing in the morning, he'd erase the whiteboard in the war room.

Rose was Sheila's nanny. Why didn't she mention it? Charlie wondered as he stared at the ceiling.

Charlie sat up and pulled a legal pad from the coffee table drawer. He wrote down a few of the facts that he needed to piece together to make sense.

There were questions about Rose's relationship with Myron and his father. Did Rose have anything to do with Elsie Wagstaff's early death? Or perhaps Myron was responsible for his mother's death, and Rose was determined to take his secret to the grave?

Charlie hoped Sheila Gerber could answer those questions since Rose refused to speak to him.

As soon as they finished dessert, Marian finished telling him the rest of the conversation. There was a falling out between Rose and Judy after Myron's mother died. Lula Belle never discovered what caused the rift in their friendship.

After the split, Judy became a semi-hermit. She lost interest in the upkeep of the house and yard. Her sour attitude and nastiness increased over the years.

Then there was the suicide of a teenage girl at the private school where Rose worked. According to Lula Belle, the young girl was one of

Rose's students. Rumor was the girl was in a deep depression after months of being bullied.

Lula Belle remembered the young girl worked at the Darlington Diner for a short while.

Frank and Peggy would be eager to dish out the answers to all the questions he had about the girl. Charlie needed their full attention. A visit after the lunch rush would be the perfect time.

Did the student's demise have anything to with what happened between Rose and Judy? Did their broken friendship have anything to do with the investigation?

Charlie yawned and stretched. Tomorrow had the potential to be an intense day. He scribbled a few more notes to his list of must achieve by day's end. The desire to snuggle with Marian hurried his pen.

Eager to get into bed, he flicked off the living room lights.

The desk.

Charlie remembered what was so special about Myron Wagstaff's desk.

When he was nine years old, a desk had been delivered to his family's antique shop in Virginia. It was exactly like Myron's. Aunt Emma had gone nuts when she saw it.

For years, she hunted for one for a premium customer but only five existed. This one showed up by dumb luck. Aunt Emma spent a whole day discovering its hidden compartments, places no one would think of looking.

Charlie slapped his forehead. "How did I forget? Got to call Thayer."

As he picked up the phone in the kitchen, he heard Marian's slippers scuffling on the wood floor.

"What are you doing?" Marian scratched her tousled hair. "Who is calling this time of night?"

He glanced at the clock above the cooktop, ten after ten.

"It's not that late for Thayer." His arm slid across her back. "I didn't mean to wake you up. Go back to bed. I'll be there right quick."

Marian leaned against his shoulder. "The boy needs to sleep. What's so urgent it can't wait until the morning?"

"Myron's desk troubled me, and I remembered why. It has secret compartments. There may be a journal or something hidden in it. I bet that's why someone broke into Myron's house."

She gasped. "A record of blackmail dirt."

He kissed the tip of her nose. "Spot on, my dear."

"Call him." Marian hurried toward the bedroom. "I'm coming with you."

"No, you're not. It could be dangerous. Understand?"

Marian's eyes narrowed. "But—"

"No."

"But I want to see the desk."

"After the case is closed. In the meantime, you'll have to wait." He held her cheeks between his hands. "No sneaking into Myron's house."

"Fine." She clutched his wrists. "I'm going to bed."

Charlie watched her retreat then looked over his shoulder at the phone.

"Ah, it can wait." Charlie went to bed.

Chapter 22

McClung rubbed his latex-gloved hands together. "Okay, Sam, video tape everything, and take lots of photos."

"Ready to roll when you are." Sam bobbed his head and stood with the camera poised over McClung's shoulder.

Thayer squatted by his boss's chair, watching every move.

McClung opened the bottom right-hand drawer, reached underneath and felt for a release. Click. He slid open a narrow drawer.

"All right." Thayer laughed.

"Did you get all of it, Sam?"

"Got it. Now for a couple of snaps." The flash brightened the contents of the compartment. "Done."

McClung retrieved a worn leather journal. "Let's see what we have here." He pinched the bottom corner of the book cover and opened it, revealing pages of notes.

A long low whistle bounced off the back of McClung's ear.

"Thayer, back up. You're breathing on me." He rubbed the side of his head.

The young sergeant covered his mouth and continued to read the pages over his boss's shoulder.

McClung turned to the middle of the journal, scanned the notes then moved to the last page. "Well, now we know the blackmailing scheme started before Myron's time."

"It must be his old man's journal. What do you think?" Thayer reached for the book. "May I, Boss?"

McClung stood. "From the dates next to the names and their sins, I agree. Do any names sound familiar to you?"

"At first glance? No, but 1936 was way before my time."

"I'd imagine most are dead."

"Yeah, or in an old folks' home." Thayer sat. He flipped to the *This Journal Belongs To* page. "There's no name."

"I'm not surprised but the distinctive handwriting should make it easy enough to verify it's Herbert Wagstaff's. See the slashes instead of dots over the letter *i*, the closed and tight loops, not much of a slant and pointed letters?"

McClung looked at Sam. "You got this?"

"Yep."

McClung patted Thayer's shoulder. "Up. There are more hidden drawers. Go ahead and bag the journal." He waited until the evidence bag was sealed.

"Okay, on to the next one." McClung glanced at the photographer. "Ready?"

"Born ready."

McClung repeated the same steps for the opposite bottom drawer and found another old journal. He searched for a date.

"This one appears to pick up where the last one ended." He gave the journal to Thayer. "Bag it. We need to take our time studying these. Best to do it at the station."

Four more secret compartments were found; each held a journal.

"Are you ready for the mother lode?"

Thayer and Sam yelled, "Yes!"

McClung grinned. "Sam, scan the top of the desk before we clear it."

The silver-haired man made two passes with the video camera and then took five photos from all sides and above the desk.

"All right, let's remove everything."

Once finished, McClung ran his fingers under the top edge of the desk. "Found it."

He grunted as he lifted the top. "Heavier than I thought it'd be. Look. What did I tell you?"

Bundles of cash, journals, and large brown envelopes filled the space.

"Holy Janey Mack!" Thayer's eyes were almost as wide open as his mouth.

"Camera's rolling. Y'all get out of the shot." Sam Goldstein circled the desk.

"That my friends, may be the answer to Myron's murder. This has to be the reason someone broke into his house."

"Done." Sam eased the video camera off his shoulder. "Let me get a few photographs before you remove anything."

Sam Goldstein took at least a dozen more pictures.

"I think that's enough." Sam swiped the back of his hand across his forehead.

McClung opened an envelope containing black-and-white, grainy, out-of-focus photographs.

"There's too much stuff to examine here. Thayer, let's get everything bagged and take it to the station." McClung gave him the envelope.

"Let me get the camera rolling." Sam hefted the bulky camera onto his shoulder.

"I can't wait to go through this stuff." Thayer shuffled through the photos then slid them into the envelope.

McClung exhaled. "As much as I'd like to, we'll leave it to Stewie and Jenny to unravel."

"What? Aw, Boss. Why?" Thayer clicked his tongue and shook his head as he bagged the cash.

"Because we need to question Sheila Gerber about Rose. And we have to talk with Frank and Peggy about the girl who committed suicide."

"Well, at least I'll get lunch."

"I don't know, it'll be almost closing time by the time we get there."

"You're killing me, Boss." Thayer's eyes rolled toward the ceiling.

McClung chuckled. "Okay, I'll buy you a late lunch."

The young sergeant bobbed his head. "Deal." He scribbled the time and date on the evidence bag.

"Tell me we'll at least look at all this stuff."

"Yep. We're coming in tomorrow."

"Tomorrow's Saturday."

"Yeah. The sooner we get these murders solved, the sooner we get back to some sense of normalcy."

"Fine." Thayer sighed. "I hope we're finished by four o'clock."

"Date with the new EMT, Leanna Wallace?"

Thayer's head snapped up. His cheeks turned bright pink. "How do you know?"

McClung slapped him on the back. "Son, you should know by now nothing gets by me."

♦♦♦♦♦♦

He walked the hospital hallway to Sheila Gerber's lab. McClung didn't know what kind of greeting he'd get from her. Who could blame her for being ill-tempered?

On their first encounter, Sheila was a suspect in the Paper Heart Stalker case, and now she's a suspect in her stepbrother's murder. Although, in his mind, McClung had cleared her of that.

When they entered the lab's empty waiting room, Sheila's cheery hello took them by surprise. Her appearance had changed so dramatically she almost looked like a different person.

"What can I help you with today?" Her smile was genuine. "Nothing can put me in a bad mood today. Not even y'all."

McClung opened his mouth.

Sheila's index finger shot up, putting his question on hold. "Buy me a cup of coffee, and I'll tell you anything you want to know."

"Deal."

"Hold on one second." She opened the door to the interior of the lab. "Hey! I'm going to the cafeteria. Hold down the fort while I'm gone."

Sheila exited the room. Her steps, quick and bouncy.

McClung caught up with her. "Why are you in such a good mood?"

Sheila hunched her shoulders.

"Is it because Myron is dead?"

"Yeah. His shadow isn't hovering over me. The bully is dead and can't hurt me anymore." She paused. "Myron wounded me in many ways."

"What do you mean?"

Sheila tapped her temple. "Myron did a number up here."

McClung heard the racket from the cafeteria.

Sheila stopped.

"Every day Myron told me I was nothing but a fat, ugly, stupid girl that nobody wanted." Sheila groaned and shook her head. "I was worthless trash."

"Those are only words. You know that."

"Yes, I know, but to a 3-year-old girl the words of an 11-year-old boy meant a lot. In my eyes, he was an adult."

McClung groaned. "So, what he said was fact."

"Exactly. Myron's father never adopted me. My last name was legally changed, but Herbert Wagstaff never adopted me. But I give him credit, he supported me financially until his death, which lucky for me was right before I graduated from college."

Sheila's story intrigued McClung.

"Why didn't he adopt you? Was your mother opposed to it?"

Sadness shadowed Sheila's face. "According to Myron, I wasn't good enough for his precious father. Of course, Herbert didn't want me as his daughter. Remember, I was fat, ugly, and stupid."

Sheila rubbed her nose. "I never asked my mother. Now I believe she didn't want me to belong to the Wagstaffs."

"I understand. The timing of Herbert's death was fortuitous."

Sheila snorted. "You got that right."

They continued their journey in silence.

As they entered the cafeteria, Sheila laughed. "After the concrete slab slid over Myron's sarcophagus, the image of King Tut popped into my head. Even in death, Myron was treated like a king."

McClung heard Thayer mumble, "good to be king."

"When we left the mausoleum, I noticed all the graves surrounding it are women. Wagstaff women. My mother. Myron's mother. Only the Wagstaff men are inside the crypt."

"That's odd."

She stopped again. "Yeah. Myron was right. The Wagstaff men viewed women as lesser beings. Not even good enough to be buried with them. The mausoleum is a club for dead men only."

Sheila shook her finger side to side. "When I woke up this morning, it dawned on me the Wagstaff women are free. Truly free from the dominating Wagstaff men. Not trapped inside with them."

"I see your point." McClung nodded.

Sheila's face brightened. "My past is buried with Myron. All the hurt, fear, and shame he caused is dead. Gone. Just like him."

She resumed the quest for coffee. "This will sound appalling, but I'd like to shake the hand of Myron's killer and say thanks for setting me free."

McClung smirked. "Have to find the killer first."

Once inside the cafeteria, they made a beeline toward the coffee station.

Sheila filled an extra-large cup then stirred in a generous amount of half-and-half.

McClung opened his wallet.

"I have another reason for my good mood."

"What?"

"Yesterday, Myron's will was read." She smiled as she sipped coffee.

"Everything as expected?"

Sheila nodded. "Even better."

"Yeah? Well, maybe you should buy our coffee."

"A deal is a deal." Sheila winked at Thayer. "What do you say, Sergeant?"

"I honestly don't care as long as someone is paying for mine."

They watched Thayer zigzag between the occupied tables until he found an empty one in the corner.

"If I may ask, what was even better in the will?"

Sheila's eyes shifted away from McClung. A blush tinted her cheeks. "You have a new neighbor."

"You're getting Myron's house?"

"Yep."

"Well, get out of the garden! Let me be the first to welcome you to the neighborhood." McClung extended his hand.

"Actually, Myron's ex-wife inherited the house but gave it to me. Too many bad memories for her. I won't be moving in right away. Even though I've never been inside the house, I'm gutting it. All traces of Myron, gone."

"I understand completely." He remembered Marian's need to remodel her house after she was almost murdered inside her closet.

"I got to rid the house of any Myron stink." Sheila's nose wrinkled. "Did you notice Myron's breath always smelled like fish? He didn't even eat fish. He hated it."

McClung managed to swallow his coffee before he snorted, thankful it didn't spew out of his mouth, or worse, his nose.

Thayer coughed, a sour smirk plastered on his face. "I'll take notes. Whenever you're ready." He held his pen over his pad.

McClung blotted the droplets of coffee clinging to his lips. "Of course. Back to business. Sheila, I have a few questions about your nanny."

"Rose? You think she has something to do with Myron's murder?"

"Maybe. Or Judy Johnson's. Possibly both."

"I find that hard to believe. Rose and Myron had a complicated relationship, a love-hate thing."

"How did Rose treat you?"

Sheila's head tilted to one side. "Interesting. She was like a mother hen, always protected me but never any warm and fuzzy moments. Rose liked me, I suppose, just not motherly, if you know what I mean."

McClung nodded. "What was Rose's relationship with Herbert?"

"I'm pretty sure Rose was sweet on my stepfather."

"Why's that?" McClung removed his cup's lid and blew away the steam snaking from the coffee.

"Rose became my nanny when I was eight years old. Her husband died two months before she took the job. The flirtations became obvious after my mother got sick with cancer."

"I'm sorry."

Sheila waved away the condolences. "Long time ago. Anyway, I was fifteen when my mother became bedridden. Rose and Herbert shared sly grins, lingering touches, and giggles behind closed doors."

McClung shook his head.

"I was young, but not so stupid I couldn't put two and two together."

McClung snapped the lid onto the coffee cup. "So, what was Rose's relationship with your mother?

"Cordial but definitely not friends." Sheila paused.

"Herbert treated Mom like a queen until the cancer diagnosis. I think he viewed her as damaged goods and that's when Rose seized her chance. In the end, my stepfather tossed Rose aside like my mother."

McClung witnessed a wave of sorrow crash over Sheila's face, so he went in a different direction with the questions. "In what way was Rose hard on Myron?"

"She never let him get away with any of the dirty tricks he pulled on me, but I never told her about his hateful remarks. No witnesses ever around to hear. It would've been his word against mine."

"Did Rose punish Myron?"

Thayer flipped the note-filled page.

"Myron got spanked at least once a day." Sheila buried her tongue in her cheek as her eyes narrowed. "Hmm, come to think of it, I believe Myron enjoyed them."

"You've got to be kidding me." Thayer snarled. "The guy's a nut."

McClung choked on his coffee as he glared at his sergeant.

"My apologies, Ms. Gerber."

Sheila chuckled. "None needed. You're right. In my opinion? Myron was a certified psychopath."

"Moving on, shall we? If I remember correctly from last year's interview, you lived at a boarding school after your mother passed away. Is that correct?"

"Thank goodness, yes. The day after the funeral."

"What did Rose do?"

"She got a job at a private school."

"Did your relationship with Rose continue after you left home?"

Sheila wrinkled her nose. "Nah. Haven't heard from her since the day stepfather's chauffeur shut the car door when he dropped me off at the boarding school."

"What about Herbert and Myron? Did they get along?"

"They had their heads together most of the time." She rolled her eyes. "I'd sit outside Herbert's office and listen to them. Finances were like a game to them. They'd talk about schemes and different ways to keep all their money and make it grow, get richer. Myron was definitely his father's son."

McClung scratched his eyebrow. "Do you know if Rose kept in touch with Herbert and Myron?"

"After I was banished to boarding school, I had no contact with Rose, Myron, or Herbert. Pfft! You know how I found out that stepfather had died?"

"How?"

"A housemaid called and told me he'd died."

Thayer dropped his pen. "Awe, nice. Myron was a piece of work."

"Yeah, a real jerk." Sheila rubbed her nose. "Can we talk about something else?"

McClung noticed her glassy eyes and moved to the second murder. "Are you familiar with all the stories about Judy?"

Sheila gawked. "Everyone in Lyman County has heard about that crazy old bat. But you want to know about Rose and Judy's connection."

"Yes."

"I'm not quite sure of the ins and outs of their relationship. When I was around thirteen, I found an interesting picture on the baby grand buried in a hundred other photos. This particular one was of Elsie, Myron's mom, Rose, and Judy dressed for a ball. They had their arms around each other's waist."

Sheila looked at her watch. "I'll need to get back to work soon."

"Do you have any inkling why they had the big falling out?" McClung bit the corner of his bottom lip.

She shook her head. "Supposedly, the three of them chased after stepfather, the most eligible bachelor at the time, believe it or not. The richest too more than likely. Elsie won his heart. The rumor was Judy poisoned Elsie. After Elsie died, Herbert went into seclusion and Rose and Judy went their separate ways."

"Interesting. Who told you that?" McClung finished his coffee.

"Myron, but he was a liar. Like I said, just rumors." Sheila glanced at her watch.

"Just a few more questions." He wondered how Sheila's mother and Herbert ended up getting married, but it wasn't relevant to the case.

"Make them quick."

"How did Herbert become rich?"

Sheila dipped her head. "Old money invested well with a little bootlegging and blackmail on the side."

"Fascinating." McClung hurried to the next question. "What was your relationship with Dr. Carter?"

Sheila snorted. "Ah. So, you know about that. Well, he helped me deal with my husband's death." She shrugged. "And we went out a couple of times, nothing serious. To be wanted by a handsome man, even for a moment, made me feel good about myself."

"Did you ever tell him about Myron or his family?"

She tossed her head side to side. "No way. I was there for my grief over Larry's death, not to relive my miserable childhood. Besides, I'm embarrassed for anyone to know I'm related to him even if it's not by blood."

McClung massaged his earlobe. "He never asked?"

"Nope, I did the talking. He'd nod and scribble on a legal pad. Why are you asking?"

"Myron blackmailed the good doctor." McClung leaned back and tapped the empty cup on the table.

Sheila's eyebrows shot up. "You're not joking, are you?"

"No."

"What secret did Dr. Carter have that was worthy of blackmail?"

"Doctors shouldn't get involved with patients."

Sheila blinked a few times. "Patients, huh? So, I wasn't the only one?"

McClung and Thayer shook their heads.

"Oh, well, I wasn't his special lady." Sheila sighed. "At least I know it's fact, the Wagstaff's were a bunch of blackmailers."

"I can't say for sure if they all were but definitely Myron." The picture of the hidden journals and photographs popped into his brain. "Do you trust your attorney, Tippler?"

"Yes, why wouldn't I? I mean, he restored my inheritance. I love the guy."

"No reason." McClung drummed his fingers on the table. "That's it for now. Let us know when you move in, and Marian will bring you some homemade goodies and a few plants for your yard. A rosebush more than likely. You may need to rein her in with the plants. Marian will have your yard looking like a botanical garden."

Sheila's eyes misted. "Thank you." She hopped up and swiped her finger under her eye. "Back to work, I guess."

Chapter 23

"Look over there." McClung pointed to a Stellar Landscaping truck parked at the gas pumps at the 7-Eleven.

"Looks like a good a time for a snack." Thayer turned in the parking lot and backed into a shady space.

Brian walked out of the store and held the door open as they neared.

"Gentlemen." Brian tipped his head. "How are y'all doing today?"

"Thank you." McClung clasped Brian's outstretched hand. "We're hard at work, believe or not. Just taking a short break."

Thayer followed McClung's lead and shook Brian's hand.

"I heard that." Brian grinned. "Doing the same thing myself. See you around."

"Later." McClung stood just inside the store and watched Brian pull away from the pumps.

"What are you going to get?" McClung grabbed a Mounds bar and wondered if they should've taken Brian into the station. But why? Because he was adopted and moved from job to job?

Thayer grabbed a PayDay and a family-sized bag of crunchy Cheetos. "This'll do for now. Are you getting a Slurpee?" He snickered.

"Kid stuff. I'm having water."

The store clerk chatted with them as he made a cherry Slurpee for Thayer.

"That guy that was just in here is a really nice guy. He paid for y'all's stuff. Left a twenty-dollar bill and said I could keep the change." The youth's smile stretched across his acne-dotted face.

"Is that right?" McClung glanced out the storefront.

"Yes, sir, he sure did."

They gathered their snacks, left the store and headed for the cruiser parked under a copse of mature pine trees.

McClung noticed something in the shadows outside the passenger door, a large pot of scarlet geraniums with a jagged piece of scrap paper nestled in the blooms. It said, *For Miss Marian.*

"Hm, Brian left these for Marian."

Thayer slurped his drink. "You think he's buttering you up? You know, to throw you off his scent?"

"Are you saying he's our murderer just because he gave my wife a pot of flowers?"

"When you put it that way, it sounds stupid."

McClung shook his head as he opened the back door and secured the plant on the floorboard.

"Let's hope we don't have to arrest anyone today."

Thayer chuckled. "We'll call Marsh to take them in."

"Yeah." McClung shut the door. "Let's sit here for a while."

A warm breeze tunneled through the car's open windows as they discussed Sheila's interview.

"You don't suppose Sheila is involved Myron's blackmail scheme?"

McClung chugged water, washing away the last bite of the candy bar. "No, for a couple of reasons. One, if Sheila wasn't good enough to be a Wagstaff, he certainly wouldn't have let her into their scheme. And two, Myron was one greedy little bugger. Why would he share with his stepsister?"

"Yeah, you're right. Sheila's not a blackmailer. But what about Rose? I mean, a teacher at a private school. Kids talk about their parents. There's money to be had there."

"I like the way you think. That could be the reason she refused to answer our questions." McClung finished the water.

"Yes! They're partners. With Robyn. Just think of all the stuff she runs across as she cleans houses."

"Yep. Maybe she had Myron killed to take over the business."

"Maybe it was Robyn who broke into Myron's house looking for the journals."

"Good. That's good. Who do you think is good for Judy's murder? McClung crushed the plastic bottle.

"Hmm. If the murders aren't related, maybe the mother of the little boy Judy shot? Or the hot-headed neighbor, Rainne Atkins." Thayer snapped his fingers. "Lula Belle. She got tired of all the nonsense. Forty-three years is a long time to put up with Judy."

McClung laughed at the mental image of Lula Belle with the BB gun slung on her shoulder.

"Nah, I don't think Lula Belle is good for the murder. Brian or Shelby, maybe? I don't know."

"Do you believe the two murders are related?"

"I haven't decided." McClung drummed his fingers on his thigh. "Let's get moving. Swing by my house so we can get rid of that bush in the backseat."

Thayer cranked the cruiser. "Think we'll be arresting somebody?"

"Yep. I feel it in the wind."

Chapter 24

McClung tapped the glass door, his nose level with a closed sign.

"Well, glory be. Frank, get out here." Peggy stuck the pencil she was using to calculate the day's receipts behind her ear.

"Three times in one week." The older woman opened the door then pulled McClung into a bear hug. "We ain't seen you that many times in a week since you got married."

McClung blushed. He welcomed the love he felt every time he entered Frank and Peggy's place. He looked around the empty diner. "You mind if we visit for a little while?"

"Don't be silly. Get up on that stool and make yourselves at home." Peggy gathered her work.

Frank appeared behind the counter. "What'll you have, boys? I ain't shut down the grill yet."

"We don't want to be a bother but since you're offering and I'm starving, I'd like a grilled cheese sandwich." McClung yawned. "It's been a long day, Frank. I'll take a cup of coffee."

"The same for me but a large Coke instead of coffee." Thayer licked his lips.

"Fries?" Frank poured a mug of coffee.

"Throw some on the plate." McClung stirred the coffee, dispelling the steam.

Peggy went around the counter opposite the two officers and leaned on her elbows. "I can see it in your eyes. You got questions, don't you?"

"I'm afraid we do." McClung heard Thayer's belly rumble at the aroma of the fries, thankful he fulfilled his promise of a late lunch.

Peggy poured herself a cup of coffee. "Still ain't solved those murders?"

"No, but I think we're close." McClung sipped the coffee. "Ah. The best."

He watched Frank slather butter on four slices of sourdough bread then layer them with cheddar and American cheese. The grill sizzled as the sandwiches hit the hot smooth surface.

Frank hummed as he flipped the toasted bread. He looked as if he didn't have a care in the world.

McClung's mind drifted as he watched the old man's fluid movements.

"Done."

Frank's proclamation jolted McClung back to the present.

"Well, we'll help you any way we can."

McClung looked at the plate laden with a golden grilled cheese sandwich, a mound of chips, and a pickle spear.

"Do you remember a girl that used to work for you around…?" McClung stared at Thayer. "When would you say?"

His sandwich was poised between his teeth. Thayer groaned and removed it from his mouth. "The early forties." He took a big bite before McClung could ask another question.

"Yeah. The story we heard was she was attended a private school. Supposedly, she committed suicide."

Peggy looked up at the ceiling as she squeezed her eyes closed and slowly shook her head. "Oh, poor child."

Frank rubbed his wife's back. "Yeah, we remember her. Sweet young thing, started working here the first year we opened."

"So it's true."

Peggy gritted her teeth and her cheeks reddened. "That mean old crow Rose Emerson is to blame."

"What?" McClung dropped the pickle.

"Frank, you tell him. I can't. I just can't. Whenever I think about it, it makes my blood boil. I just want to strangle that woman."

"Her name was Charlotte, but everyone called her Lottie. She worked here for about a year before it happened."

"Tell me the story." McClung leaned across the Formica countertop.

"Eat your food before it gets cold. I'll tell you everything I know, then you can ask your questions."

McClung picked up a few chips.

Frank clutched Peggy's hand. "Hon, will you get me a diet Coke?"

She shuffled toward the ice bin as she pulled the hem of her apron to the corner of her eyes.

"On second thought, I'll get my Coke if you get me a big slab of apple pie and if you don't mind, heat it up then put a scoop of vanilla ice cream on top."

Peggy disappeared into the kitchen.

"As I was saying, Lottie was a sweet beautiful young girl. Shy but a hard worker. Some people would say she was from the wrong side of the tracks. Just poor that's all."

McClung wiped his mouth. "Poor? How was she able to attend a private school?"

"Her mama and daddy worked two jobs each so their only child could get on up in the world."

Frank tapped his temple. "Lottie was a smart girl. Brought in her report card once. All A's. Anyway, all the boys were gaga over her. Even the well-to-do ones and that ticked off old Rose Emerson."

"Lottie came in one day. Eyes all red and swollen. Peggy finally got her to tell her what had happened. That Rose woman told Lottie that she weren't good enough for them boys in her school. That she needed to find a dumb hick like herself."

Peggy burst from the kitchen. "I told Lottie I was going to go up to that high and mighty scrawny old shrew and give her a piece of my mind."

"She begged my Peggy not to. Afraid she'd get kicked out of that fancy school." Frank snaked his thin arm around his wife's thick waist. "Poor Lottie. We'd find her crying in the back almost every day. She wouldn't say why, but we knew it was that snotty Rose."

"Oh, fuff! I thought only kids were bullies, but Rose Emerson was the biggest bully ever. A grown woman picking on a sweet innocent child like Lottie." Peggy balled up her fist and shook it. "One day. Pow! Right on her long, stuck-up nose."

Thayer swallowed hard. "Worse than Judy Johnson?"

"I think those two harpies were in competition. At least I never heard of Judy mean-mouthing kids. Telling them they were no good." Peggy fanned herself with her food-stained apron.

"Yes, sir. I gotta agree with Peg. But then one day, Lottie comes in and tells us that she's going away for a while."

"That's the last time we saw her." Peggy sighed heavily. "Lottie didn't say why, but I know. I heard her a few times in the bathroom throwing up and her skirts were getting tighter."

Thayer gawked. "No. Pregnant? By who?"

They both shrugged.

"Don't know. She never talked about a boyfriend. All the boys that came in fought for her attention, but she never paid no mind to them."

McClung finished the sandwich. "Did she have the baby?"

"We heard that her parents made her give it up." Frank clicked his tongue. "Lottie went into a deep depression."

"I guess Rose Emerson's soul-crushing insults and the loss of her baby had poor Lottie believing she wasn't fit for this Earth."

Peggy sniffled and snatched a napkin from its dispenser then pressed it to her nose. "Poor, poor child."

"Are her parents still living in Lyman County?" McClung now believed Rose Emerson was capable of murder.

"Nope, moved away after they buried their Lottie. Heard it was somewhere in South Carolina."

Peggy tapped her chin with her finger. "No, pretty sure it was Tennessee."

The hair on McClung's neck jumped up. The birth certificate.

Frank hiked up one shoulder. "Peggy's probably right."

McClung slid off the stool. "We've got to go." He removed a twenty and a five from his wallet and laid them on the counter.

"Your money ain't good here. You know that." Frank pushed the bills away.

"Peggy, tell Frank what I always say."

She tucked a strand of dyed black hair behind her ears. "It's for your favorite charity."

Thayer stood. "What's your favorite charity, Frank?"

The old man winked. "My retirement."

McClung returned his wink. "Thanks for the information. Thayer, let's go." He paused at the door. "What was Lottie's last name?"

Frank and Peggy chimed. "Banks."

Chapter 25

McClung jogged to the cruiser. "Get to the station, pronto."

After a quick glance from left to right, the cruiser shot forward. Thayer was glad he'd taken the time to back into the slanted parking space.

"What's got you fired up, Boss?"

"Charlotte."

Thayer wrinkled his nose. "I don't get it."

"You will soon." McClung was thankful the police station was only five miles from the square. He jumped out of the car before Thayer turned it off.

McClung rushed through the double doors, waved at Penny, swiped his badge and jogged to Stewie and Jenny's office.

Empty.

Thayer caught up. "Where are they?"

"That was a lot of stuff we brought in to process." McClung took off and yelled. "War room."

McClung came to a sliding stop, grabbed the doorjamb, and flung himself into the bright room. "They're here."

Jenny jumped and squealed. "Jeeze! You scared me half to death."

"I see the ten cups of coffee and five diet Dr Peppers you've had so far today have had no effect on you." Stewie grunted.

"Oh, shut up."

"Sorry, Jenny. Didn't mean to scare you." McClung eyed the Wagstaff's journals spread out on the long conference tables. "Have you found anything about Judy Johnson or Rose Emerson in those?"

"Yeah." Jenny made a beeline toward the books.

"What about a Charlotte Banks or Brian Lane?"

Stewie picked up a folder. "We have most of them categorized. And so far no Brian Lane or Charlotte Banks mentioned."

McClung pulled out a chair and straddled it backward. "What have you discovered about Rose and Judy?"

"Let me tell them, Stewie." Jenny bounced on her toes. "Judy Johnson apparently was a murderess times two. Her fiancée and Elsie Wagstaff."

"No way!" McClung slapped the back of the chair.

"Rose ratted her out." Stewie picked up one of the journals. "All in here."

"Apparently, Rose got a cut of the blackmail for every secret she gave to Herbert and Myron." Jenny glared at Stewie. "Rose is the snitch. Not a victim."

"Now it's beginning to make some sense. I can feel it coming together." McClung nodded. "Do you have Brian's adoption records here?"

"No, I thought you had it on your desk. All of this is the evidence from Myron's desk."

McClung snapped his fingers. "That right." He hopped up. "No mention of anyone named Banks?"

Stewie and Jenny shook their heads.

"But we still have two more journals to process." Stewie picked up two plastic bags. "These are more recent years."

"Thanks, guys. Let me know if you find anyone named Lane or Banks." McClung walked out of the war room, then jogged down the hallway to the stairwell.

Thayer chased after him. "What is it with Brian and Charlotte?"

"I think I may know who'll be next on the murderer's list."

"What?"

McClung plopped into his desk chair and unlocked the bottom desk drawer. "I have a theory, Thayer."

"Enlighten me, Boss."

McClung smirked as his sidekick used one of his own favorite expressions. His fingers ran across the files then he yanked out Brian Lane's file. "There's a pattern to the two murders."

Thayer scrunched his eyebrows together. "A man. A woman. Dead. One killed by drowning. The other by a BB gun." He threw up his hands. "I don't see a pattern."

"Think, Thayer. Think." McClung tapped the side of his head. "Study the victims. What do they have in common?"

The young sergeant gaped. "I'm clueless."

"Personalities."

Thayer sighed and scratched his chin. "Mean people?"

McClung's thumb popped up as he stared at the papers in the folder.

"They were killed because they were ornery?"

"Found it. Brian's birth certificate." McClung held it out to Thayer. "Look." He beamed. "Oh, and yes. Because they were ornery."

Thayer perused the document. His mouth dropped open. "No, way. Banks. Brian's adoptive mother. Her maiden name was Banks, and she lived in Tennessee."

"If I'm correct, Brian's mother was Charlotte and his great aunt adopted him."

Thayer laid the certificate on the desk. "I still don't get the connection."

"I'm going to make a few calls to verify my hunch. In the meantime, ask Penny to send out an *Attempt to Locate* for Brian Lane and have him brought in."

"Right on it, Boss."

The phone rang.

"Yes, Penny." McClung covered the receiver. "Thayer." He waved him back.

"When?" McClung stood. "Got it. Penny, issue an ATL for Brian Lane." He nodded. "Yes. Have him brought in."

McClung hung up. "We're too late. Rose Emerson is dead."

Chapter 26

"You want me to go where?" Thayer lifted an eyebrow.

"The cemetery. The one where Myron was buried."

Thayer pulled out of the precinct parking lot. "You're telling me Rose Emerson was found dead in the cemetery."

"No. Robyn found her grandmother in their sitting room."

Thayer huffed. "Then why are we going to the cemetery?"

McClung turned in his seat. "Marsh and Henry are at the scene with Robyn. I feel pretty sure Sam Goldstein is on his way there, too. He has a nose for this sort of thing."

"We'll find Brian at the cemetery." McClung's adrenaline plummeted as he thought of breaking the news to Marian.

"How can you be so sure, Boss?"

"Yesterday, when we were staking out Myron's funeral, remember the Stellar Landscaping truck parked in the distance?"

"Yeah."

"I believe it was Brian visiting Charlotte Banks' grave."

◆◆◆◆◆◆

Brian knelt on the ground, planting Forget-Me-Nots around a grave covered with multi-colored, earth-tone pebbles. A freshly scrubbed tombstone read, *Charlotte Paige Banks*. Underneath her name were the words, *Beloved Daughter,* and the dates *June 25, 1926–September 16, 1943.*

"How did you figure it out?" Brian kept his gaze fixed on the ground, plunging the trowel in the earth then placing a flower in the gaping hole.

"It doesn't matter." The lines on McClung's face deepened, his lips pressed together. How could a man so kind be such a brutal murderer? Looking down on Brian's hunched back, he appeared to be an old man ready for the grave.

McClung knelt beside Brian. "I'm sorry for what happened."

Brian's hand hesitated as he dug another hole. "You don't know the half it." He sat back on his heels after he filled the hole with the last plant.

"Happy Birthday, Mama." His whispered words trembled.

"Mama would've been 56 years old today. Only seventeen when she died." Brian sniffed and ran the cuff of his shirt across his cheeks. "It's so dang hot. Sweat's running down my face."

He faltered as he stood.

McClung and Thayer, on each side of Brian, steadied him by his elbows.

"I feel like my soul is ready to be taken. I'm tired. So…" Brian's rough hands cradled his face, smothering a heavy sob.

"Yeah, the heat can do a number on a body." McClung gave him a tissue. "Why don't you come with us? We'll get you something cold to drink and a cool place to rest."

"Sounds good." Brian shuffled to the cruiser, eyes cast to his feet. Stopping, he looked back to his mother's grave. "Goodbye, Mama."

Brian pressed the tissue on his closed eyes. "Dang, heat. Sweat's getting in my eyes."

McClung was conflicted. A grieving man needed comforting. A murderer needed to be punished. "I'm sorry, but we have to handcuff you."

"I understand." Brian's feet scraped the ground as he continued toward the police cruiser.

"Chief, may I ask a favor?" Brian's glassy eyes searched McClung's face.

"Sure."

"Do you think Marian would mind looking after my mama's grave?"

McClung's eyes felt full and he swallowed hard. "I don't think she'd mind at all."

Brian bit his lip and looked away. "I'm so sorry to disappoint her."

Once in the car, Thayer turned on the air conditioner, full blast.

"How's that Brian?" McClung glanced over his shoulder.

Brian nodded as he stared at his dirty fingernails.

"Straight to the station?" Thayer mumbled.

McClung motioned his index finger forward.

They rode in silence.

McClung couldn't recall a time when he felt sorry for a murderer. He was angry three people had died. Yet, the man sitting in the backseat may have had a different life if his mother had not been bullied to the point where she felt the only way to end her misery was death.

It was a short ride to the station, only ten miles, but it seemed like a hundred.

Thayer escorted Brian to interview room one and left him alone with a bottle of water and a cup of ice. Thayer watched him from the viewing room as he waited for McClung.

McClung appeared thirty minutes later with Brian's dossier. "How's he been?" He observed Brian with his head buried in his arms resting on the table.

"Quiet. Every now and then his body shutters." Thayer looked at McClung. "Crying, I suppose."

"I called my contacts in the city where Brian grew up and a few others where he worked to confirm my suspicions."

"What did you find out?

McClung cupped his hand over his mouth. "I think it's best to hear it from Brian. But I'll tell you one thing, it's bad."

McClung and Thayer entered the room.

Brian sat up. His eyes were bloodshot.

McClung pushed the cube of tissues toward the middle of the table.

Brian ran several tissues over his damp face and under his nose.

"All right. Brian, do you want to tell us your story?"

His shoulders bunched up then his whole body sagged. Brian's elbow banged on the wooden table and his forehead fell into his palm. "Why? You probably know everything."

"We need to hear your story."

Brian's lips quivered. "How long you got?"

"Take all the time you need." McClung thought about Marian and their date at the Chinese restaurant. He'd have to call her.

As if Brian had read his mind, he stared at him with dull eyes. "You'll probably need to call Marian then." He fumbled with the half-empty bottle. "Did she get the scarlet geraniums?"

McClung again struggled with his feelings. A serial killer was friends with his wife. He guessed, maybe, if he'd spent more time getting to know Brian, he may have spotted something. Then again, Marian didn't.

"Yes. Planted it right away. Marian said red geraniums meant comfort."

Brian nodded. "Other meanings, too." He snatched a tissue and blew his nose.

"I knew it would be a matter of time before you figured it all out. You're a smart man. I wanted her to have something to remember the better part of me."

McClung pressed his lips together and gave him a quick smile. "Ready to tell us your side of the story?"

Brian sighed. "I knew I was adopted, but I didn't know my adoptive mother was my great aunt. She said my mama couldn't take care of me and that my mama loved me so much that she wanted me to have the best home possible."

Brian paused. He licked his lips then look up with eyes watery. "She never told me my mama was dead."

He chuckled sadly and wiped away the tears from the corners of his eyes.

A vision of Ma popped into McClung's mind and he found it hard to keep a stoic expression.

"When did you find out?"

"About six months ago when the only mother I ever knew died. I had to clear out her house and sell it. My father, adoptive father, died a few years back. So, it was left to me to settle the estate."

Brian ran his fingers through his thick, unruly hair. "That's when I found letters from my real grandmother to my adoptive mother. The first letter was about my mama getting pregnant. Another one begged my great aunt to adopt me. Then the hardest one to read told her my mama was dead."

Brian's tongue ran around his gums as he stared at the corner of the table. He shook his head and sighed heavily.

McClung leaned forward. "I was under the impression Charlotte's parents moved to Tennessee right after she died."

"Yeah. Yeah, they did." Brian sat up and poured the rest of the water into the cup.

"I called them Uncle Sunky and Auntie M. They both passed away years ago. They were good to me. I wished I had known then who they really were instead of six months ago."

Brian held the empty bottle. "But you're probably wanting to know about my descent into madness."

"I wouldn't say madness, more of a vigilante on the road of revenge." McClung clasped his hands and lightly tapped the table.

Brian shrugged. "Sounds more, uh, heroic, I suppose." He tugged the hair on the nape of his neck.

"I was thirteen when my best friend died right in front of me." Brian pushed out his lips. "Protecting me. Ronnie was his name. Only sixteen."

Thayer exhaled. "That's rough."

The plastic bottle crunched in Brian's fist. "It was an accident, but it wasn't an accident what I did to that boy who shoved him."

"Walk us through it." McClung sat back.

"I was big for my age. Clumsy. Real shy. Never looked at anyone. Always kept my head down. I'd been teased since the first day of school because I was adopted. I was awkward and never felt I was good enough for nothing. I don't know why. Just didn't."

Brian tapped his forehead. "Not right in here, I guess."

He grabbed the hair on either side of his head. "This mangy hair didn't help."

McClung said nothing.

Brian's hands fell to his lap. "Anyway, Ronnie moved next door when I was seven. Like a big brother to me from day one."

Thayer cleared his throat. "That was a good thing."

Brian smiled sadly. "Ronnie and I were walking home from school. We passed a group of boys. The biggest one stuck out a foot and tripped me."

Brian's fingers rubbed the hump on the bridge of his nose. "Fell flat on my face. Blood everywhere. The boys all laughed and called me a clumsy wooly booger bastard."

Brian shifted in the seat. "Ronnie popped the bully in the jaw. The bully shoved Ronnie really hard, and he fell backward."

He ran hands over his ears. "I can still hear the crack of Ronnie's skull as his head hit the curb. I crawled to him. His eyes were wide open. Just stared at nothing."

Brian threw his head back then it flopped forward and he stared directly at McClung. "I'd never seen a dead person before, but I knew Ronnie was dead."

McClung swallowed hard. "What happened next?"

"Not exactly sure how, but I ended up with a pipe in my hand and I beat that bully within an inch of his life. He never recovered. Died a few months later."

McClung flipped open the manila folder. "You only spent a few months in juvenile detention?"

"My adoptive parents got me a real good attorney. Spared no expense." Brian chuckled. "Never knew they had so much money until six months ago."

He glanced sideways. "You'd never know from my looks, but I'm a very rich man. Money-wise that is, but other than that…" Brian grunted. "I've got nothing. Nothing at all."

Brian gritted his teeth. "The day Ronnie died, I swore as long as I was alive I wouldn't let another bully hurt anyone else."

"How many bullies will never hurt anyone again?"

"Lost count."

McClung pushed away from the table. "I need to step out for a few minutes."

"I understand."

McClung walked out with Thayer close behind.

They went into the break room.

"Is he telling the truth?" Thayer squawked.

"I told you it was bad." McClung dropped a few coins into the vending machine. A can of Dr Pepper rattled down the shoot.

"Going for the hard stuff, huh?"

McClung opened the can. "I need it."

Thayer leaned against the counter. "How many are dead?"

"Hard to say. I asked my counterparts how many unsolved murders of known thugs they had." McClung held up his hand. "Before you ask, I can't swear that Brian was responsible for any of them. All I know is Brian was working in those cities at the time of the murders and he left town soon afterward."

A low, slow whistle eased from Thayer's lips. "You're thinking he's good for Myron and Judy's deaths?"

McClung nodded. "Don't forget Rose."

Thayer crossed his arms. "Are you going to call Marian and tell her about Brian?"

"I'll call her, but I won't say anything about Brian. Best to do that in person." He picked up the phone in the break room.

"Hey, sweetie, I'm going to be later than I thought."

Marian exhaled softly. "Okay, but I still want Chinese tonight. I have an idea. I'll get takeout say around six-thirty and keep it warm. Date night will be at home."

"Sounds great. I'll call you when I'm ready to head home."

"I love you, Charlie."

"Love you, too."

◆◆◆◆◆◆

McClung and Thayer sat across from Brian.

"Brian, there are unsolved murders in every town you worked. I'm not going to ask you about those."

"Best you didn't."

"I want to know about Myron Wagstaff, Judy Johnson, and Rose Emerson."

Brian sniffed loudly. "So, you know about Rose already?"

"We got the call right before we found you at the cemetery."

"I see."

McClung rubbed the top of his ear. "Do you know anything about the blackmail scheme Myron and Rose were running?"

"Nope."

"Why did you kill them?" McClung knew the answer, but he wanted to hear it from Brian.

"I didn't want to, not after I'd met your wife."

McClung's nostrils flared. He hadn't expected that response. "What do you mean? What's Marian got to do with this?"

Brian sat up straight, his hands hung between his knees. "Don't mean no offense, Chief McClung."

"I'm listening." McClung balanced his fists on the edge of the table.

"Marian was one of the first people I met in this town." The crow's feet around his eyes softened. "There's something about her." Brian shook his head. "Don't mean nothing bad by that. No disrespect. Everything above board."

Brian smiled. "She has a good soul. Treated me with respect. Like I was somebody. Not just some old man who tended her yard. She only saw the good in me."

McClung unclenched his hands. "She does have a way about her. Everyone is special, important to her."

"Yeah, I never felt like a no nobody around her." Brian shrugged. "I didn't want to disappoint her or make her think less of me. But then…"

McClung waited for Brian to finish.

Brian rubbed his hands on his thighs. "You see, I couldn't take it anymore, Myron's hate. He was filled with it. His core was rotten with it. Everyone has a bad day and acts like a jerk every now and then."

He tossed his head side to side and shook his finger at McClung. "But Myron." Brian grimaced. "He was evil. Pure evil. And when he assaulted that defenseless old man, the one who delivers papers. I snapped."

Brian's outstretched finger curled, his hand became a white-knuckled fist, and his face turned crimson.

McClung was afraid the man was going to have a stroke.

Brian exhaled and shook his body. "I'm sorry."

"Thayer, go grab a couple of bottles of water."

The sergeant left.

Brian pulled a red bandana from his shirt pocket and ran it over his face.

The door opened. Thayer entered with three bottles and set them on the table.

Brian took one. "Thank you, son. Thank you."

"Do you want to continue?" McClung wondered if they should call it a night and let Brian rest. In a cell.

"Yes, I want to get it over."

"All right, but whenever you need a break, let me know."

"Thanks. You're a good man."

McClung tipped his head.

Brian continued. "I'd gotten my anger under control after Myron grabbed the old man. I let him know I was none too happy. Just grabbed his arm. Didn't hit him. Said my peace and went on my way."

Brian's gaze wandered beyond McClung. "But that morning, the morning I killed Myron was my breaking point."

He stabbed the air with his finger then tapped his chest. "Myron asked me to do his yard first thing Monday morning. He knew exactly when I'd be there. He knew."

Brian grunted. "And do you know what I find when I get to Myron's house?"

McClung mumbled. "Myron watering his lawn."

Brian's hands flew up in the air. "Right. Everyone knows you don't mow wet grass."

Thayer chimed. "You don't get a clean cut."

"I asked him what on Earth he was thinking? Myron snarled, '*I'm paying you to cut my grass not question my intelligence, you stupid oaf*.'"

McClung witnessed the metamorphosis as Brian's face transformed from that of a sane guy to a madman.

"When I turned to leave, Myron sprayed me and yelled he's going to have me fired. And then he said those words. *Clumsy wooly booger bastard.*"

McClung groaned and wondered if Myron had somehow gotten his hands on Brian's juvenile records. "How did Myron know to call you that?"

Brian heaved a few deep breaths. "I have no idea, but you know what happened next."

"We know Myron was drowned by a garden hose that's about it. Tell us how it happened."

"Myron continued to squirt me as I charged him. Fuff! Like a little bit of water was going to stop me."

"The guy's a nut." Thayer muttered.

Brian's nails raked across his forearm. "I wrapped my arms around Myron. He back peddled all the way to the pool still hanging on to the hose."

McClung held up his hand. "Where did the scuffle begin?"

"The patio. Plowed right through it."

"That explains the jumbled furniture, Boss."

McClung nodded. "Brian, what happened by the pool?"

"The hose must have wrapped around Myron's ankle. He lost his balance. I let go and watched him fall. Myron's head bounced on the concrete, I sat on him and kept jabbing his mouth with the hose until I got it down his throat. When he stopped struggling, I rolled him into the pool. His precious pool."

Brian grabbed a bottle of water and drained it.

"Why put Myron in the pool?" McClung held out the last bottle.

Brian took it and shrugged then his face crumbled. "Never meant for poor, sweet Marian to find Myron. I'm really sorry about that. Deeply sorry. She's been through enough this past year."

Tears rolled down Brian's wrinkled cheeks. "I'm so, so sorry she had to see that. So sorry."

McClung pulled his earlobe. "Yeah. I know."

Brian scrubbed his rough hands over his face and mouth. "I best get on with Judy Johnson. Told you most everything last time I was here. In the beginning, I felt sorry that she was old and alone. Had nobody to look after her. But then she started killing poor little animals who weren't doing her no harm. When she shot that little boy picking a pretty little weed for his mama, well, you know."

"You had enough of Judy's tormenting the neighborhood." Thayer stared at him.

Brian shifted his gaze from McClung to Thayer. "That's it in a nutshell, son. I wanted her to know what it felt like to be threatened by the BB gun. How it felt to be shot. I wanted to rid Lyman County of her."

"And Rose Emerson? What did she do to you?" McClung glanced at his watch, five o'clock, and thought the interview was going so smoothly that he may get home before seven o'clock.

Brian's eyes narrowed. "There was another letter among the ones I found six months ago. One my mama wrote to my great aunt. Mama said she was happy that her little boy was going to them, that she knew they'd love me and give me a good home. She said tell my little boy Brian that his mama loved him deeply."

McClung swallowed hard as a tear clung to Brian's weathered cheek.

"Mama said she didn't feel worthy to be a mother. That maybe Miss E was right that she didn't deserve to breathe God's good air."

A chill slithered down McClung's spine.

"Mama wrote that letter the day she died." Brian wiped his eyes with the bandana. "It took me a while, but I finally found that woman who drove my mama to do what she did."

"I'm curious. How did you figure out Miss E was Rose Emerson?"

Brian looked at McClung. "Like you, I asked questions. Miss Lula Belle gave me the missing pieces."

McClung's head jerked back. "I thought her sons cut her grass."

"Yes, she's got good kids." Brian's face brightened. "She'd invite me in for cake and coffee sometimes when I'd attempt to mow Judy Johnson's yard."

"I guess seeing Rose Emerson at Myron's funeral must have made your blood boil."

A sad, lopsided grin pulled at Brian's lips. "Grieving over a piece of trash like Myron Wagstaff."

His back straightened. "I watched her townhome to figure out Robyn's schedule, when Rose would be alone. Even though Robyn's a mean girl, my beef was with her grandma."

"How did you get in?" McClung couldn't believe Rose Emerson would invite Brian into her pristine white living room.

"Easy. Knocked on the door, she opened it, and I pushed my way in." Brian's fingers curved as if wrapped around Rose's neck.

McClung noticed deep scratches on the back of Brian's hands and wagered they weren't from rose bushes but from Rose Emerson's fingernails.

"I grabbed her pencil-thin neck, forced her into a snow-white chair. As I squeezed the life from Rose Emerson, I looked down on her and said, '*I'm doing this for my mama. Miss E, you don't deserve to breathe God's good air*'."

A loud laugh rolled up from Brian's gut. "Her eyes bugged out when I said that. She croaked, '*No. It. Can't. Be.*' I grinned as big as I could and said, '*Yes, Miss E, Charlotte Banks was my mother*'."

Chapter 27

McClung sat at his desk. Not yet seven o'clock but he was ready to go home. Brian was sitting in a cell. Robyn was home alone. She refused a family liaison.

During Robyn's interview, she claimed she knew nothing about the blackmail scheme. She said gossip was the only thing that made her grandmother happy.

Robyn rustled up all the tittle-tattle she could to make her life with Rose tolerable. Cleaning houses was the perfect job for that.

She swore she didn't know beans about Myron's criminal side until her grandmother had her search his desk for a journal. A journal her grandmother said was hers. Stolen by Myron.

When the fact sunk in that Myron was using her for information as well as was her grandmother, Robyn's face drooped like a deflated balloon.

McClung squeezed the back of his neck. Marian was good at working out the knots. He gazed at his wife's picture sitting on his desk.

Gathering all the papers and files on his desk, the weight of the day drained his energy. He longed to be home with Marian leaning on him as they watched television. But he knew he'd be consoling her after he explained that Brian, her garden buddy and friend, had confessed to the three murders.

McClung heaved a sigh. "It is what it is. No sense worrying about what might happen." The twenty-minute drive home would be plenty of time to figure out how he'd tell Marian about Brian.

◆◆◆◆◆◆

Charlie placed his hand on the hood of Marian's Mercedes. Warm. "Hm, the food should still be fairly hot."

He called out as he entered the kitchen. "Hey, sweetie."

Marian ran to him and buried her head in his chest.

He kissed the top of her head. "You know."

Marian's hot breath filtered through Charlie's shirt as she murmured *yes*. She pulled back and looked at Charlie. "I saw Penny and her boyfriend at the Chinese restaurant."

"Oh." He studied her face. Reddish nose. Glassy eyes. Smudged mascara. "Do you want to talk about it?"

She hiked up her shoulders and turned away. "You must be starving. We'll talk later."

Charlie gathered dishes for dinner. "Do you want wine?"

"Yes. Riesling." Marian removed the food warming in the oven.

"Do you mind if we eat in the living room? The Braves are playing the Reds tonight."

Charlie smiled as Marian passed by with a tray loaded with food. "Sure. You're a woman after my own heart."

He paused in the doorway. Marian sat on the sofa, her elbows on her thighs, her hands covered her face.

Charlie set the wine glasses on the coffee table. "Marian? Honey?"

She fell into his arms. "Why did he kill them?"

Her tears dripped on his chest.

"It's complicated but, in his mind, Brian was ridding the world of bullies."

She raised up. "What?"

"It's a long story."

"Well, I want to hear."

"Now?"

Marian picked up a glass of wine. "Uh-huh."

◆◆◆◆◆◆

Marian blotted her eyes with a well-used tissue. "I know I shouldn't be so upset about Brian. It's just…" she paused, "he was always a gentleman. He kinda reminded me of my daddy."

Her lips trembled as stared at her hands lying on her lap.

Marian shook her head. "I can't believe I was fooled." She looked at her husband. "My friend is a murderer." A sob took control of her face.

"Shhh." Charlie wrapped his arms around her. "It's okay."

He stroked the back of her head. "By all accounts, he was a nice guy. But something snapped inside his head. He couldn't control the darkness."

Marian gasped. "Do you think he could've hurt me?"

Charlie used his thumb to wipe a wet spot from her cheek. "No, baby. Bullies were his target. Brian respected you."

Marian bit her bottom lip. "I don't know what to think. Will he get the death sentence?"

"It depends on his lawyer." Charlie gave her a clean tissue.

"I hate to say it, but Rose Emerson got the sentence she deserved. An adult tormenting a child is worse than evil." Marian blew her nose.

The harsh ding of the doorbell echoed around the living room.

Marian's hand landed on her chest. "Gah! That scared the bejeezus out of me."

Charlie went to the door and pressed his eye to the peephole. "It's Joan and Jack. Were you expecting them?"

"No. Let them in."

The warm summer night air wafted in as Charlie opened the door.

Jack and Joan stood grinning like two jackasses eating briars.

"Are you two drunk?" Charlie stepped aside. "Get in here."

They rushed inside still wearing silly grins.

Marian, infected with Joan's euphoria, giggled. "What's up with y'all?"

Joan danced on her toes. "Get over here."

Marian hurried over. "What is it?"

Joan squealed as she shot out her left hand and wiggled her ring finger.

Marian squealed at the sight of the giant sparkling diamond.

"We're getting married!"

About the Author

I am the author of The Charlie McClung mysteries, including *Brilliant Disguise, A Good Girl, Criminal Kind, Sins of My Youth, and Flirting with Time*. Although I was born in Mercedes, Texas, I have lived most of my life in Georgia. I live in Smyrna with my husband and our ill-tempered Tuxedo cat named Gertrude.

Thank you for taking the time to read *How Deep is the Darkness*. If you enjoyed it, please consider telling your friends about it. Word of mouth and reviews are an author's best friends and are very much appreciated. Reviews are precious to me.

The seventh book in the series, *Complex Kid*, will be released next.

You can find me on Facebook, Twitter, Instagram, Pinterest, LinkedIn, and Goodreads. I invite you to visit my website:

www.MaryAnneEdwards.com

Charlie and Marian look forward to seeing you again as they journey together through mystery, murder, and love.

Made in the USA
Columbia, SC
· 13 June 2020